The
EMPEROR of
MARS

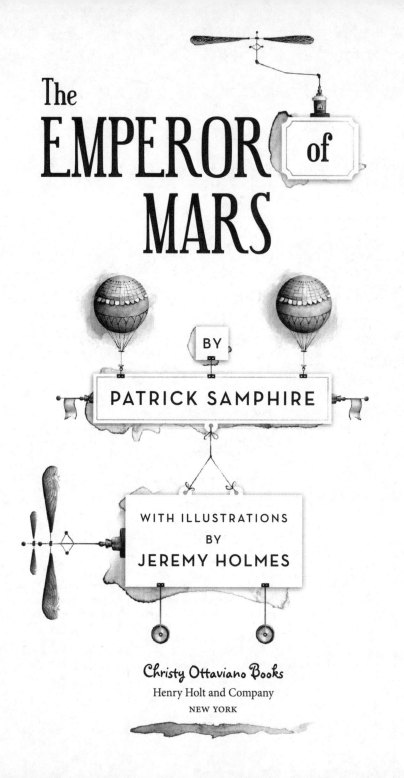

The
EMPEROR of
MARS

BY

PATRICK SAMPHIRE

WITH ILLUSTRATIONS
BY
JEREMY HOLMES

Christy Ottaviano Books
Henry Holt and Company
NEW YORK

Henry Holt and Company, *Publishers since 1866*
Henry Holt® is a registered trademark of Macmillan Publishing Group, LLC
175 Fifth Avenue, New York, NY 10010
mackids.com

Library of Congress Control Number: 2016953765

ISBN 978-0-8050-9908-9

Our books may be purchased in bulk for promotional, educational, or business use.
Please contact your local bookseller or the Macmillan Corporate and Premium Sales
Department at (800) 221-7945 ext. 5442 or by e-mail at MacmillanSpecialMarket@macmillan.com.

First Edition—2017

Printed in the United States of America by LSC Communications, Harrisonburg, Virginia

1 3 5 7 9 10 8 6 4 2

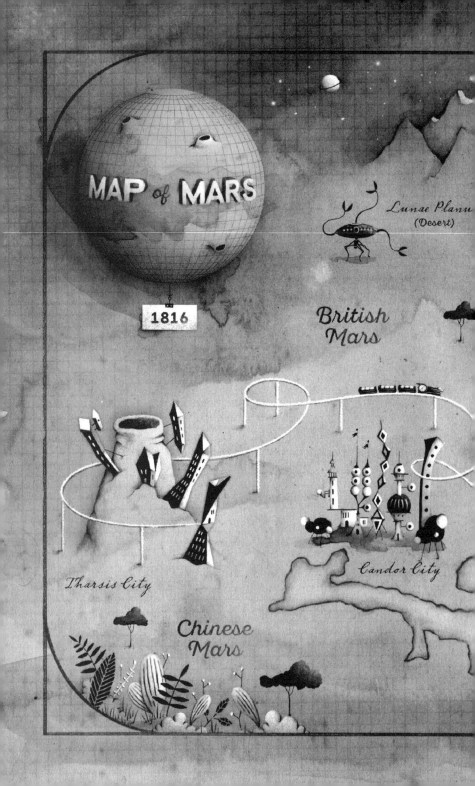

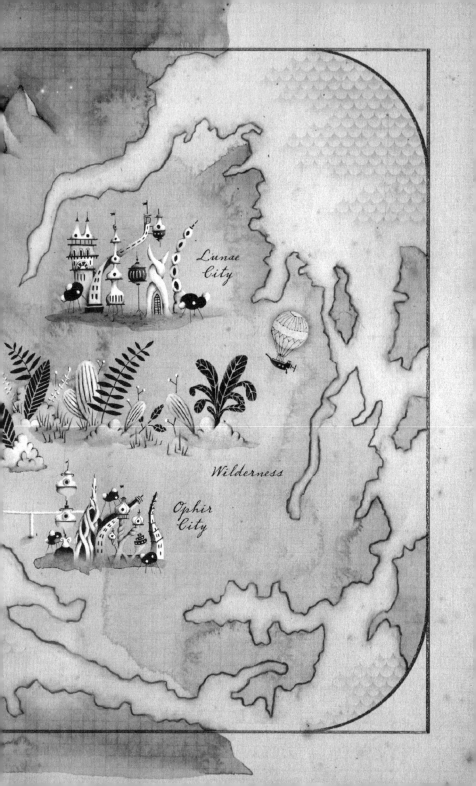

Lunae
City

Wilderness

Ophir
City

PART ONE

*The Missing
Martian*

The Trouble with Vine-Mining

Mars, 1817

I was twenty feet underground, surrounded by glowing blue sandfish crystals, with my head jammed in a beetle-vine warren, when I realized that vine-mining wasn't for me.

I had seen the notice pinned up outside the local office of the Imperial Martian Airship Company:

VOLUNTEERS NEEDED!

ROOT OUT BEETLE-VINES! SAVE LUNAE CITY!

SIGN UP TODAY!

BEFORE IT'S TOO LATE!

Perfect, I'd thought. *What a great idea.*

I had never been so wrong.

You might have thought that living in the middle of Mars's biggest desert would mean that you never got wet. You would have been wrong. Once a year, it rained for a solid month in the wilderness hundreds of miles upstream. The Martian Nile rose, and the river valley turned into a gigantic lake. The Inundation, they called it, and it was very, very wet indeed.

That would be all right if you didn't mind a bit of water. Or it would have been, if not for the beetle-vines. All year they had been burrowing away under Lunae City, sending out satellite clusters through their tunnels. When the Inundation arrived and water rushed into the tunnels, the beetle-vine clusters would erupt like fireworks made of multicolored toffee. The whole city would end up covered in bright, sticky string.

It was a crisis, but I was ready.

We'd been in Lunae City for eight months, and the truth was, I was bored. So when I'd seen the advertisement for vine-miners, I'd thought this was it: something fun to do at last.

I managed to believe that for almost half an hour. Then I found myself wedged upside down, dangling over a particularly ripe beetle-vine cluster, while sweat dripped onto the disgusting-smelling thing.

Water was what made the beetle-vine cluster think the Inundation had arrived, and here I was, dripping on it like a leaking pipe. I wondered what would happen if it exploded right in my face.

Beetle-vines were semidormant at night, so the mining

took place after dark. I'd had to wait until my entire family had gone to bed before I could sneak out. Now I was wishing I'd stayed in bed.

"What the devil are you doing?" a voice snapped out.

I twisted around and saw that a tall, thin man in a long, black coat had emerged from a side tunnel and was peering up at me through thick lenses. My shoulders were still jammed tight, so I indicated the beetle-vine cluster with my head.

"Trying to clear that out."

The man adjusted his lenses with a small lever set into the side of his glasses and squinted up at me again.

"And this is the way you propose to do it?" he demanded. "If you damage it, you'll drive it further underground, and then who will go after it, boy? You?"

"This wasn't exactly my plan," I muttered.

"Amateurs," the man said under his breath. He reached into one of his many bulging pockets and pulled out a small clockwork saw. "Don't move."

"Um, about that . . ." I said.

The man knelt beside the beetle-vine cluster and began cutting one of the tendrils that joined the satellite cluster to the other parts of the vine.

When I'd received my instructions, I'd been told that I would need to slice through every tendril before I touched the beetle-vine cluster itself.

Something crunched where my shoulder pressed into the

tunnel wall. Sand and fragments of sandfish crystal powdered down over my face.

"You might want to hurry," I said.

The man ignored me.

The sand shifted and I felt myself slide an inch down. I still couldn't move my arms. I scrabbled about with my fingers, but there was nothing to grab hold of.

"Seriously," I said.

"Please stop talking," the man said waspishly, without looking up. "I've a good mind to leave you hanging up there all night."

More sand trickled past my ear.

"Somehow I don't see that happening," I said.

The man straightened then moved around to the second tendril. In the pale blue glow of the sandfish crystals, I could see eight or nine tendrils snaking away into little tunnels.

I tried to slow my breathing so as not to dislodge any more sand. My left arm was itching like mad, and I was starting to feel dizzy from the blood going to my head.

Something gave way, and I dropped almost a foot before my arms jammed again.

"Keep still!" the man barked.

I bit back a reply. A knot of sandfish crystals pressed hard against my lips. If I spoke, they'd end up in my mouth.

The man stopped cutting to wind his clockwork saw. I wanted to scream.

"Use a knife!" I hissed through tight lips.

The man didn't bother to answer.

Sand slid against my arms. I pushed them outward to hold myself in place. Hard crystals pressed into my shoulders.

"Oh, God," I mumbled.

The sand crumbled. The sides of the tunnel gave way. With a yell, I dropped like a plunging crash-eagle.

I barely had time to get my arms in front of my face before I hit the beetle-vine cluster with a *splat*!

Sticky, stinking fluid sprayed across me. The smell was like rotting meat. I gagged and spat and clawed the stuff from my eyes.

"You imbecile!" the man screeched. "You useless, careless, dangerous imbecile!"

I pushed myself up just in time to see the vine tendrils whipping away into the tunnels, carrying fragments of the beetle-vine cluster with them. Within hours, each of them would have grown into a new beetle-vine cluster deep beneath the city.

"Get out!" he screamed, waving the clockwork saw at me with a shaking hand. "Get out, and never, ever come back!"

Aching, covered in reeking, gluey beetle-vine goo, I limped out of the tunnels and into the evening streets.

Vine-mining had turned out to be as big a disaster as everything else I'd tried here.

Eight months ago, I'd been caught up in the villainous Sir Titus Dane's scheme to rob a dragon tomb. It had taken an airship full of clockwork crabs, being lost in the Martian wilderness, and a terrifying fight against Sir Titus's minions in the middle of the desert for me to understand something important: most of the time, when they weren't being kidnapped or attacked by deadly hunting machines, my family could look after themselves. It didn't matter how terrible the disasters or how awful the scandals they got into, they could usually find a way out.

Which meant I didn't have to spend my entire life keeping them out of trouble.

On the other hand, I had absolutely no idea what to do with myself anymore. I was like a swarm of Martian slug flies, bouncing off walls and going nowhere.

Out here, surrounded by the tombs of the old Martian emperors and thousands of years of Martian history, it should have been like an adventure out of my favorite magazine, *Thrilling Martian Tales*. I should have been fighting off smugglers and tyrants, and uncovering amazing relics, just like Captain W. A. Masters, British-Martian spy, did in every issue. Instead, I'd been reduced to burrowing after beetle-vines in the middle of the night.

I was seriously thinking about canceling my subscription to *Thrilling Martian Tales*.

The desert chill had seeped into the city, leaving a thin layer of dew on the dusty streets. Years were twice as long on Mars as they were on Earth, and we were now well into the six-month Martian autumn. While the days were still baking hot, the nights often got cold. My clothes were soaked in beetle-vine sap and I was starting to shiver.

"Blasted beetle-vines," I muttered to myself. "Stupid city." Papa might be happy here with all his ancient artifacts to play with, but I'd had enough. More than enough.

I could just make out the sound of the Martian Nile lapping at the docks several streets away as I trudged through the city. Moored boats creaked on the water, and the faint, eerie songs of the native Martian sailors drifted through the night air. Maybe I should just get on one of those boats and go sailing away. I bet sailors never got bored.

The moons were high in the sky, wreathed in a faint mist, but still bright enough to light the cobbled street. I'd been told that Earth's moon was much larger and brighter than either of Mars's moons. That must be weird. I wondered if I'd ever get to see it.

I was still aching from falling into that beetle-vine cluster, and sandfish crystals had gotten into my socks and pantaloons. I glared at the moons, wondering exactly what they had to be so cheerful about.

And that was when I saw the fourth-floor window of Lady Harleston's enormous town house shoot up and a figure dressed all in black emerge, carrying a sack over one shoulder.

I didn't often go wandering about in Lunae City at night, but even I knew that this wasn't usual.

A rope uncoiled and snaked down the wall to end five yards short of the ground. Then the figure swung over the ledge and scrambled down.

I had lived long enough with my little sister, Putty, to see a disaster when it was coming straight at me, and I'd learned not to hesitate.

I launched myself forward just as the figure reached the end of the rope and lost their grip. Feet crashed into my outstretched arms, the sack hit my head, and we both collapsed to the hard road with an explosion of breath. The stranger leaped up and I stumbled after, still half tangled with their arms and legs.

"Are you . . . ?" I started, but I didn't have time to finish.

The figure whipped away the scarf that had been tied around their face and let long, brown hair fall free. I found myself looking up into a girl's dark eyes.

"Oh," I said, letting go quickly and stepping back. At a guess, she was about a year older than me, but she was much taller, and I could see she was part native Martian.

She looked completely furious.

"What do you think you're doing?" she demanded.

"What do I think *I'm* doing?" I spluttered. "What do you think *you're* doing?"

She looked at me like I was an idiot. "I'm escaping. What does it look like?"

I glanced over her shoulder at Lady Harleston's house. "Who are you escaping from?"

The girl gave me a pitying look. "From whoever owns this house. Obviously."

This conversation was getting away from me. My mouth opened and closed like a hungry fish. "Were you robbing it?"

"Let's think," she said. "You caught me climbing out of a house on the end of a rope in the middle of the night with a bag over my shoulder. What did you think I was doing? Cleaning the windows?"

"That's wrong," I said, realizing how stupid I sounded. I didn't normally get this flustered, even when arguing with Putty. But Putty didn't make me feel sweaty and fidgety, like I was wearing a shirt made from squeezethorn fibers. I wondered if falling into the beetle-vine cluster had made me sick.

"So what are you going to do?" she said. "Report me to the militia?"

I kept catching myself staring at her, then having to look away quickly.

"You'd be arrested," I said.

She glanced around. "Look, where are you going anyway?"

I pointed up the road with a shaky hand. "Um. To the Flame House," I said, giving the name the locals used for our new home.

"Well, I'm going the opposite direction. You can make yourself useful and help me with the bag if you like. I can't wait here all night."

I gawped like a confused marsh bat. "I'm not going to help you carry stolen goods."

"Fine, then." She hoisted the heavy bag onto her shoulder. "If I'm caught and hanged it'll be your fault."

I spluttered. "My fault? I saved you! You'd have broken a leg if I hadn't caught you."

"Don't be absurd. I've done that a thousand times." She sniffed and wrinkled her nose. "You smell really bad. Now, good-bye!"

"It's the beetle-vine," I mumbled, but she'd already turned on her heel and jogged away down a nearby alley, into the concealing darkness.

I stared after her. I wanted to say, *Don't go,* but I knew how ridiculous I would sound.

Almost as ridiculous as I looked standing here, mouth hanging open, as though I were trying to catch glow moths.

My head hurt.

I backed away, and my foot hit something. It skidded across the cobbles, glinting metallically. I followed, then crouched to pick it up, frowning.

It was some kind of mechanical device—but old, like something that had been pulled out of a dragon tomb. It was cylindrical, the size of my fist, and cleverly made. I peered at it. Through a dozen small holes in the side, I saw fine brass cogs and levers, and the hint of a coiled spring deep inside.

I had no idea what it was. The thief must have stolen it from Lady Harleston's house and dropped it when we got all tangled up. The thought made me feel uncomfortably hot in my jacket again, despite the cold air.

Perhaps she would come back for it.

I dithered, peering into the alley, the device clutched in my hands.

And a hand closed tight on my shoulder. "Got you!" a voice exclaimed.

I nearly jumped out of my skin.

My little sister, Putty, was standing right behind me, grinning. "You shriek like a girl, Edward." She was wearing the loose, native Martian robe that had been driving Mama crazy all week. Putty changed her obsessions even more often than my oldest sister, Jane, changed suitors, but this particular obsession had been one of her more frequent ones since we'd traveled on a native Martian boat across the desert.

"What are you doing here?" I hissed.

She waved a hand casually in the air. "Oh, I was just delivering a forged letter for Jane."

"You were just . . . Never mind." Putty had come up with some unlikely stories in her time, but the idea that Jane would send her out in the middle of the night to deliver a *forged letter* was beyond absurd.

"Actually, she wanted you to deliver it, but you were too busy playing at vine-mining, so she sent me instead."

I frowned. "How did you know I was going vine-mining?"

"You talk in your sleep. That's how I know all your secrets."

"Are you telling me you've been standing in my bedroom listening to me sleep?" That was . . . disturbing.

Putty looked offended. "That would be silly. I simply fitted a speaking tube between our rooms when we first moved in. I attached it to a silent alarm so it would wake me whenever you said anything or went sneaking about. It's very clever."

"You bugged me?" I demanded, trying desperately to remember everything I'd said and done in my bedroom since we'd moved in.

"Of course. I'm surprised you didn't notice. You're the one who wants to be a spy. You'll have to notice that kind of thing, you know. Cousin Freddie would have found it in minutes."

I ground my teeth.

"Anyway," Putty said, "it was for your own good. If you'd been captured by villains again, I'd have been able to rescue you. Again. Who was that you were talking to?"

I blinked at the sudden change of direction. Putty's brain was like a rubber ball shot from a steam cannon: I could never tell where it was going to bounce next.

"A thief," I said, as calmly as I could, even though just

mentioning her made me feel strange. "She was stealing from Lady Harleston's house."

Putty's jaw dropped. "I can't believe you arranged a rendezvous with a thief and you didn't invite me."

My face turned as hot as a steam boiler. "It wasn't a rendezvous. She was trying to escape."

Not that I'd been trying to stop her. Maybe just delay her a bit.

Putty's eyes bugged. "We should catch her! Maybe Lady Harleston will give us a reward! Maybe she'll let us use her library."

As usual in conversations with Putty, I lagged several steps behind. "Why on Mars would we want to use her library?"

Putty put her hands on her hips. "She's a collector. She's got the biggest collection of Ancient Martian documents in the city. Imagine if she let us read them!"

I shuddered. The Ancient Martian language used impenetrable symbols called ideograms instead of proper writing. I'd never managed to get the hang of them. A whole library of them sounded like a nightmare.

"What's that?" Putty jabbed a finger at the device in my hand.

I shrugged. "No idea. The thief dropped it."

"Good." Putty smiled. "We'll give it back to Lady Harleston. I'm sure she won't mind being woken in the middle of the night if we're returning her artifact. She'll definitely let us use her library."

I looked down at the strange device in my hands and realized I didn't want to give it back. This was the most exciting thing that had happened to me in eight months. It was an *adventure*. If I gave the device back, it would be over before it began. I didn't even know what it was. Anyway, maybe it didn't belong to Lady Harleston.

"I'm not giving it back to her," I said, making a decision. "I'm giving it back to the thief." I wondered what she would think when I did. I realized I was grinning and straightened my face.

Putty stared at me. "You want to give it to the thief? After she stole it?"

"We don't know she stole it," I said. "All we know is she dropped it. It might have been hers."

"Really? What would she be doing with something like this?"

I peered at it again. "Using it to break in?" I hazarded.

"Well, we should definitely give it back to her, then," Putty said sarcastically. "In case there are some more houses to burgle. Maybe you two can run away together and live a life of crime."

I glared at my little sister. "You know—" I started.

But I didn't get a chance to finish.

Above us, a window shot up, and Lady Harleston's head appeared, her long, graying hair loose and tangled over her nightdress. She stared down at us, and we gaped back up at her.

"Thieves!" she shouted. "Thieves!"

Hellfire! Hellfire and damnation!

I put down my head, and we ran.

The Missing Martian

By the time Putty and I got home, it was nearly three in the morning. I was exhausted and stinking, I felt like I'd been stamped on by a pack of tramplebeasts, and I was pretty sure I had sandfish crystals stuck in my ear. I bathed as quickly as I could and fell into bed.

I could have slept most of the morning, but of course I didn't get the chance. The morning light was barely working its way through my thick curtains when someone hissed "Edward!" in my ear.

I rolled over and buried my head back in my pillow. "Too early."

A hand shook my shoulder. "You have to wake up!"

I blinked until I could make out the figure leaning over me.

"Jane?" Why was my oldest sister waking me up so early?

Jane *never* came into my room. I tried to free my legs from the twisted sheet. "Is the house burning down?"

"You have a new tutor." She threw a nervous glance across the room, toward the door.

I let my head flop back on the pillow.

My tutor's name was Mr. Davidson, and Papa had employed him yesterday. Until then, I'd been sure I'd gotten away with it. After all, we'd been living in Lunae City for most of an Earth year, and nobody seemed to have noticed that I wasn't going to school. Papa spent most of his time with his head stuck inside one of his inventions or over at the museum examining the devices we'd found in a dragon tomb. Mama had thrown herself into planning Jane's social season in Tharsis City like a rhinoceraptor charging into a cluster of grass eels. I'd thought they'd forgotten about me.

No such luck.

"I'm going back to sleep," I croaked.

"I saw you with him yesterday, but I have not been introduced. Do you not think it wrong that I should not have been introduced?"

"Oh, you don't want to know what I think is wrong about this," I said.

"He seemed like an amiable young man, did you not think?"

No, I didn't. I'd stood there in Papa's study as Mr. Davidson had recited his qualifications in Latin, Ancient Greek, algebra, and literature, and all I'd been able to imagine was

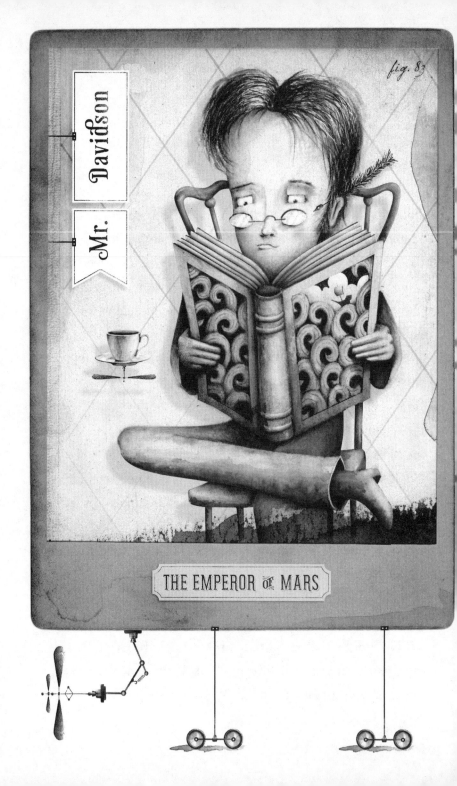

my life being drowned in a sea of books and chalk dust. I might have been bored, but I wasn't *that* bored.

I pushed myself upright.

"You can't be in love with him already," I said. "You haven't even met him."

Jane blushed. "I didn't say I was in love with him. I said I thought he seemed amiable."

I didn't believe a word of it. Jane fell in love as easily as anyone else would fall over a trip wire. Personally, I couldn't understand the appeal. Love scrambled people's brains. Take Olivia—my next-oldest sister—and Cousin Freddie. Cousin Freddie was a secret agent for the British Martian government. He'd been tasked with stopping the machinations of the evil Sir Titus Dane. But the moment he'd set eyes on Olivia, his brains had begun to dribble out of his ears. And Olivia had been just as bad. One second, she was the most sensible, proper person on Mars. The next, she was fighting off thugs and hiking through the Martian wilderness. Love was like a disease, and I was enormously relieved to be immune.

Jane was showing no signs of leaving.

"Why exactly did you have to wake me up to tell me this?" I said.

"You will have to introduce me," Jane said. "It's only proper. If a gentleman is to be coming and going in our house, I must be introduced. Imagine what people might say otherwise."

All I could imagine was the wonderful sleep I wanted to get back to. I'd been dreaming about something, and it had been a good dream, but now I'd forgotten it.

"He's not coming until next week," I said. "Thank heavens." I slumped down into my bed again and closed my eyes, hoping that was enough of a hint. "I'll introduce you then."

Jane let out a martyred sigh. "By then he may have met someone else!"

I grunted and turned my face into the pillow. "That would be tragic."

"I'm so glad you agree!" Jane said brightly. "I knew you would understand. That is why I went to Papa's study, borrowed his paper, and wrote a message asking Mr. Davidson to attend this very morning."

My eyes popped open again and my mouth worked soundlessly. Jane had snuck into Papa's study and forged a letter? *Jane?*

"Parthenia delivered it last night," she said.

"But . . . No . . . What?" I stuttered. "I thought Putty was making that up."

"Come on, Edward!" Jane said. "You have to get up."

I stared at her. My brain was *not* working properly this morning. "Why do I have to get up?"

"Because Mr. Davidson will be here in fifteen minutes, and you have to introduce me right away." She looked mutinous. "I'm not leaving until you agree."

I let out an exhausted sigh. "Fine. You win. But I'm not going to forget this. Now, at least let me get dressed?"

⊰◈⊱

When we'd moved to Lunae City, Papa's business had been struggling. He was very good at making machines but not much good at making money from them. He'd spent most of what we had rebuilding our house at Valles Marineris after Freddie and I had blown it up. The only place Papa had been able to afford in Lunae City and which was big enough for Mama was this one, and that was only because absolutely no one else wanted to live in it.

Most people called it "the Flame House," because it looked more like a fire than a house. Or maybe because the best thing anyone could have done with it was to burn it down. It had been built by a wealthy Englishman, Sir William Flanders. When Sir William had first arrived in Lunae City, he'd been so impressed by the native Martian buildings with their twists and spirals and jutting spines that he'd decided to build a house just like them. Unfortunately, he had absolutely no idea what he was doing, and he hadn't noticed that most of the elaborate twirls on native Martian buildings were up on the roofs, where they wouldn't get in anyone's way. By the time it was finished, the Flame House was a complete disaster, and Sir William had run out of money to do anything about it.

Nothing in the Flame House made any sense at all. No two rooms were on the same level, corridors ended abruptly in walls (and, in one unfortunate case, in a door that opened into thin air four floors up), and every single room was a different shape. To get from my room to Olivia's room next door, for example, I had to go along a wobbly, sloping corridor in the wrong direction, up a ladder to the attic, back down some stairs, along another corridor, and squeeze through a narrow gap into an abandoned music room, before I could finally reach her. Generally, the best way to get anywhere was to go back to the front door and start over again.

By the time I'd gotten dressed and made it safely to the entrance hall, I was in no mood to meet anyone. My stomach was rumbling like a land shark and I could still feel the sand-fish crystals in my ear. I should just skip this whole ridiculous plan of Jane's and get some breakfast. I licked my lips. Eggs. Kippers. Toast. Fried slumber-plant. I could *smell* them. I headed for the breakfast room.

But I'd only made it two steps when a hand reached out from behind a pillar and grabbed me. I stumbled back, right into Jane, who was skulking in the shadows, a nervous expression tightening her face.

"I thought you weren't going to make it!" she hissed.

I shot a longing look toward the breakfast room. Those eggs weren't going to eat themselves.

The doorbell sounded, loud and clear. *Too late. Blast!* I grimaced as our new ro-butler glided smoothly past. No getting away from this now.

My tutor was a thin man with a too-small face and dirty

brown hair. Every time he glanced at me, he made a face like he'd looked down and realized he'd forgotten to put on his trousers that morning.

"Mr. Tobias Davidson," the ro-butler announced. "Tutor. To see Professor Sullivan."

I stepped out in front of him and cleared my throat.

"May I introduce my sister, Miss Sullivan? Jane, this is Mr. Davidson."

"I am so pleased to make your acquaintance, Mr. Davidson," Jane said, curtseying. She offered him her sweetest smile, the smile that had made a hundred young men fall instantly in love with her.

Mr. Davidson glanced distractedly around. "Delighted," he said. "Please excuse me. I am summoned to see your father." With that, he tipped his hat at her, stepped past, and followed the ro-butler.

Jane stared after him, aghast.

I'd never seen anything like it. Jane trapped young men like a sky-spider trapped bear-snakes. Young men met her. They fell in love. That was it.

But not Mr. Davidson.

The moment he disappeared, Jane was at my side.

"Oh, Edward. It's over!" She grabbed my jacket. "He didn't notice me. I am too old. I shall die a spinster."

"You're only twenty," I said, wriggling free of her grip.

"Twenty!" she cried. "Mama always said this would

happen. She said I must capture a gentleman before it was too late, or I should be forced to settle, like she did."

"Mama didn't *settle* for Papa," I said. "He was the only one of her suitors who ever really loved her. And she loves him, too. Anyway, I'm sure Mr. Davidson just wanted to make a good impression on Papa. What did your letter say?"

Jane straightened. "It was rather urgent."

"There you are. I'm sure he'll pay you more attention next time, when he's not so worried about what Papa wants. And at least you've been introduced now."

With luck, by the time Mr. Davidson took up his duties next week, Jane would have fallen in love with some other young man instead.

"There, there," I said helpfully.

Now, *at last*, I could get some breakfast.

But when I reached the breakfast room, Putty was crouched on the window ledge, staring in through the glass at me. I thought about ignoring her, but Putty was a very hard person to ignore. With a sigh, I crossed to the window and pulled it up.

"What are you doing?"

Putty slid in and dropped to the floor. "Looking for you. I knew you'd be here."

"Brilliant deduction. And at breakfast time, too. Is there something wrong with the door?"

"I'm avoiding Miss Wilkins."

Miss Wilkins was Putty's governess. Putty had had a dozen governesses since we'd come to Lunae City. Most of them hadn't lasted more than a week, but Miss Wilkins had been here over a month and showed no signs of giving in. I'd never met anyone so strict. Miss Wilkins was about as movable as a granite wall, and Putty had been butting her head against her without making a dent. All I could say was that I was glad she wasn't *my* governess.

"Are you coming?" Putty said, bouncing impatiently from foot to foot.

"Coming where?" Had we agreed to go somewhere? I didn't remember it, but I'd been distracted by my run-in with the thief last night.

Putty rolled her eyes. "To see Captain Sadalius Kol, of course. He's in the garden."

"He is?"

Captain Kol owned a riverboat that carried goods up and down the Martian Nile and along the network of ancient canals that crisscrossed the Lunae Planum desert. When Sir Titus Dane had kidnapped my parents and Jane, he had sent his accomplice, Dr. Octavius Blood, to prevent any pursuit. Captain Kol and his crew had saved us from Dr. Blood's hunting machines. They had taken us on board their boat, fed us, and carried us all the way to Lunae City so we could rescue Mama, Papa, and Jane.

"I didn't even know he was back in town."

"That's because you were too busy vine-mining." She

Miss **Wilkins**

THE EMPEROR OF MARS

fig. 87

shot me a hard glance. "Without me. Anyway, if he wasn't back in town, how would he be in the garden? Mama won't let him in the house."

I stared at her. "Mama won't let him in?"

"She said we couldn't have his sort here in case Mrs. Lewis saw him."

Mrs. Lewis was Mama's biggest rival in Lunae City, and they were constantly trying to outdo each other. But this was too much.

"*His sort?*" Captain Kol was a native Martian, and I knew how most British Martians treated the native Martians, but even so, didn't Mama have any shame? We'd all be dead without him.

"Come *on*, Edward. It's urgent."

I shot a last, longing look at the breakfast. "I don't suppose we could use the door, could we?"

Putty swung her legs back out over the windowsill and dropped to the red Martian grass below.

"No, well, I didn't think so," I muttered.

I followed her awkwardly out and across the lawn.

Captain Kol was waiting in the small, artificial Martian wilderness by the river. He rose from the bench as we approached.

Even though we'd lived in Lunae City for eight months, I still hadn't gotten used to how tall the native Martians were. In the unknown thousands of years they'd lived on Mars, with its weak gravity, they had become a race of tall, elongated people. They looked as though they might snap in two at the slightest breath of wind, but I'd seen Captain Kol and his crew haul about boxes and bales with ease. When I'd tried to shift one myself, I'd scarcely been able to move it.

I'd been trying to learn the dialect of native Martian spoken in Lunae City, but I still hadn't managed to pick up more than a couple dozen phrases. Captain Kol's English was better than when I'd first met him, but even so, we had to rely on Putty to translate.

Captain Kol looked grave as we exchanged greetings.

"I had hoped to find your cousin here," he said.

"Freddie?" I said. "I think he's still trying to track down Dr. Blood. I don't know where he is."

Freddie had gone after Dr. Blood the moment Sir Titus Dane had been defeated, but as far as I knew, he still hadn't caught him. Dr. Blood had seemed harmless, just a small, fussy, pedantic little man obsessed with his rocks and Ancient Mars. But he'd been ruthless. He'd crashed our airship, then his machines had pursued us relentlessly, and he was still out there.

"Then I must ask you for help," Captain Kol said.

I frowned. "You know we'd do anything for you. What is it? Putty said it was urgent."

Captain Kol nodded. "You remember my crewman, Rothan Gal?"

"He was the one who told us all that history of Mars," Putty said.

I did remember him. While we'd sat recovering on the deck of the boat on the long journey on Martian canals and down the Martian Nile, Rothan Gal had often sat next to Putty, telling her elaborate tales of Ancient Mars. His English had been much better than most of the sailors, but I hadn't really paid attention. We'd only just survived an airship crash and fleeing across wilderness. All I'd wanted to do was rest.

"I suppose," I said.

"Did you know," Putty said, "the old emperors of Mars used to build barges, and then when the Inundation came, they would float downriver with their dragons at their feet to intimidate people? That's how they kept their power. Rothan Gal told us, don't you remember?"

I looked blank.

"I knew you weren't listening!"

"I was half drowned at the time," I said. When Captain Kol and his crew had dragged me out of the canal, I'd swallowed more water than a whale. "Anyway, don't get ideas. There aren't any dragons or Martian emperors anymore, and when the Inundation comes, all we'll get is wet feet."

Putty pouted, and I turned back to Captain Kol. "Has something happened to Rothan Gal?" I hadn't listened much to his stories, but I'd liked him. I'd liked all the native Martian sailors. We might only have spent a week with Captain Kol and his crew, but they were like family.

"I fear it has," Captain Kol said. "Two days ago, Rothan

Gal entered the Museum of Martian Antiquities. Nobody has seen him since."

"You think something happened to him there?" I said. "Something bad?"

The captain shrugged. "I do not know. I have been to the museum. The curators there will not talk to a native Martian about his missing friend. But I know that he entered the museum and I know that no one saw him emerge. I had hoped Freddie could ask questions there."

"I'll do it," I said. "I know most of the curators." Papa worked part-time at the museum researching the artifacts from our dragon tomb.

The museum was never busy, but there were plenty of curators and it was a public place. Why would someone do something to Rothan Gal there, where anyone might see them? If I wanted to jump someone, I'd do it in a dark alley or in the crowded streets of Lunae City, where no one would notice in the crush of bodies.

"Why was he in the museum?" I said.

Captain Kol frowned. "Why would he not be?"

"I just . . . I mean . . . I didn't think he'd be interested." I grimaced. I was sounding like an idiot.

"The Museum of Martian Antiquities contains the history of the native Martian people," Captain Kol said. "The artifacts are the artifacts of our people. Those great empires, they were the empires of our people. The figures you see laboring in the fields in ancient pictures and the emperors you place on high thrones, they are native Martian, not British or Chinese or French or Turkish. Why should Rothan Gal not wish to study the remains of our civilization?"

"I didn't mean . . ." I mumbled.

Except I had. I hadn't realized it, but somehow I'd thought native Martians wouldn't be interested in the museum or history. I felt my face turn a bright, burning red. I hated that I hadn't known better. I was no better than those curators who wouldn't talk to Captain Kol.

"I thought he was a sailor," I said.

"He is. How else would he earn a living? None of your universities would employ a native Martian. The museum certainly would not. Besides, there are secrets about native Martian history that we choose not to share with outsiders."

Putty's eyes bulged at this. "Secrets? You have to tell me!"

Captain Kol smiled. "When you come to work on one of my boats, Rothan Gal may choose to teach you. But first we must find out what happened to him."

"I'll get you an answer," I promised. "If they won't tell me, they'll tell Papa. We'll find him."

I owed Captain Kol that. I owed his whole crew.

— 3 —

The Clue in the Museum

The Museum of Martian Antiquities was an enormous red stone building near the river, built around the remains of an Ancient Martian temple.

Once, thousands of years ago, there had been temples all along the banks of the Martian Nile. We had passed dozens of ruins on our trip down the river. They had been ridiculously big. I had no idea where they had found enough people to fill them all or even build them. I guessed the Ancient Martians hadn't figured it out, either, because the temples had collapsed and now there were only lines of broken pillars, looking a bit like snapped-off fingers sticking out of the ground, and giant chunks of wall.

Except for here, where the museum had been constructed from the ruins.

"You know," I said to Putty as we slipped through the press of bodies on the way to the museum, "you don't have to come. Miss Wilkins is going to be furious you snuck out. You'll be confined to the nursery for a week."

Putty shot me a furious look. "You'd like that, wouldn't you?"

I missed a step and someone jostled me. "What?"

"You're always trying to leave me out of things these days."

"No, I'm not."

"Yeah?" She narrowed her eyes. "So why did you go vine-mining without me? *I* wouldn't have gotten fired for messing it up. And why did you go to meet a thief without telling me?"

I felt my cheeks turn hot. "I didn't go to meet her! And there was no way Miss Wilkins would have let you go vine-mining."

Putty glowered. "Don't even talk about her. She never lets me do *anything*. Anyway, I think she's a French spy."

"You think your governess is a French spy," I said slowly, letting every word fall clearly from my lips.

"Yes! She took my whole collection of experimental photon emission globes. Only Papa and I know how they work."

"They are rather dangerous," I said. "And you did break a couple of them in the kitchen while Cook was preparing dinner."

"I was researching them," Putty said with dignity. "Even Papa says I understand photon emission and capture devices better than anyone else on Mars. Or he *would* say it if he thought about it. Anyway, I have a plan to get them back.

It'll hardly cause any damage. Nothing that can't be repaired. And she is a spy. I can prove it."

"Right," I said. "And it's got absolutely nothing to do with the fact that you haven't been able to scare off this governess like all the others?"

"Don't you think that's suspicious? I've been really awful, and she's still sticking around. I was right when I said those men wanted to steal Papa's water abacus last year, and you didn't believe me then. Imagine all the secrets she could be passing on to the French if she were a spy. Napoleon is already the emperor of half of Earth. Do you want him to be the Emperor of Mars, too? He totally could invade if he got Papa's secrets."

"She's still not a spy."

She glowered. "And you still could have invited me vine-mining."

I sighed. "It's not that I didn't want you to come. It's just that . . ." How was I going to explain this so that Putty would understand it? Hell, even I didn't really understand it. "It's just that I've spent most my life chasing around after everyone else in the family. I've never really *chosen* what I wanted to do. I just end up doing whatever you or Jane or Olivia or Mama or Papa wants me to do. I just want to find out what *I* want to do."

"You're not making any sense, Edward."

"No," I said. "No, I don't suppose I am."

We turned off the main street, down a narrower street

lined with shops and stalls, before coming out onto the wide square in front of the Museum of Martian Antiquities.

From the top of one of the largest columns that fronted the museum, a half-crumbled dragon's head leered down. I always shivered when I walked under it. I knew it was just a carving, and anyway, its eyes had been worn away ages ago, but I still felt like it was watching me. A large banner had been slung above the doorway reading, "New Exhibition: The Glories of the Emperors of Mars."

Putty snorted. "Oh, please. That's completely untrue. There was only one emperor in our tomb."

In two days, the museum was opening a new gallery stuffed full of the amazing artifacts we'd found in our dragon tomb. Well, most of them. Putty had snuck out a fossilized dragon egg without anyone except me and Freddie noticing. But most of the rest of the stuff would be in there.

We pushed our way through the heavy, iron-studded door, and deafening noise immediately washed over us.

"Look out!" Putty shouted.

I ducked just in time as something swooped by, almost taking my head off.

The entrance hall was in chaos. For a moment, I thought the museum had been attacked. But it was almost worse: Dozens of junior curators were rushing around the lobby in panic, shouting and waving, while a cluster of automatic servants strained to carry a large, elaborate artifact toward a nearby gallery. One of the curators had even put on a pair of pneumatic wings and was flapping around, out of control, almost crashing into the other curators, the artifact, the walls, and us. The automatic servants wobbled, the curators shouted contradictory instructions, and any moment the whole thing was going to end in disaster.

"Hey!" Putty shouted. "That's our artifact! You'd better not drop it!"

I'd never quite figured out what the artifact was supposed to be. It was made of hundreds of brass balls, each the size of Putty's fist, all connected together with thin brass rods. We'd found it in the dragon tomb when we'd been taking shelter from Sir Titus. Before I'd had a chance to look at it, he'd smashed it to bits with his excavator. The museum had spent the last few months restoring it, but I still didn't know what it was, and no one else seemed to, either. It looked a bit like a man crouching, ready to jump up. Or maybe like a bowl of noodles tipped over a sculpture made of marbles.

"Look," Putty said. "There's Dr. Guzman. Why don't you ask him about Rothan Gal?"

I eyed the small, dust-smeared junior-under-curator standing on the far side of the lobby. "Why don't *you* ask him?"

"He's awfully boring. You deal with boring better than I do."

"Thanks?" I said. Personally, I'd rather have my toes chewed off by a swarm of gator-bugs than talk to Dr. Guzman, but I'd promised Captain Kol. *Hell.* I gritted my teeth.

"If he goes on about his pottery again, though, I'm blaming you," I told Putty.

We dodged past the struggling automatic servants, ducked the flying curator again, and finally reached our target.

"Dr. Guzman!" I called.

He looked around and rubbed his smudged eyeglasses. "Oh. It's you. This is all your fault, you know."

I started. "Mine? What is?"

Dr. Guzman sniffed heavily. "The new gallery. I was all ready to present my pottery collection to the world and then *you* had to find that dragon tomb and my pottery is forgotten. And now," he said, looking like he'd bitten into a thorn lemon, "it seems that I am no longer junior-under-curator but junior-under-curator, *second class*. I have been forced to abandon my own studies to dance around this new gallery. Perhaps the senior curators imagine my pottery will interpret itself? It is a disgrace. Your father is not here, I am afraid. You would think he would be, with this being his gallery, but no. I believe he is in his office."

"Actually, we had a question for you," I said.

He brightened immediately. "About pottery?"

"No."

His shoulders fell. "Oh. Well, out with it. It is not as though I have anything better to do. Not now that I am junior-under-curator, *second class*. Pottery is of no importance, you see. This is only a museum."

fig. 67

Dr. Guzman

THE EMPEROR OF MARS

"Have you been here all week?" I interrupted before he could really get going.

"And the week before, and the week before that. Every day of every week for the last seven years. And now I am *second class.*"

I gritted my teeth. Every time I didn't see Dr. Guzman for a few weeks, I forgot how annoying he was. "A man's been visiting the museum. A native Martian. I wondered if you'd seen him."

Dr. Guzman's face twisted. "I do not understand why the senior curators allow such people in. Criminals and vagabonds, the lot of them. But the curators say that the museum must be open to all." He sniffed again. "If I were in charge, things would be different. Has the fellow been arrested? Did he steal something?"

Putty's jaw dropped. I pulled her back quickly. *We need answers,* I told myself. *Don't kick him!*

"No," I said, "I want to know what he did while he was here."

Dr. Guzman straightened. "How would I know? Why would *I* talk to the man? I am a junior-under-curator for Third Age antiquities." He cleared his throat. "Second class. I am not some native guide. Ah . . . But, I, ah, did have a question for you." He looked awkward. "Will your sister be coming to the gallery opening?"

"Me?" Putty said indignantly. "Of course I will!"

Dr. Guzman shuddered. "No. No, indeed. Not you. The oldest."

"Jane, you mean?" I said. "I expect so."

Dr. Guzman made an attempt to straighten his dusty jacket. "Ah. Excellent. Excellent. A most . . . perceptive young lady."

I resisted the urge to roll my eyes. I was used to young men falling in love with Jane, but for some reason I didn't really think of Dr. Guzman as a young man. Or any sort of man at all. More like a forgotten, dusty artifact from an old tomb that no one knew what to do with. Well, Jane deserved this after dragging me out of bed so early this morning.

"She was asking about you," I said.

"When?" Putty demanded incredulously. I kicked her. "Ow!"

Dr. Guzman brightened. "Ah! Capital! She showed a quite sincere interest in my pottery last time we met."

"So, um . . . the native Martian?" I prompted.

Dr. Guzman's face crinkled in distaste. "That fellow. Well, all I can say is that each time he came, he visited the same gallery and stayed for several hours before he left."

So he hadn't just been looking around the museum. He'd come here for something particular. Something important enough to return repeatedly. Something important enough to get him into trouble?

"Could you show me?" I asked.

Dr. Guzman cleared his throat. "My work . . ."

"And I'll be able to tell you what Jane said about you on the way," I said. "She was so hoping to meet you again."

"No, she wasn't!" Putty objected. "She—"

"Yes," I said firmly. "She was."

Dr. Guzman straightened himself and brushed at his jacket. "Then follow me, young man. And, ah, all the details, if you please. . . ."

He led us through the museum to a small, long gallery in the west wing. It actually looked more like a corridor with a few display cases shoved in than an actual gallery. Surely there wouldn't be anything important left here? On the way, I made up all sorts of stories about things Jane had said. I managed to make her sound actually interested and intelligent about Third Age pottery. All I had to do was repeat back everything Dr. Guzman had said to me over the last few months, and by the time we got there, he'd convinced himself that Jane was a genius *and* absolutely fascinated by his bits of old pottery. He was going to be in for a shock next time he talked to her.

I peered into the display cases as we made our way up the corridor gallery. All I could see were old stone tablets carved with ideograms. Most of them were badly damaged, and only a few had translations above them. Mostly they seemed to be about crops and harvests and bags of flour or other equally exciting things. Life must have been *really* boring back then if people bothered to carve these kinds of things into rock.

"If it were up to me," Dr. Guzman said, "I would replace all of these with pottery. I have a very fine jug from the beginning of the Third Age, from the reign of the minor emperor Gel-ib-Nar. It would look quite fine here."

"You don't know what the Martian was looking for, do you?" I said.

Dr. Guzman peered down his dusty nose at me. "I have better things to do than follow such people around. Perhaps he was just keeping out of the sun. These fellows are singularly averse to work, you know, and rarely labor in the middle of the day."

I almost laughed but managed to turn it into a cough at the last moment. Was he serious? I'd have liked to see him hoeing a field in the midday Lunae Planum sun, or hauling bales of cotton onto a boat like Captain Kol's sailors did.

I moved on to the next display. "What was in this case?"

The small wood-and-glass case had been set into the wall and something mounted inside it. But now it was empty. The irregular shape of the artifact had left a dusty outline against the white board behind it.

"Ha!" Dr. Guzman exclaimed. "I knew it! He has stolen something! I told the curators that we should not let native Martians into the museum."

I knelt beneath the case. There, on the floor, up against the wall, where the automatic cleaners had missed it, was a dark, brown stain.

I peered closer.

"Look," I said to Putty.

It was blood. Dried blood.

"He didn't steal it," I said.

Rothan Gal had been standing in front of the display case, studying the artifact, and he had been attacked. Now the artifact was gone, and so was Rothan Gal.

"What happened?" Putty said, crouching down beside me.

I shook my head. "Someone attacked him. Or maybe he was just in the way. They obviously wanted whatever was in that display case."

"So where is he?"

"They must have taken him with them." But why? Unconscious or a prisoner, getting him out of here without anyone noticing would have been an enormous risk.

I straightened. "I need to know what was in this display case."

Dr. Guzman heaved a sigh. "It will be in the records. But I cannot find out today. I have already spent far too much time away from my work. You must come back tomorrow."

Tomorrow? Rothan Gal had already been missing for two days. Every hour that passed reduced our chances of finding him. But I knew Dr. Guzman. If I pushed him too far, he'd refuse to help at all. I dug my fingernails into my palms.

"Have you seen anyone else around this exhibit in the last few days?" I asked.

Dr. Guzman straightened his jacket. "I am a junior-under-curator, second class. I am not a museum guard."

"Fine. I'll tell Jane how helpful you've been," I said, managing to keep the sarcasm out of my voice.

I watched Dr. Guzman go, then turned back to the display case.

"It doesn't make any sense, Edward," Putty said. "If they wanted to steal something, why not wait until Rothan Gal was gone? He wasn't here all the time. Edward!" Her hand landed on my sleeve just as the sound of a footstep made me look up. At the far end of the gallery, someone was watching us. He was a tall, broad-shouldered man with dark brown skin, wearing a long, green greatcoat. A wide hat shadowed his face, and his eyes were fixed on us.

"Hey!" I cried out.

The man turned on his heel and strode away. I took off after him.

But by the time I reached the end of the gallery, he was gone. I stared down the corridor. Had he been watching us? If not, why had he fled when we spotted him?

"You lost him," Putty said, coming up behind me.

I cursed silently. "Come on," I said. "I want to talk to Papa."

Papa's office was on the second floor of the museum, above the main galleries. When I pushed open the door, he was leaning over his desk, peering through an elaborate arrangement of lenses at a fine device that lay dismantled in front of him.

"Edward!" he said, looking up in surprise, as I shut the door behind us. "Parthenia. Did I forget my lunch again?"

"We were just in the museum," I said. "We thought we'd stop in to ask you something."

"Dreadful things have been happening!" Putty blurted, looking delighted.

Papa picked at his cravat. "Ah. How unfortunate. Er . . . Wouldn't you prefer to deal with that yourself, Edward?"

I rolled my eyes. Papa was expert at avoiding dealing with problems.

"Don't worry," I said. "That's not why we're here."

"It's not?" Putty said.

"No."

"Ah. Good. Good. In that case . . ." Papa frowned suddenly. "Actually, now that you *are* here, Edward, a peculiar thing happened this morning."

I knew what this was about. I put on my most innocent expression.

"Oh?"

"Your tutor came to me. You remember the chap? Mr. Davidson."

"Of course."

"It appears that I wrote to him, summoning him to meet with me at his earliest convenience. But I had absolutely no recollection of writing the letter, and I had no idea what I wanted with him. It was most awkward."

I kept my face carefully neutral. "Did he bring the letter?"

Papa pushed it across the desk to me.

Jane had done a fantastic job of imitating Papa's scrawled

handwriting. I wouldn't have been able to tell the difference, and clearly neither could Papa.

Most gentlemen these days used auto-scribes to set down their messages. The auto-scribe had a large, trumpetlike opening into which you spoke. Then there was a whole jumble of cogs, springs, levers, and the rest that looked a bit like the inside of an automatic servant's brain, and at the far end, a pen. When you spoke into the trumpet, the device wrote out your words. But whenever Papa tried, it always came out with so many *oh*s, *ah*s, and *er*s that it was almost incomprehensible. He was always promising to invent a better one that missed out the *oh*s, *ah*s, and *er*s, but he'd never gotten around to it, so he still wrote his messages by hand.

"I don't know what Mr. Davidson must have thought of me." Papa smiled. "But all was not lost! Mr. Davidson has agreed to start your lessons tomorrow rather than wait for next week!"

I closed my eyes. "Tomorrow."

"I knew you'd be pleased. I feel guilty that I left you without a tutor for so long. Indeed, I was under the impression that you already had a tutor, if you can believe it." He beamed widely. "But I trust you have been educating yourself on your own?"

I cursed Jane silently. This was absolutely the last time I was going to help one of my sisters with anything. Ever.

I pulled from my pocket the device the thief had dropped. "Do you know what this is?"

"Honestly, Edward," Putty huffed.

Papa took it and studied it for a moment. Then he gave it a twist. Several dozen tiny levers appeared from the side of the cylinder, rotating and moving in and out, like the legs of a strange deep-sea creature.

"It's a key," Papa said. "Fourth Age manufacture, certainly. You can tell from the fine engravings on the metal. It is almost as though the mechanicians of the age were attempting to deny their civilization's impending collapse through the art of their creations." He looked up. "It is a fine souvenir. However, the lock it fits is undoubtedly lost beneath the desert sands."

"So it's not something you would use to break into a house, or something like that?"

Papa squinted at me. "What a peculiar idea. No. This would have been designed for a specific lock."

I took it back and replaced it in my pocket. "Thank you."

So had the thief stolen the key from Lady Harleston because there was a particular lock it fitted? Or had she brought it along knowing the lock was in Lady Harleston's house?

And what exactly was hidden behind that lock?

Doom

Putty and I spent the next few hours quizzing as many of the museum's curators as we could, but even though a few had seen Rothan Gal in the museum, no one had seen what had happened to him and no one seemed to have noticed the man with the broad hat who had been watching us in the gallery.

When we got home, Olivia was waiting for me in my bedroom.

"There you are," she said as I pushed the door open. "You missed all the excitement." She was sitting on the chair next to my window, reading a letter, which she folded up quickly when I entered. Another letter from Freddie, I guessed. I had no idea what he found to write about so often. Certainly it wasn't about catching the elusive Dr. Blood.

I shrugged off my jacket. "You have no idea," I said. "What happened?"

Olivia grinned. "Mrs. Lewis called on Mama."

I groaned. Mrs. Lewis, of all people. Whenever Mama's biggest rival called, it was always a disaster. "What happened this time?"

Olivia's grin widened. "We're going to the ball."

"Good luck with that." I didn't know what Olivia was smiling about. "I thought you hated balls?"

"You and Putty are coming, too."

I gaped. "I beg your pardon?" How on Mars were *we* going to the ball? Children never went to balls. They were strictly for adults. "How did we get invited?"

"Oh, we didn't. Mrs. Lewis was crowing about being invited to more events than Mama, so Mama said we'd been invited to Lady Harleston's ball, and Mrs. Lewis said, 'Oh, everyone's invited to that,' and Mama said actually our whole family was invited, including you and Putty, which is ridiculous. Of course, none of us was actually invited at all, but Mama's not letting that stop her. I hope you like dancing." She stopped. "Are you all right, Edward? You look pale."

I felt pale. In fact, I felt paler than a frightened ghost fish in a snowstorm.

"Whose ball did you say it was?" I stammered.

"Lady Harleston's. You must know of her."

"Oh, yes," I croaked. "I know of her." Only too well. After all, I'd stared right into her face just last night as she'd bellowed *thief* down at me. "Do we have to go?"

"Are you going to argue with Mama?"

No one argued with Mama. Not when she was on one of her missions. I could have my leg torn off by a sea serpent and Mama would still make me go. She'd just make me hop. . . .

Maybe it would be all right. Maybe Putty and I could keep out of Lady Harleston's way. Maybe we could wear disguises. Maybe she wouldn't recognize us after all. She wouldn't expect to see a pair of thieves turn up at her party. Would she?

Oh, God. This was *not* going to end well.

⸺◆⸺

When I'd seen Lady Harleston's grand town house last night, it had been in shadow, lit only by the stars and the glow of the Martian moons and with a thief shinning her way down a rope. Now, though, it was almost as bright as day. Photon emission globes in dozens of colors, floating on balloons or swooping about on small spring-powered propellers, filled the air above it, and thin laces of light had been strung over the whole façade.

When we'd uncovered the dragon tomb, it had been lit by webs of these glass fibers. It hadn't taken Papa long to unlock their secrets, and within months his new manufactory at the edge of Lunae City had begun to churn them out. Now they were the latest fashion, and Lady Harleston was clearly trying to outdo her social circle with this display.

Our automatic carriage waited in line with two dozen others to draw up to Lady Harleston's house. It would have been quicker to hop out and hurry along the street on foot, but apparently that would have been a dreadful breach of etiquette. Although, turning up without an invitation and with your children in tow was apparently all right in Mama's book.

No, I didn't understand it, either.

"Lady Harleston is supposed to be ridiculously rich," Olivia said from the other side of the carriage.

"Olivia!" Mama said, fanning herself. "That is entirely improper."

"Everyone says she inherited a fortune from her late husband," Olivia continued. "Although they also say that her husband lived like a pauper, which either means he was squirreling his fortune away or that she has another source of income that no one knows about."

"Olivia!" Mama snapped. "Enough!"

Olivia winked at me. "Forgive me, Mama. But did you hear the news? Lady Harleston's house was broken into last night. Thieves raided her study and stole her Ancient Martian artifacts."

"That is not a proper topic for conversation," Mama said. "Thieves, indeed!"

"She's offered a reward for their capture and the return of her property," Olivia went on, unbowed. She grinned at Putty. "I'm surprised you're not already out hunting down the perpetrators."

"Parthenia will do no such thing while she is *my* charge," Miss Wilkins said coldly. She was sitting as straight as a rod opposite Putty. "She might have been allowed to run wild while under the care of others, but I am *quite* a different proposition. It is not in me to indulge such nonsense. A young lady does not speak without first being spoken to. She does not leave the house unaccompanied and without permission. She does not fill her mind with mechanisms or science. She sews. She plays music. She sings. She dances when asked to. She engages in polite but inconsequential conversation. I *will* make a proper young lady of Parthenia."

Mama nodded approvingly.

Putty gave me a pleading look. I cleared my throat awkwardly. "Did it say anything about the thieves or what they took?"

"Just a description," Olivia said. "There were two of them. Children, the witnesses said."

"I do not know what their parents could be thinking," Mama said, with a sniff. "I have always believed that a firm hand and a necessary intolerance will soon put an end to such nonsense. You may see the results in Jane."

Jane's cheeks reddened and her gaze dropped.

"You are so right, Mama," Olivia purred. She pulled out a flier. "The older thief is described as about twelve years of age, with light brown hair and a nondescript face. It says the younger was ratty and pinched of face."

"Ratty?" Putty squawked. "Edward, that's—"

I kicked her.

"Do you recognize the description?" Olivia asked sweetly.

"No," I said.

"Indeed, why should we recognize such miscreants?" Mama said.

She drew herself up as the carriage moved forward again. If it hadn't been for the nervous flutter of her hands at her waist, I would never have guessed she wasn't as confident as a king. Her fan trembled against her reticule.

We were almost at the steps of Lady Harleston's house now. Even though this was all Mama's fault, my stomach tightened in sympathy. There was no way we would be allowed in. All the ladies in Mama's social circle would be there to witness it. She would be humiliated.

I had no idea how she would stand it.

With a deep breath, Mama swept out of our automatic carriage, followed by Papa and the rest of the family. All around, carriages and personal fliers were disgorging beautifully dressed guests. I felt shabby and drab by comparison. Right at the foot of the steps, I saw the Chinese consul and his retinue making their way up to the wide-open front door.

I'd managed to persuade Putty to wear a too-large bonnet to cover her features, and I'd found the largest hat I could to shade my face from view. I tugged it lower and hoped I wouldn't run into Lady Harleston.

Mama surged through the press, pulling us in her wake like flotsam caught in the wash of a big ship. Putty was complaining of something behind me, but I shut out the noise.

We took our place in the line making its way up the steps.

"Professor Sullivan, Mrs. Sullivan," Mama announced to the butler standing at the top of the steps. "And children."

A titter ran around the crowd at that last bit. I stared straight ahead.

The butler looked impassively down at Mama. "I am sorry, madam. Your names are not on the list."

Mama reddened, but she stood her ground. "Then your list is incorrect. Lady Harleston herself expressly invited us. Please check again."

The conversations around us quieted to excited whispers. I could feel dozens of eyes on us. I bit my lip and forced myself not to reach out to support Mama. A nest of claw-worms churned in my stomach. Mama's shoulders were rigid.

The butler did not move. "I would remember, madam. I must ask you to leave."

"Do you not know who I am?" Mama said, her voice cracking on the last word. "I am a personal friend of—"

"If you were invited, madam, I would know who you were."

My nails bit into my hands as we stood there, immobile. Everyone was looking at us. I could hear laughter like breaking glasses around us. If I could have sunk into the ground, I would have.

Still Mama didn't move. I wasn't even sure she could.

The butler raised a hand, and a couple of footmen moved forward. We were going to be thrown out bodily. The humiliation in front of the whole of Lunae City society would kill Mama. She already looked ready to shatter.

"Is that Professor Sullivan?" a voice called from the doorway.

I glanced up. Lady Harleston had appeared to investigate the disturbance. I scarcely recognized her from last night. Her long hair had been elegantly pinned up, with curls falling to either side of her face, and she was wearing a bright green gown. I quickly looked down to hide my face beneath my hat.

"Madam," Papa said stiffly.

"I have been meaning to consult with you, sir," Lady Harleston said. "I have come into possession of some particular artifacts that I am struggling to understand. I had hoped to ask for your assistance."

Papa bowed. "I am at your service, madam."

Lady Harleston waved a hand. "Then please come in. We are having a ball. I am sure your family will find it diverting while I show you my devices."

The footmen stepped back. I had to grab Mama's elbow to support her as her knees gave way.

It was her only moment of weakness before she straightened her spine and stepped past the butler, barely favoring him with a look.

⊷◈⊶

The ball was already a mill of noise and light. Dozens of guests drifted from room to room, admiring the displays of Ancient Martian artifacts. A delicate flier hung from the ceiling of the entrance hall, suspended by wires. Half a dozen wings spread, as fragile and glittering as dragonfly wings, above a scooped body. In one corner, one of the original, hulking automatic servants stood, its innards laid open for the guests to poke at.

I found a secluded corner and dragged Putty into it.

"Stay here and keep your head down," I told her.

Miss Wilkins settled close by, just out of earshot, and fixed Putty with an unwavering gaze.

"I want to see Lady Harleston's collection," Putty protested.

Papa was already accompanying Lady Harleston up the grand staircase.

"If she catches sight of you, the only thing you'll see is the inside of a militia cell, and believe me, that's not much fun."

"She'd have to catch me first," Putty said.

Olivia slid in beside us. "I see you've found somewhere to hide."

"Shouldn't you be dancing?" I said.

"Jane will dance enough for all of us."

"If you two are going to talk about dancing and romance and suchlike all night, I'm going to be sick," Putty said.

Olivia stuck out her tongue. "You wait three or four years. You'll be worse than Jane."

Putty glowered back. "No, I won't. I'll be a sailor on Captain Kol's boat. Or maybe I'll join the British Martian army and fight Napoleon."

"You'll only be thirteen."

"I'll be almost fourteen. I think I'll be a captain. I'd be jolly fierce, and my company would capture every one of the emperor's eagles. So there."

"Except Napoleon is not going to invade Mars," I said. "The only way here is by the dragon paths, and the Martian governments have surrounded them with gun platforms. His ships would be blown to pieces."

Putty gave me a furious look. "If *I* were Napoleon, I could figure out a way past the gun platforms."

"Well, it's a good thing you're not," I said.

Olivia looked down. "Let's talk about something else, shall we?"

Her voice had shaken and she looked nervous. Her hands were clasping and unclasping.

"What's wrong?" I asked.

"Nothing. I'm just worried about Freddie."

I peered at her. "Why?"

She looked away. "He's on Earth. In England. Napoleon might not be able to invade Mars, but he *will* invade England. When you start talking about the emperor, all I can think is about Freddie getting caught up in the war. I couldn't bear it."

I frowned. "What's he doing in England? Did Dr. Blood flee to Earth?"

Olivia glanced around and her voice dropped. "The British-Martian Intelligence Service gave him a new assignment. They said Dr. Blood wasn't a priority anymore."

I knew I must be turning red, but I couldn't help myself. "Not a priority! He killed people. He almost killed us!"

"I know. Freddie didn't have a choice. He kept going as long as he could, but . . ." She shrugged helplessly. "He said he'd get someone to keep an eye on us in case Dr. Blood came back."

"Well, it doesn't look like his friend has turned up," I said. "Why didn't you tell us?"

If anything, Olivia looked even more miserable. "I couldn't. You know his missions are secret. He shouldn't even have told me. He made me swear I wouldn't tell anyone else, but I'm worried, Edward."

"Freddie can look after himself," I said. "Anyway, he's a spy, not a soldier. There's no reason for him to get involved in fighting."

Olivia's head drooped. "I hope you're right. I really do." She looked back up. "Edward, Putty. You must mention nothing of what I said. Do you understand? Freddie's mission is top secret. I shouldn't have said anything to you, and you mustn't repeat it."

"I am excessively good at keeping secrets," Putty said. "Edward never knows what I'm up to."

I stood. "Don't worry about it. Really. He'll be safe. Now, I'm going to find something to eat." I glared back at Putty as I made my way through the crowd. "Don't move."

⬥

The party had spread beyond the ballroom. Loud groups stood in every hallway and room. Automatic footmen moved almost silently, driven by the flat springs in their chests, carrying drinks, but I couldn't see food anywhere. Putty and I had missed lunch while we interrogated the museum curators, and Mama had hurried us so quickly through dinner I'd hardly had a chance to snatch a roasted stemfruit before the automatic servants had cleared it all away again. My stomach rumbled so loudly I should have been able to detect food through echolocation, like a bat.

I headed for the back of the house. Maybe there would be a way down to the kitchens.

The sounds of the party faded away. Apart from the odd echoing laugh or shout, and the faint music from the small orchestra in the ballroom, this part of the house was silent. Even the clockwork moths that flitted endlessly back and forth, carrying messages among the partygoers, were absent. I poked my head into various darkened rooms, even rooting around what looked like a private dining room, but there was nothing.

Eventually, though, I came across a narrow servants' door that opened onto darkness. I peered into the gloom, trying to see if it led down to the kitchens. If I didn't get something to eat soon, I'd start gnawing on my own arm.

Yes! That was the smell of something baking. I licked my lips hungrily.

A single footstep sounded behind me, then a hand shoved me so violently I fell through the doorway. I stumbled, almost losing my footing. Steep, shadowed stairs dropped away before me. I teetered, grabbing for support, but before I could, more hands grabbed hold of me and pushed me back against the wall. My head bounced off the plaster, sending stars shooting across my vision.

I tried to pull my arms free, but someone was holding them. I blinked furiously to clear my eyes.

When I could see again, Lady Harleston was staring impassively down at me. Two of her footmen stood, one on either side of me, pinning my arms back.

"Well," Lady Harleston said. "I am impressed. I really had not expected to see your face again. You show courage, if not sense." She smiled serenely. "Now I have you."

A Desperate Plan

There was hardly any room on this narrow landing at the top of the dark stairs. I was shoved against the back wall, held tight by the footmen, while Lady Harleston pressed in far too close. All they would have to do was give me a quick shove and I'd go tumbling down the steps.

I'd probably break my neck.

"What do you want?" I demanded. I was sweating and my chest felt tight. The footmen had forced my arms too high, and they hurt. I was half dangling like a badly stuffed scarecrow. It was hard to look innocent like that. I gave it my best shot, though. "You've got the wrong person."

Lady Harleston laughed. It didn't much sound like she found it funny. "You know, because I am a woman, some men think that I must be weak or stupid, or that they can take advantage of me. I have had to teach those men some very painful lessons." She leaned closer until I could feel her breath brushing against my cheek. It was hot and damp, like the breath of a trapdoor-wolf. "Do not take me for a fool, boy. I already have your accomplice."

"What?" I pulled against the footmen, but it was no good. I couldn't get free.

While I'd been wandering around like an idiot, looking for food, they must have isolated Putty somehow then grabbed her. Maybe she'd slipped away; she was good at that. *Hell!* I should have stuck to her like glue-ant spit.

"I saw you both sneak in behind Professor Sullivan's party," Lady Harleston said.

"Let her go!" I said, struggling uselessly.

"I don't think so. You stole some things from me, and I would very much like them back."

"You're got it all wrong!" I said. "We didn't steal anything. We're not thieves. We're . . ." I didn't really want to say this, not here, like this. "We're Professor Sullivan's children. Ask him!"

Lady Harleston's face darkened. "You still think I'm a fool, don't you? You still think you can take advantage of me. Maybe you think I'll become distracted and you'll get a chance to run. Or maybe you think I'll just let you go." She snorted. "Maybe I need to convince you how serious I am."

"It's the truth. Fetch him and you'll see."

"I have a better idea," Lady Harleston said. "I will bring

fig. 13

Lady ⟷ Harleston

THE EMPEROR OF MARS

you your accomplice's finger instead. How about that? The little finger first, I think. Then maybe you'll believe that I'm serious."

"No!" I shouted, bucking against the restraining hands. "I'll get your stuff. I will! I promise."

Lady Harleston tilted her head and gazed at me with cool eyes. "That's better. Then go. Your time is growing short, and I am not a patient woman."

She stepped aside, and the footmen half pushed, half carried me toward the door. My feet scrabbled for the floor like I'd been electrocuted.

"If you do not return, boy," Lady Harleston called after me, "trust me, I will find you, and we will not have a happy reunion."

⊰◈⊱

The hulking footmen hauled me through a servant's corridor, avoiding the party, and shoved me down the steps to the street outside. They stood with their arms crossed, faces impassive, as I picked myself up and looked around.

There was no way past them back into the house, no way to tell Papa or even Olivia what had happened and get their help. *Damnation!* Putty and I should never have come. Why hadn't we thought of a way out of it?

Despite the noise spilling from Lady Harleston's party, I felt like I was walking in an underwater bubble as I stumbled across the street. All the sounds were dulled and muffled.

I wouldn't be able to track down the thief in time, and even if I could, why would she hand over everything she'd stolen?

And what if I found her, got everything back, and gave it to Lady Harleston? Would she just let Putty and me walk away? Any other Society hostess like Mama might. They'd probably hand us over to the militia, but that would be all right. Papa would sort things out. Lady Harleston was different, though. I couldn't imagine Mama threatening to cut off someone's fingers. There was a very good chance Lady Harleston wouldn't let either of us go.

An automatic carriage swerved around me, its cogs clashing. The driver shouted something at me. I had no idea what. I staggered out of the road and leaned heavily against the wall of a house.

Why had I been so stupid? Why had I kept the key cylinder? Why had I stood outside Lady Harleston's house chatting to Putty right after it had been burgled? Why had I stared up at Lady Harleston so she could get a good look at my face? What had I been *thinking*? This was my fault, all of it.

Every window of Lady Harleston's house was brightly lit, and the street was full of people coming and going. I'd lurched past them, hardly noticing them pointing and laughing as I went. Not a single one of them would believe Lady Harleston had kidnapped my little sister.

I had no choice. I was going to have to rescue her all by myself.

I slid into a darkened alley, then started to run.

—◆—

It took me almost an hour to get everything I needed. The party was louder than ever when I got back. Several of the windows had been thrown open, and the sound of conversation and laughter, and the faint strains of music, drifted into the street.

I was still in time. That might be my only stroke of luck. This plan was so full of holes, I could have used it as a sieve. If I'd had a week to prepare, maybe I'd be ready. But if I'd had a week to think about it, I'd never have had the courage to do something so stupid.

I settled my sack on my shoulder, took a deep breath, and started up the steps to the house.

One of the footmen was waiting. This one looked like he spent his spare time fighting with scorpion-bears. Either that or banging his face against walls. If I tried to hit him, I'd break my hand. Lucky my plan didn't involve a punch-up.

The footman grabbed my arm and pulled me into the shadows beside the door.

"Show me," he snarled.

I opened the neck of the sack just wide enough to show him the key cylinder. If he asked to see more, this would go horribly wrong. I'd shoved a few of Papa's old manuscripts in there to maintain the illusion, and I doubted the footman could read the ideograms on them. But I had no idea what else the thief had stolen, and there were things in there that I didn't want the footman to see.

He reached in and shoveled through the papers. I stood motionless, not daring to breathe. There would be no point running. Not while Lady Harleston still held Putty.

With a grunt, the footman let the papers fall back. "Follow me."

A servants' staircase led up to the fourth floor. The footman followed close behind me.

"If I was going to run away, don't you think I'd have done it outside?" I muttered.

The footman shoved me so hard I tripped over the next stair.

"All right," I said.

I wouldn't feel any sympathy for this one.

I slipped on the brass goggles with the thick, dark lenses that I'd borrowed from Papa's workshop. In the darkness of the stairwell, I could scarcely see a thing. I stumbled on.

Lady Harleston was waiting for us in her study, sitting behind her desk, working on some papers. She looked up, removing a pair of eyeglasses, as we entered. At one end of the desk, the skeleton of a rotary eagle had been posed on a bare branch in a glass case. Its head moved jerkily under the control of a tiny clockwork motor, turning to follow my movements as I was pushed into the room. The walls were lined with polished wormwood shelves and every shelf was packed with manuscripts, books, and fragments of stone-work carved with ideograms. A dozen mysterious Ancient Martian devices stood in cabinets and display cases around the room.

Apart from a second footman, Lady Harleston was alone. When the heavy door closed behind us, the sounds of the party were cut off. No one would hear any shouts or screams through it. The windows were firmly closed and shuttered, despite the heat in the room. Lady Harleston didn't want anyone to know what she was doing here. I shivered. That wasn't good. It meant she had something nasty in mind.

So did I. I just hoped it would work.

"Where is she?" I demanded.

Lady Harleston looked up at my goggles in amusement. "Is that supposed to be another disguise? It's no better than your ridiculous hat. Have you brought my property?"

I reached into the sack and pulled out the key cylinder. Lady Harleston nodded.

"Good. Now the rest of it. Not the toys. The valuable artifacts and papers."

I kept my face blank. The key cylinder was just a toy? Maybe the thief hadn't been after it at all. Maybe she'd just grabbed it on the way out. Maybe she didn't even realize or care that she'd lost it. *Blast.*

"Show me my friend," I said, forcing my voice to stay steady. I'd spent the whole time while I was preparing for this worried about what they might be doing to Putty. I'd been scared that I might be too late. "I want to see she's all right."

Lady Harleston's expression didn't change. "That's not how this works. The way this works is that you hand over what you stole. What happens to you afterward is entirely up to me. You don't really have any options here."

Yeah? We'd see about that. I moistened my lips. "This had better work."

Lady Harleston's head rose. "What's that?"

I pulled back my hand. "Catch."

I tossed the key cylinder into the air. Lady Harleston came out of her chair, her eyes following the arc of the key cylinder as it flew across the room. My hand darted into the sack again.

"Sorry, Putty." I pulled out one of her experimental photon emission globes. It was dull and dark, but inside, the focused brightness of the sun had been captured. If I flicked the switch, it would send an electrostatic charge across the surface of the device, changing the properties of the enclosing glass, allowing the sunlight to leak out in a gentle glow.

I didn't flick the switch. As Lady Harleston grasped for the falling key cylinder, I flung the photon emission device against the wall.

The glass shattered and the stored sunlight erupted in a single burst. Even through my darkened goggles, the light was painfully bright, but I was expecting it, and I was already racing across the carpet.

Lady Harleston screamed and her footmen shouted in agony as the light burned into their eyes. The key cylinder clattered to the floor. I scooped it up as I ran.

A small door had been cut in the wall behind Lady Harleston's desk, then partially disguised with the same wallpaper as the rest of the room. It had clearly been meant for the servants, but Lady Harleston's footman had brought me through the main door. That meant the servants' door was used for something else.

Lady Harleston stumbled past, shouting with pain. Her long dress tangled around her legs and she sprawled onto the floor.

It was dark behind the servants' door. I pulled off my goggles. Narrow stairs led both up and down. Which way? I'd only get one chance.

Lady Harleston would want Putty as far from the party as possible. I muttered a prayer for luck. *Up.*

I took the stairs three at a time.

Behind me, I heard Lady Harleston shouting, and voices calling back, questioning.

A door loomed out of the dark above, blocking the stairs. My shoulder thumped into it, and I bounced back. I grabbed the handle and shook it. The door was locked.

I reached into the sack again.

Papa had always refused to work on weapons, no matter how much pressure the British Martian government put on him, but with the right imagination, anything could be turned into a weapon.

The mechanism I brought out had originally been designed as a safety device for workers on high buildings. It could clamp tight on to any surface and easily support the weight of several men. Unfortunately, construction bosses had little interest in spending money on safety. Labor was cheap and mechanisms were expensive, so Papa's invention had languished in a corner of his laboratory.

I fixed it over the lock and tested the seal. A land-whale couldn't have pulled it free. Which was good, because on the strong ceramic ring that jutted from the back of the clamp, I fixed one of Papa's other inventions. The elephant-lifter was no bigger than a football, but the tightly wound springs within it drove a propeller with such power it could lift a block of stone the size of a carriage.

I stepped back, and turned the device on full.

The elephant-lifter blasted away with the force of a cannon-ball. The thick wooden door was no match for it. The clamp ripped the lock from the door and the door half from its hinges. The blast of air made me stagger.

The elephant-lifter crashed into the ceiling, then clattered and spun down the stairwell, smashing the wooden stairs, while its gyroscopes struggled to steady it. I heard a shout of alarm from below, but I was already running through the doorway.

I came out into the attic. Old furniture, trunks, and packing cases were stacked nearly head high. And there, tied to a heavy chair, which itself was bolted to the floorboards, was Putty.

Her eyes boggled as I came racing in.

"Where have you been?" she demanded as I pulled her gag off. "Honestly, Edward. This is the slowest rescue I've ever seen. If I were rescuing you, we'd be home already."

"Well, we're not," I said, tugging at the knots binding her. "And we're about to have company."

"I was starting to think I was going to have to free myself. Which I would have done, and with less noise."

"You never did anything with less noise," I said.

Putty shook her wrists as I finally freed her. "So, what's the escape plan?"

"Yeah," I said. "About that . . ."

I had planned to use the elephant-lifter to send us soaring out of one of the windows and away over the rooftops.

"I didn't exactly have much time," I mumbled.

Putty looked superior. "You should never enter a building unless you have your escape route planned."

"Did you read that in one of my magazines?"

"Yes. And it wasn't a very believable story. If I had been Captain Masters, I would—"

"You do know we're about to be captured?" I said. There were voices on the stairs now. Lots of them.

"Throw something at them," Putty suggested.

"Let's just look for a way out," I said.

There was a shuttered gable at one end of the attic. Thin Martian moonlight slipped through the slats in dusty lines. I squeezed past the mounds of furniture and clambered up.

The window protested as I hauled it open, and I had to kick the shutters to free them. The rooftops of the town houses stretched away to the north. To the south, the twisting, organic native Martian buildings looked like strange, thin arms reaching up to the dark sky.

We were five floors up, and the street below was still full of light and people. Voices approached from the stairs.

I had a steel-worm rope coiled in the bottom of my sack, but I'd intended to tie it to the safety clamp and attach it to a wall if we needed it, and the clamp was gone along with the elephant-lifter. I couldn't see anywhere I would trust to support our weight.

"They're almost here, Edward!" Putty hissed.

Our pursuers must have realized there were no more projectiles coming down the stairs at them. Feet thumped up the last few steps.

I gave Putty a push. "Get out on the roof."

I pulled the last of my borrowed devices out of the sack. It was a metal container not much bigger than a jam jar. I flipped off the lid and tossed it into the attic.

Cloud mites were another one of Papa's inventions that had never really caught on. These miniature devices, almost too small to be seen with the naked eye, carried a powerful electric charge. As they erupted into the attic, they spread in a cloud, and the electric charge pulled the dust from every surface. They'd been intended to clean a room, but the effect as the dust was ripped into the air from packing cases and furniture was thicker than smoke.

The last thing I saw before the room went dark was one of Lady Harleston's footmen watching us from the entrance to the attic. Then the dust grew too thick, and our pursuers were hidden from view.

— 6 —

The Thief

Unfortunately, we hadn't gotten away with it quite that easily.

When we finally reached home, Mama and Miss Wilkins were sitting in the entrance hall, perched stiffly on hard-backed chairs like a pair of furious dragon statues guarding a temple.

"I know," Putty said brightly as we hurried in the front door. "Why don't I go to bed! I am tired, and I'm quite young to be up this late." She yawned theatrically.

"Oh, no," I said, taking her shoulder. "You're not escaping." This might be my fault, but I saw no reason to face Mama and Miss Wilkins on my own.

Mama's face was like stone. "What," she demanded, "is the meaning of this?"

I put on my most innocent expression. "Did no one tell you, Mama?" I said, trying to sound surprised.

Mama drew herself up. "Tell us what, pray?"

"That Putty was feeling sick so I decided to take her home."

"But—" Putty started. I kicked her shin. "Ouch! You kicked me! Mama, Edward kicked me!"

"You should have come to me." Miss Wilkins's voice was colder than a glacier. "It would have been proper for me to have taken Parthenia home in the carriage."

I could have argued. I could have told them the truth, that Lady Harleston had kidnapped us and almost tortured Putty. But Mama would never believe us. Even *I* found it hard to believe.

"Forgive us, Mama," I said. "I didn't want to interrupt the ball. I knew how important it was to you."

Mama's eyes narrowed, but I kept my face downcast and my shoulders slumped. Eventually, she nodded imperiously, and we slunk away.

Exhausted from the long day, I fell into bed without even bothering to get undressed.

Which turned out to be a good thing, because it seemed like only a few minutes later that I awoke and knew there was someone in my room.

——◆——

I rolled over, letting my hand drop over the far side of the bed. It closed around the cudgel clipped to the frame. The weapon had a lead core and was heavy enough to fell a charging fire-bull. I pulled it free and came up into a crouch.

"Are you really going to hit me with that?"

Whose voice was that? I recognized it, but . . . I snatched up my auto-flint and lit a candle.

The thief was sitting in a chair a couple of feet from my bed.

"Do you know you snore?" she said.

I grabbed my sheet and pulled it over me, then felt ridiculous because I was still fully dressed.

"What are you doing here?" I demanded. "How did you even find me?"

The window was ajar, and the faint sounds of the Lunae Planum night drifted through: strange shrieks of hunting dart-bats, the low, distant singing of the native Martian boat crews, and the barking howl of a sand otter. Maybe that was what had woken me. The thief hadn't made any noise, even though she'd crossed my cluttered floor and settled in my old chair. I grimaced as I caught sight of the piles of clothes heaped on the floor. The automatic servants had obviously gotten lost in the Flame House again and not tidied. Now I wished I'd taken a few minutes to do it myself.

"You told me where you live," she said. "And you have something of mine. You must do."

"Something of yours?"

She looked away. "Yeah."

"Something you stole, you mean."

She looked back at me with those incredibly dark eyes, and I felt my mouth turn dry. "You have it, though, don't you? It wasn't where I must have dropped it. I went back to check."

I worked my mouth to bring moisture to my lips. How did she manage to make me feel like this? It had been the same last night. One look and I lost all my sense.

"I was going to look for you," I said. "To give it back, I mean." Only I'd had no idea how to find her.

She cocked her head to one side. "Really? Why? I wouldn't have given it back to you."

I squirmed awkwardly. "It just . . . seemed like the right thing to do."

She frowned at me. "I don't understand you. You're different. Strange." She shrugged. "So where is it? I tried searching your house while you were asleep, but it is kind of a maze. Did you know one of your rooms is missing a floor?"

I looked at her curiously. Lady Harleston had said the key cylinder was just a toy, but the thief had gone to a lot of trouble to get it back. She'd even risked waiting for me to wake up when I could have turned her over to the militia.

"What's so important about this? I mean, it's just an old key, right? What good is it to you?"

She passed a hand over her face, and for a moment she looked exhausted. "I can't tell you. Really. I can't. I don't even know."

"Someone paid you to steal it?"

She shook her head. "Look, do you have it? Do you want me to pay you for it?" She looked around my room. "Although I don't suppose I could pay you enough. You've got

fig. 02

Mina

THE EMPEROR OF MARS

everything. You could fit a whole family in this room and still have spare space."

"I can't imagine my mother being happy with that."

She laughed, then her hand flew to her mouth and she looked around guiltily.

"Don't worry," I said. "No one will hear." Not since I'd stuffed a pair of socks in the speaking tube Putty had fixed between our bedrooms.

"It must be strange," the thief said. "Living with your family, I mean."

"You don't?"

She shook her head. "It was just me and my brother. We had a room in the orphanage, but when he got too old, they threw him out. He had to leave Lunae City to find a job. They wouldn't let me go with him, so then it was just me." She looked awkwardly away. "Until a few months ago, anyway. Then our dad turned up, but you know, it's still just me."

"I'm sorry," I said.

"It doesn't matter. We had each other. You have to trust your brother, don't you? Or your sisters, I suppose, for you. No matter what. Anyway, we did a lot better than most people. I'm not complaining."

"I guess." I swung myself out of bed and padded across the room.

When Sir William Flanders had designed the Flame House, along with all the other bad decisions he'd made, he'd forgotten to fit furniture until it was almost too late. He hadn't left any space for a wardrobe in this room. He had, however, accidentally left an enormous empty space under the floor in the corner of my room. So my wardrobe was actually beneath my washstand. I hinged the washstand into a gap in the wall, then tugged on a pulley system to raise the wardrobe out of the floor.

The key cylinder was no use to me, and after the way she'd acted, I wasn't going to give it back to Lady Harleston. If the thief needed it, then as far as I was concerned, she should have it.

I had buried the key cylinder beneath a pile of my clothes at the foot of the wardrobe so that no one would see it even if they glanced in. I dropped to my knees and pulled the clothes away.

The key wasn't there. I burrowed through the clothes, throwing them aside.

Nothing. *Damnation.* What had happened to it?

I turned back to the thief. She was gazing at me with a desperate, unguarded expression. My throat tightened. It actually hurt when I tried to speak.

"I . . . I think it's been stolen."

Her eyes widened as though I'd slapped her. "Are you trying to be funny? Is this just a game to you?"

"No," I protested, jumping up. "I left it here. Right before I went to bed. It's gone."

The thief's face whitened. "It can't be." Her hands clenched into fists. "I have to have it. I *have* to."

I stared helplessly at her. "Couldn't you . . . I don't know . . . pay back the person who paid you to steal it? I could help," I hurried on. "With money, I mean, if you need it. If you can't afford it."

She was already shaking her head.

"You don't understand. It's not for a client. It's for my father. He needs it." She pushed her fists into her eyes. "He really needs it. I . . . I didn't even know I had a father until a few months ago. I can't let him down." She shook her head. "You don't know what it's like not having parents."

I pushed the wardrobe back into the floor. It closed with a *thunk* that sounded like my whole mood turning to stone and falling down between my feet.

"I'll find it," I said. "I promise. I'll get it for you." Somehow.

She took a deep breath and rubbed her hand across her face. "Thank you. You don't have to. I know that. So thank you."

"Let's meet again," I said. "Tomorrow. If I've got it, I'll bring it. Not here. How about outside the museum? At one o'clock?"

"I'll be there," she said. "I'll be waiting."

I was having trouble breathing, so I just nodded.

On soft feet, she padded to my window and swung it open. She looked back at me.

"I'm Mina," she said.

"Edward," I croaked.

"I know," she said, and then she was gone.

⤙◆⤚

The first thing I did the next morning—after having breakfast, anyway—was to go looking for the key cylinder, and I had a pretty good idea who might help me find it.

Putty wasn't in her room, and she wasn't in the nursery. Eventually, I found her skulking under a cluster of mirror bushes near the wall where our small estate bordered the river.

"If Miss Wilkins finds you've snuck out of the nursery again, she'll use your skin for a new hat," I said.

"Oh, don't worry," Putty said airily. "She went out on an errand. I have several alarms set up around the house in case she gets back, and a rope ladder up to my room. And this."

She pulled up a strange device. It looked like a spyglass that tapered to a narrow rubber tube, which in turn disappeared into the red Martian grass.

"Er . . . good?" I said.

Putty rolled her eyes. "You don't recognize it, do you?"

"Not personally."

She sighed, then passed it to me. "Take a look."

I put the device to my eye and squinted into it. It was like looking at a picture by candlelight through a dirty window. Except it wasn't a picture, because it showed the gate to our estate, and the balloon-palm trees were swaying in the light breeze. Clouds drifted across the scene. When I moved the device about, the scene stayed fixed.

"Is it a spyglass?" I said. "How does it stay fixed on the gate?" I lowered the device. "In fact, how does it even see the gate?" The house was between us and it.

"Sometimes I wonder what you do with your time, Edward," Putty said. "Papa and I have been working on this for the last three months." She picked up the rubber tube. "This is an optical cable." I must have looked blank—I did that a lot around Putty—because she went on, "You remember those threads of light in the dragon tomb and on Lady Harleston's house? They're made out of flexible glass that lets light travel along the inside. Well, Papa and I modified them so that the light wouldn't come out the sides but would travel all the way down the cable."

I gave her a blank look. "What's the point of that?"

She stared at me. "Isn't it obvious?"

"Not really."

"You're very exasperating. Think about it. When you look down this end, you see the light that's come in the other end. You see what the other end is pointing at. We thought that it would be a good communication device. The person at one end writes a message on a piece of paper and holds it up to the lens. Then the person at this end looks in and can see the message. Only, the light seems to fade with distance, so it's not much good after a couple of miles. We're working on improving the glass."

"So, let me get this straight," I said. "You and Papa spent three months inventing this incredible, magical communication system—"

"It's not magic, Edward. That would be ridiculous."

"And you set it up so that you could spy on our gate and see Miss Wilkins coming back. You know. Instead of doing something useful with it."

"Of course."

"And instead of spending your time in the nice, comfortable nursery with whatever books or inventions you fancy, you have to lurk in the bushes, peering at the gates through cloudy glass."

"It's the principle of the thing. I'm not going to be beaten by her. This is war, you know."

I peered down the device again. The view was still fixed on the front gate. Putty was going to give herself eyestrain if she kept this up. It wasn't even particularly well focused. But something looked off. Something looked different. I screwed up my eyes, trying to get a better look.

Leaning against a tree, hidden by the shade beneath a balloon-palm on the far side of the road, was a man.

He wasn't doing anything much. Just leaning casually against the tree. But he was clearly watching the estate, and anyone who entered or left would have to do so right in front of him. I squinted harder. Although the view was murky, I could make out the wide hat and the dark brown skin.

"That's the man from the museum!" I said. My heart was

suddenly pounding like I'd run a mile. "How long has he been there?"

"Since I got up," Putty said. "He's not doing anything. He's just watching."

"Why didn't you warn me?" I demanded. "I might have walked out there without realizing."

He must have followed us back from the museum. If he'd been involved in Rothan Gal's disappearance, maybe he thought we were onto him. I didn't like that he knew where we lived.

Putty looked at me in astonishment. "I didn't think anyone used the front gate. I always climb over the wall."

"We could creep up on him," I said. "Capture him. Ask him questions."

"He'd see you coming," Putty said. "He's in a pretty good position. He's exactly where I would have stood. Anyway, he's much bigger than you. He'd knock you silly. Most people do. I could probably capture him, but I'm busy defeating Miss Wilkins, and he's not really doing anything much. We don't even know that he's got anything to do with Rothan Gal."

I shook my head. I'd worry about our watcher later. Putty was right. He wasn't a problem just now.

"Look," I said. "That's not what I want you for."

She perked up. "You wanted me for something? Are we off on an adventure? Are we sneaking into someone else's house? I thought we did pretty well last night."

"We got caught. She was going to kill us."

Putty waved a hand. "I would have gotten us out. Anyway, it was only our first try."

I rubbed a hand across my face. "We're not sneaking into anywhere. No. You see, I was up half the night wondering, and you know what I thought? I thought there was only one person it could possibly be."

"I have no idea what you're talking about, Edward."

"My key cylinder was missing from my wardrobe," I said, "and I couldn't think of anyone who would be poking through my stuff while I was asleep except you. So hand it over."

Putty waved a hand. "Oh, that. It's in my bedroom. I wanted to figure out how it worked. I knew if I left it with you, you'd just give it back to the thief before I had a chance, because you're in love."

I turned red. "I am not! And her name's Mina."

"Of course you're not." She peered into her device again. "Now you'd better get going. Your tutor's on his way and he's carrying *lots* of textbooks."

—◆—

We studied Latin verbs all morning.

I'd never realized just how many of them there were. Hundreds and hundreds of them, like a swarm of dust moths all trying to eat their way into my brain and turn it to powder. Still, if I ever met an actual, live Roman, I would be able to conjugate verbs at him until he thought I was completely mad and left me alone. Which was more than could be said for Mr. Davidson, who seemed determined to stay around and plague me, no matter what.

It was nearly eleven o'clock before my rumbling stomach and drooping head finally registered on Mr. Davidson's consciousness.

"Ten minutes," he warned as I hurried for the door. "Then perhaps we can study some Greek, if that would please you."

"Oh, that's not what would please me right now," I muttered, then headed for Putty's room, taking the shortcut through the crawl room and along the hanging corridor that dangled on ropes above the ballroom.

Putty's bedroom was always a confusion of half-finished projects and dismantled devices. The automatic servants had been banned from it, to avoid unnecessary damage to their mechanisms, and Mama hadn't dared enter any of Putty's rooms for years. Even Miss Wilkins hadn't made any difference to the chaos.

Luckily, Putty hadn't had time to start work on Mina's key cylinder. It lay on her desk among a jumble of tools, hastily scribbled diagrams, and the dead body of a strange deep-river Martian fish.

I shoved the key cylinder into my jacket pocket and hurried off to grab something to eat on the way back to my lessons.

The fastest way to the kitchen took me into Putty's closet, then down a pole between two walls. Gritting my teeth,

I lowered myself through a tangle of squirt-spider webs, then pushed past a wormwood panel into the third-floor hallway, and straightened.

Just along the hallway was the door to Papa's study, and crouched in front of it was a man. He wasn't knocking, and he certainly wasn't just peeping through the keyhole. He was picking the lock.

Bright light streamed into the hallway from the large window at the far end, making me squint, and the figure was dressed in a long coat and drooping hat, so I couldn't make out who it was. The only thing I was sure was that it wasn't Papa or any of my sisters.

"Hey!" I shouted.

The figure jerked back, then spun and ran from me. I took off in pursuit.

A servants' staircase cut down from the far end of the hallway. The intruder snatched open the door and threw himself in. I was there in time to catch the door before it closed completely.

The intruder was already leaping down the uneven stairs, taking them four at a time, risking his life with every leap. I raced in pursuit, one hand on the smooth banister.

We were three floors up, and when the intruder reached the ground floor, he would have a direct route through the kitchen to the gardens. He was taller than me, and faster. If I didn't catch him before he reached the gardens, he was going to get away.

He passed the second-floor landing and flung himself down the next step of stairs. I leaped after him.

I hit the landing just as the door beside it opened. My shoulder slammed into the door, crashing it back. I tried to grab the banister, but I was off balance and already falling.

The floorboards came up to meet me, knocking the breath from my lungs and the sense from my head.

I flailed to pull myself up, but my knees wouldn't hold me and everything was whirling around me.

"Stay still," a voice said.

I slumped back on the floorboards. When I could see again, I saw Jane kneeling over me, looking worried.

"Are you all right, Edward? What's going on?"

I groaned. "I was chasing an intruder. They were trying to break into Papa's study."

"I heard a noise," Jane said. "In the servants' staircase. I opened the door to see what was happening . . ."

"And I ran straight into it," I said. "Give me a hand up. Did you see who I was chasing?"

She shook her head.

"Hellfire."

"Edward!"

I looped my arm around Jane's shoulder for support and let her help me up.

"Come on." At least I could make sure the intruder was gone.

At the bottom of the stairwell, I found the hat and cloak abandoned. The man from the museum, the man who had been hanging around outside our house, had been wearing a wide hat. This one was blue, though, and floppier. Maybe the man had changed it. Maybe he had been someone else entirely. I cursed again. I'd been so close. If I'd been faster, I could have had him. We could have settled this. Instead, all I'd gotten were more bruises.

I turned too quickly for my dizzy head and stumbled into Jane. Something fell from under her jacket with a *thump*. She snatched it up, but not before I saw it.

"Is that a *book*?" I said. And not just any book by the look of it. A solid, heavy book on Ancient Martian history. "When did you start reading books?"

Jane's face turned as red as a sunset. "Don't tell Mama! She says that if you spend all day with your head in a book, you'll never attract the right kind of gentleman. Gentlemen don't want wives who think, she says."

I shook my head, still too stunned from my tumble to think of anything to say.

How had I missed Jane starting to read academic books? *Jane!* And what else had I missed?

7

An Indecipherable Clue

Even at midday, when the heat from the desert gathered like an oven between the tall buildings of Lunae City, the streets were packed, dusty, and chaotic. Native Martian men and women stood by little squares of cloth they had laid out on the street, selling everything from sweetmeats and little fried birds to pots, pans, and shoes to the crowds that swirled around them.

It was lunchtime, and I'd finally managed to escape Mr. Davidson's lessons. Now I was picking my way through the packed bodies, and I felt like I was a prisoner who'd been let out after being locked up for years in a horrible dungeon. Even the heat and dust felt wonderful.

Every now and then, someone of European, Turkish, or Chinese descent would pass, sitting on the back of a lizard-donkey led by native Martians or carried by automatic servants in elaborately carved palanquins. Wide, thin cloths dyed in swirling green and blue stretched across the streets, protecting us from the direct sun. In the dim light that filtered through the cloth, it felt like I was swimming through a deep ocean.

I'd lived in Lunae City long enough that I was getting pretty good at slipping through the hordes of people. There was no point fighting the crowds; you had to slide through them like a fish.

An enormous, old, two-legged machine, shaped like a giant bird and spouting steam and smoke, thumped down the middle of the street. The gentleman riding it kept his nose turned up as it plodded forward, scattering the pedestrians. I darted around it and hurried on.

I reached the Museum of Martian Antiquities almost half an hour before I was due to meet Mina. The weight of her stolen key cylinder pushed against my hip as I made my way up the three low steps to the museum's door.

Last night, I'd been ready to hand back the key cylinder, no questions asked. Today, I wasn't so sure. I understood that Mina wanted to impress her father—I really did—but this was a man who'd left his children as orphans for years, and when he finally turned up, he sent his own daughter out to steal for him. What kind of father did that? If I gave the key cylinder to Mina, I would be giving it to him. I didn't know the man, but I didn't trust him and I didn't like him. He'd treated Mina badly.

If anything, the museum was in even more of a flap today than it had been the day before. Under-curators scurried in every direction like digger ants in a rainstorm. I found Dr. Guzman in the middle of a shouting match with another, even more dusty junior-under-curator. The two were pressed almost nose to nose, yelling and waving hands just outside the new gallery.

I stepped close to get Dr. Guzman's attention.

"Oh," he sniffed when he saw me. "You again. This imbecile wants to place a Third Age statuette next to a pair of Fourth Age suction boots."

The other curator bristled. "It is a thematic connection, you miserable amateur! If you cannot see it—"

"Amateur? Me? Why, I was educated in the great universities of Heidelberg and Vienna—"

"Educated? Is that what they're calling it now?"

"Dr. Guzman," I said, before they could start hitting each other. "You had something for me."

Dr. Guzman blinked. "I did?"

"You remember," I said. "When I was telling you yesterday about how much my sister Jane admired you, you offered to find out what had been stolen from the small gallery."

"You . . . ah . . . mentioned me to your sister?"

"Of course," I lied. "She's looking forward to seeing you at the gallery opening tomorrow."

He perked up. "Indeed! Indeed! I have the record in my storeroom. Please come with me." He shot the other under-curator a bitter look. "But I must not be away long. *Some* people cannot be trusted, you understand."

Dr. Guzman's storeroom was in a basement beneath the main body of the museum. I followed him through the maze of narrow galleries and hallways, then down a set of stone stairs.

"My entire collection," Dr. Guzman grumbled as we walked. "Consigned to shelves that no one may see. It is a disgrace! I can tell you far more of interest from a single potsherd than you would get from any mechanical artifact."

The door to his storeroom was made of thick steel set into a solid wall. A lock larger than my head fastened the door. There was no space for a key, just seven small holes in a semicircle. Carefully, Dr. Guzman inserted both thumbs and five of his fingers into them.

"A fine needle traces the unique patterns on my skin," Dr. Guzman said, "while another measures the pulse in my thumbs. If the patterns do not match what is recorded in the lock, it will not open. Ah!" With a *clank*, heavy metal bolts retracted from the door. Dr. Guzman flung it open.

"At least they're concerned enough to give you a secure storeroom," I said. "I mean, no thief is going to get in here."

"Ha!" he snorted. "It was the only free space. None of the other curators wish to use it. They do not approve of the stairs. And, see! Even one storeroom is considered too much for my collection. I am forced to share it with whatever junk was deemed too worthless to show in your father's new gallery."

He swept a dramatic arm at the heaped shelves. Most of them were stacked with thousands of fragments of pottery, interspersed with the odd complete specimen.

"See the variety!" Dr. Guzman exclaimed.

Personally, I would have struggled to tell one broken pot from another.

Several of the shelves had been cleared, and some of the smaller artifacts from the dragon tomb we'd uncovered had been placed on them. Most were pretty basic devices, the kind of things you'd find in any dragon tomb, or even in the ruins of Ancient Martian cities or temples. Little clockwork toys and tiny fragments of ideograms. There were also smashed pieces of artifacts that had been destroyed when Sir Titus Dane had driven his excavator right into the tomb. I even spotted the miniature stone sarcophagus that had held Putty's dragon egg. It was shoved right at the back of a shelf and had been filled with loose cogs and springs.

Dr. Guzman crossed to his table in the center of the room and plucked off a sheet of paper.

"The stolen artifact was a section of ideograms on a broken stone tablet," he said. "Not large, nor greatly significant. No doubt the fellow intended to sell it for a few pennies in the market."

"Do you know what was on it?" I said.

Dr. Guzman drew himself up. "I have better things to do with my time than read lists of grain or cattle owned by some minor emperor." He shoved the paper at me. "You may see for yourself. The ideograms were copied for the archives, as all such ideograms are. Good record-keeping is the basis for a civilized approach to history. These ideograms were never translated, however."

I took the paper and peered at it. It might as well have been in Ancient Greek. Mr. Davidson would have been ecstatic.

"As you can see," Dr. Guzman said, "the tablet was badly damaged. The curator who cataloged it noted that the ideograms would likely be impossible to translate. With so many of the ideograms missing or damaged, there would be no way to retrieve the meaning. I do not suppose the fool who stole it was aware of the fact, nor cared. No doubt the artifact even now decorates the dusty corners of some tourist's drawer." He sniffed. "It is of little loss to the museum."

Maybe Papa or Putty would be able to decode the ideograms. I certainly couldn't. I turned to head out, but Dr. Guzman cleared his throat.

"Ah . . . I have been thinking about what you asked yesterday. You asked if I had seen anyone else in the gallery from which the item was stolen, and I have not. However, something peculiar did happen a few days before. I was approached by a man who wanted to talk to me about artifacts in the museum. Although I was off duty, I always consider it my obligation to inform the public about our collections, particularly the pottery. Unfortunately, it soon became apparent that this man did not have an academic interest.

He was, in fact, asking me to obtain an artifact from the museum. I made it quite clear that I would not do so, and I bid him what I fear was a rather short good evening. It occurs to me that this man may have been involved in the theft of the fragment of ideograms."

"Thank you," I said, and I meant it. Excitement was flooding through my body. This was a clue. A real clue. "What did he look like?"

Dr. Guzman frowned. "Small, I would say, and fussy. I found his mannerisms irritating. He was accompanied by two other men. Rough sorts."

"Was either of them a tall man with broad shoulders and dark skin?" I said, thinking of the man I'd seen at the museum and outside our house. "Maybe wearing a wide hat?"

Dr. Guzman shook his head. "No. Now, I must get back. I cannot trust my fellow junior-under-curators. They are incompetent!"

"One last question," I said. "Where did this man approach you?"

"It was at a coffee house many of the junior-under-curators frequent," Dr. Guzman said. "It is called The Snap-jackal. Now, good day!"

I still had ten minutes until I was due to meet Mina. The dim light and stale heat of the museum basement were giving me a headache, so I decided to take a stroll around the square outside to clear my head.

A swarm of sky-seeds had found their way into the

museum, and their drifting tendrils had gotten entangled in the aerofoils of a large spring-powered heli-lifter the curators were using to move exhibits. The heli-lifter lurched back and forth across the foyer, trailing the squealing sky-seeds. Under-curators chased after it, shouting and tripping over each other. I slipped past and out of the museum.

The dry desert heat brought sweat to my hands right away. But at least it was a clean heat. What with Mr. Davidson's unending lessons in the tiny schoolroom and Dr. Guzman's sweltering basement, I felt like I'd been boiled in a pot all day long. If I was going to meet the thief—if I was going to meet *Mina*—again, I didn't want to look and smell like an overcooked cabbage.

I'd passed a native Martian selling slices of piranha-melon on the main street only a block from the museum. I checked my watch. Just enough time. I hurried across the square. My mouth was already watering.

But I'd barely made it halfway when a voice rang out. "You!"

I turned to see Lady Harleston emerging from an alley not twenty yards away. She was wearing dark, smoked eyeglasses, but even so, I could see the sunlight was making her wince.

Hellfire and damnation! How had *she* found me?

Her thuggish footmen followed her out of the alley, carrying cudgels. They looked like they were suffering from the aftereffects of the photon emission globe I'd exploded in front of them last night, too. They were squinting and shading their eyes. *Serves you right!*

"Get back here!" Lady Harleston bellowed at me.

Not likely. I put my head down and sprinted in the opposite direction. Behind, I heard the two footmen set off after me.

It took me almost twenty minutes to shake off my pursuers in the crowds, and even then, I didn't dare go back to the museum with Lady Harleston looking for me. Mina would think I wasn't coming.

The thought made my chest so tight I could scarcely breathe. She would think I had betrayed her. She would think I had let her down. I trudged slowly back home, the weight of the key cylinder banging against my hip with every heavy step.

The man was still waiting outside our gates. He was partially hidden by the thick shade of the balloon-palm, but now that I was seeing him up close rather than through Putty's invention he was unmistakable.

I slipped over the wall and hurried back to the house, where Mr. Davidson was waiting to torture me with a pile of old Greek books. I almost wished I'd let Lady Harleston capture me after all.

⊰◆⊱

I didn't get free again until six o'clock, and then only because I told Mr. Davidson I had to get changed for dinner.

Tomorrow I'd been promised algebra. I didn't think I could

cope. I staggered back to my room, ready to flop on my bed. But Putty had beaten me to it. She was sitting on my bed, flipping through a notebook.

"What are you doing here?" I demanded.

She looked up. "There aren't any ice caves in Xanthe Terra, you know. This isn't very realistic."

"Hey! That's mine." I lunged for the notebook, but she snatched it behind her back. I growled at her.

I'd been using that notebook to write my latest Captain W. A. Masters adventure. Captain Masters had been caught by the high priest, Karman Kel, and imprisoned in a pit of dragons in the ice caves of Xanthe Terra, and I hadn't figured how I was going to get him out again.

"I hid that," I said indignantly.

"I wouldn't have bothered finding it if you hadn't hidden it, would I?" She closed the notebook and tossed it over. "It's not very good."

"It's a first draft," I mumbled. "What do you want?"

"Jane said someone tried to break into Papa's study."

"Jane should know better than to tell you about that kind of thing."

Putty waved a casual hand. "People tell me everything. They know I'm going to find out in the end." She narrowed her eyes. "*Most* people. Anyway, I know who tried to break in. It was Miss Wilkins."

I stared at her. "What?"

"She's a spy. I told you. She's probably stealing secrets to give to Napoleon. Then he'll invade Mars and we'll all be enslaved."

"She's not a spy. Anyway, Papa doesn't work on weapons. Papa doesn't have anything Napoleon would want."

Putty gave me a pitying look. "You are naïve, Edward. I could turn half of Papa's inventions into weapons, and Napoleon has some quite brilliant mechanicians." She looked thoughtful. "Not as brilliant as me, of course. But I bet they'd still be able to work it out. Imagine if you put Papa's water abacus inside one of Napoleon's great machines of war. It wouldn't even need a driver or gunners. It could be automated. Imagine a thousand of them coming toward you on a battlefield. It would be a massacre."

"Except he'd have to get them to Mars," I said, "and he can't do that. Why are we even talking about this? Miss Wilkins is *not* a spy."

"She *is*," Putty said. "And I'm going to prove it. It's her evening off, and I'm going to follow her. I know where she goes on her evenings off. You should come, and then you'll see."

"I don't have time for this," I said. I still didn't know who had taken Rothan Gal, Lady Harleston was searching for me, the man in the wide hat was still spying on our house, and I'd missed meeting Mina.

Putty's face fell. "You always used to."

"And you hated it," I snapped. "You said I got in the way and wouldn't let you do anything."

"I looked for you at lunchtime," Putty said. "I suppose you were hiding from me then, too."

"Actually, I was helping Captain Kol. I went back to the museum and found out what Rothan Gal had been looking at when he was attacked."

If anything, Putty looked even more miserable. "And you didn't take me? Captain Kol is my friend, too."

"Well, you can help now," I said. I passed her the sheet of paper Dr. Guzman had given to me. "The missing item was a fragment of ideograms. This is a copy of them. I have absolutely no idea what they mean."

"I'll try," Putty said doubtfully. "They're kind of damaged." She looked up. "Did you find out anything else?"

"Maybe." I frowned. "Dr. Guzman said someone approached him to steal something from the museum. It could be the same person. He didn't know any names, but he said they'd approached him in a coffee house called The Snapjackal."

Putty's eyes widened. "But Edward! That's where Miss Wilkins goes on her evenings off. I knew it! I knew it! She's up to something!"

That couldn't be a coincidence. Could it?

I took a deep breath. "I guess we're going there together after all."

— 8 —

Eaten Alive

We waited until the house was quiet. Mama, Jane, and Olivia were in the drawing room, Olivia writing yet another letter to Cousin Freddie, care of the British-Martian Intelligence Service, and Papa had retreated to his laboratory to tinker with one of his inventions.

"I always thought there was something suspicious about Miss Wilkins," Putty crowed as we dropped over the garden wall onto the quiet street.

"We don't *know* that," I said.

"Oh, please. Don't you think it's suspicious that she would come to a coffee house on her evenings off?"

I picked myself up and dusted off my jacket. "Native Martian women do it all the time."

"But she's not a native Martian."

I gave a reluctant nod. A coffee house wasn't the kind of place a respectable lady would visit on her own. If Miss Wilkins had been married, it might have been different, but Mama would never let a married woman be Putty's governess. It would simply be too improper.

"It doesn't make her a spy."

Putty gave a long-suffering sigh. "Edward, Miss Wilkins has free run of our house and easy access to Papa's inventions. Every week she comes to the same coffee house and disappears into the same private room. What else could she be doing?"

Sighing, I gave in. "What exactly is the plan?"

"We'll wait near the coffee house," Putty said. "She normally arrives about nine o'clock. Then, when she goes in, we can sneak around the back. I found a way to climb up to the room she always uses to meet that Frenchman—"

"Have you ever seen this Frenchman?"

"Well, no. But I did hear him once. He wasn't speaking French, but then he wouldn't if he was a spy, would he? Anyway, who else would she be selling secrets to? So we climb up and listen in on the conversation. Then we can confront her, capture her, and turn her over to the British-Martian Intelligence Service. We'll be heroes, and Mama will never dare get me another governess."

"We're supposed to be looking for the man Dr. Guzman told us about," I said. "Remember?"

"I expect he's the one Miss Wilkins is meeting. We'll get

him, too, and he'll tell us where Rothan Gal is. You wait and see. I'm always right. It's down here."

She led me along a series of tight alleys before stopping at the edge of a square. On the far side, a wide, three-storied building spilled light across the dry earth. People were entering and leaving in a steady stream, laughing and chatting. A sign hung above the door showing a picture of a large, high-shouldered animal with a scaly tail and enormous jaws.

Even though it was late, lights shone through the windows of The Snap-jackal. A large scorpion-crawler was parked outside, its eight articulated legs bent so that the cabin was lowered almost to the ground. The boiler at the rear was damped down, only allowing a few wisps of steam to escape into the chill night air. Beside it, a couple of cycle-copters bobbed on top of their balloons, tethered to the rail. A larger two-person airship was anchored firmly to rings on the outside of the coffee house.

Putty and I crouched in the alley on the far side of the square, watching. We hadn't been there for more than ten minutes when Miss Wilkins appeared and strode confidently across the square. Putty leaped to her feet.

"Are you sure about this?" I said. "If we're caught, you're going to be in an awful lot of trouble."

She gave me a fierce look. "We have to prove it, Edward. I *have* to get rid of her. She's a monster. If your tutor was a spy, wouldn't you want to get rid of him?"

I groaned. I almost wished Mr. Davidson were a spy. Then maybe he'd spend more time spying and less time torturing me with Latin verbs. But if I had it hard, Putty had it a hundred times worse. At least I had *some* freedom. Putty had done exactly as she pleased for most of her life. Now Miss Wilkins had arrived, and she treated Putty like a little automaton who had to do exactly what she was told all the time. It was no wonder they were clashing so badly. But that didn't mean Miss Wilkins was a spy.

Up above, a flock of moon birds had formed a perfect circle around the outline of Phobos, Mars's largest moon.

"I knew you'd understand," Putty said. She stepped out of the alley. "Follow me! I know just the place. Even you'll be able to climb it."

A man slipped out of the coffee house and headed for the small airship. He was short, no taller than I was, and he moved with a fussy haste, like a nervous bird.

"Wait!" I grabbed Putty's arm and dragged her back into the alley. She stumbled against a wall.

"Ouch! What was that for?"

My heart was thumping so loud I could hardly think. How could this be happening? *How?*

"Look!" I hissed, jabbing my finger toward the small man.

Putty's eyes widened. "It's Dr. Blood! What's he doing here?"

I could hardly force the words out. "I don't know." My throat clenched and every muscle in my body tensed rock hard. I was sweating, even in the cool night air. Dr. Blood was here. *Here!*

I'd been so *stupid*. Dr. Guzman had talked about a small, fussy man who had asked him to steal something from the museum. Why hadn't I suspected that might be Dr. Blood?

Hellfire and damnation!

Dr. Blood was supposed to be fleeing or hiding, not hanging around Lunae City trying to get hold of artifacts. Not approaching people out in the open in coffee houses like this one. Yet here he was. No wonder Freddie had been worried enough to ask someone to keep an eye on us. He must have suspected Dr. Blood might come back. If only Freddie's friend had shown up.

When Dr. Guzman had refused to steal the ideograms for Dr. Blood, Dr. Blood must have sent his own men to get them. They must have come across Rothan Gal studying them and attacked him. They must have taken him with them.

But why? Dr. Blood had helped Sir Titus Dane try to loot the dragon tomb we'd found. Maybe he was still after something from it. So why had he taken those damaged ideograms that Rothan Gal had been so interested in instead and not something from the new gallery?

And why had he kidnapped Rothan Gal? None of this made any sense.

"We can't let him get away," Putty said. "Not if he's got Rothan Gal. Not after what he did to us."

"No," I said grimly. "We can't." Dr. Blood had tried to

kill us. He'd attacked the airship we'd been traveling on and crashed it, and when we'd survived that, he'd hunted us across the Martian wilderness with his deadly machines. He was a murderer and a villain, and now he had our friend.

Dr. Blood stopped at the two-man airship and unclipped it from the wall anchors. Once he was in the airship, he would fly off into the Martian night. This might be our only chance to capture him and find out what had happened to Rothan Gal.

I held on to Putty's vibrating shoulder until Dr. Blood had his back to us.

"Now!" I said.

We raced across the square as Dr. Blood clambered into his little airship. Without any hurry, he engaged the propellers, angled them down, and the ship began to rise, turning away from us. Dr. Blood settled on the upholstered double seat, control levers in his hands.

I lengthened my stride. The airship was climbing slowly, still only a couple of feet above the ground. I put my head down and raced toward it.

I was less than a dozen feet away when a red-faced man stepped out of the coffee house and right into my path. I didn't have time to dodge. We collided and tumbled to the ground. I scrambled to my feet, but my legs were tangled in the man's stick and he grabbed at my jacket. I fell back. I saw Putty's legs flash past.

I twisted my neck. The airship was already six feet off the ground.

Putty leaped. Her fingers caught on a metal bar beneath the airship's seat. The airship swung under the impact, but it kept rising. Putty clung on.

I shoved the red-faced man away from me and sprinted for the airship.

It was too high. By the time I was beneath it, Putty's feet were well above my head.

Let go! I mouthed.

She shook her head.

Dr. Blood must have known something was wrong. His airship swung awkwardly from Putty's attempts to pull herself up. Brass flying goggles appeared over the edge of the seat.

I ducked my head so he wouldn't see my face. He twisted, trying to look beneath his airship. He must have known someone was hanging on from the way the airship was rocking, but the seat hid Putty from view.

I spun and ran back to where the cycle-copters were tied to the rail.

The red-faced man made it to his feet and came stumbling toward me, stick raised.

I grabbed the first cycle-copter, pulled myself astride, and flicked off the restraining rope. The cycle-copter's balloon beneath me took my weight, and it began to float up. I engaged the springs. The blades above my head started to rotate.

"Thief!" the red-faced man bellowed, swiping at me with his stick. I fended him off with a foot.

Dr. Blood had reached the rooftops, with Putty still dangling beneath. I grabbed the cycle-copter's steering levers and directed it in pursuit. It wobbled horribly. I started to pedal as fast as I could, increasing the spin of the blades.

I'd only ridden a cycle-copter once before, and it had been a disaster. I'd ended up trapped in the branches of an outraged fern-tree, and after that, everyone said I should stay on the ground.

This was really hard to control! The cycle-copter dipped and bobbed and spun like a duck in a whirlpool.

A building shot toward me. I jerked one of the levers and the cycle-copter swiped away.

I fired a glance at Dr. Blood's airship. It had risen above the buildings, but now it was swooping down again. The spiky rooftops jutted at Putty's dangling body like a forest of spears.

Desperately, Putty flung herself to one side. The rooftops swished by, barely missing her. Dr. Blood brought his airship up and around, ready to come in for another pass.

I urged the cycle-copter on. I was beneath the airship now and climbing toward it. But now I saw another problem. I couldn't come up directly beneath Putty. The beating blades of the cycle-copter would be in the way. Putty would be chopped to bits. And I couldn't get in close enough to the airship to leap onto it, because its egg-shaped balloon covered it entirely.

I swung the cycle-copter away, still pedaling, bringing it higher and higher.

I would only get one chance.

The airship swept across the rooftops again. Putty twisted between two sharpened spirals of wood. Her foot smacked against the shingles, and a spike caught on her jacket. For a second, she was stretched between the airship and roof, as taut as a fishing line. Then, with a rip of fabric, she came free from the roof.

As Dr. Blood's airship flew out over the street, I pushed both of the steering levers forward and sent the cycle-copter into a dive.

I plunged beneath the airship and jerked the levers back. The cycle-copter leveled out, and I jammed the left lever forward.

The effect was like a slingshot. Momentum threw the cycle-copter into an almost horizontal curve beneath the airship. I felt the cycle-copter slip down, no longer supported by its whirring blades.

"Let go!" I shouted to Putty.

I shot past under her, lying nearly flat. She glanced down then released her hold. She dropped onto me with the force of a falling rock.

Wind whooshed from my body. Instinctively, I grabbed Putty with one hand.

The cycle-copter tumbled. The balloon wasn't enough to lift us both by itself. As the cycle-copter flipped, the street and the buildings whirled past me.

"Grab the lever!" Putty screamed in my ear. She was dangling from the edge of the cycle-copter, her body being thrown this way and that as we spun, her arms tight around my waist.

I gritted my teeth, released her, and snatched the steering lever.

A building loomed up before us. I hauled back, and again the cycle-copter swung.

We were too close. The tip of one of the blades screeched across the stone wall. For a moment, I thought the whole copter would shatter, sending metal blades ricocheting across the street, but then we were clear again and still flying.

Putty swung her leg up behind me to straddle the cycle-copter. With a sigh, I pushed the levers gently forward and the machine dipped toward the ground.

"What are you doing?" Putty demanded beside my ear.

"Going down," I said. "Before I kill both of us."

"Down? Chase him!" She jabbed a finger toward Dr. Blood's little airship. It had passed over the rooftops of Lunae City and was now beating its way slowly north, angling over the river and into the desert.

"We'll never catch him," I said.

"Of course we will. You just need to pedal!"

I groaned. She was right, of course. Nothing had changed. We still needed to catch Dr. Blood before we lost him for good.

I angled the levers back and started pedaling again. The copter blades spun faster. Ponderously, the machine lifted into the night sky.

Ahead of us, Dr. Blood's miniature airship floated elegantly and effortlessly onward. Behind him, I pedaled and panted, my legs burning. Sweat dripped off my face and down my back. Putty leaned over my shoulder, whacking me enthusiastically.

"Faster! He's getting away!"

Faster? My legs were ready to drop off.

We flew out over the fields, leaving the city behind. Several miles away, on the far side of the Martian Nile, the vast, dark desert mesas rose. Deep canyons cut through them. There was nowhere out there for Dr. Blood to flee.

I heaved a breath and pedaled faster. Our little craft surged forward. We were going to catch him.

"Edward!" Putty shouted. "Watch out!"

I twisted around. Looming over us was the enormous balloon of a giant airship. It was bigger than a whale and a hundred times more scary. It was so close and so big it completely blotted out the stars and the Martian moons.

Where the front of the airship's gondola would normally have been were two huge brass-and-steel jaws, stretched wide. Metal teeth glistened in the starlight. It had crept up on us on silent propellers while I'd been too busy panting and sweating to notice.

It was going to swallow us!

I smashed the steering levers forward. The cycle-copter dropped toward the desert, spinning out of control.

Too late.

The airship's jaws closed with a *snap* around us.

PART TWO

Betrayal

Prisoners

We plunged into darkness. One moment it had been stars and the faint glow of Mars's tiny moons and the lights of Lunae City way behind us, then nothing. It was as if we'd flown into a giant inkwell and someone had slammed on the lid.

I wrenched back on the cycle-copter's control levers before we could smash headfirst into the floor. The cycle-copter swirled around, bouncing and lunging in every direction.

"Watch out for the walls!" Putty shouted in my ear.

"I can't *see* the walls!"

I stopped pedaling and hit the switch that disengaged the spring. The copter blades sighed to a halt and the cycle-copter fell again.

We hit the floor with a jolt. The cycle-copter tipped. I tumbled to the floor with Putty on top of me. I snatched for the cycle-copter, but it was already rising away from us.

At least we were down safe. I just didn't know *where* we were down.

I stretched out a hand and felt rough wood beneath my fingers. We must be on floorboards, but they were covered in a thin layer of sticky dust or pollen. Putty scrambled up, managing to jab me in the neck with her elbow. I grabbed hold of her jacket to stop her from disappearing off in the dark.

"Let go!" she hissed.

"Not a chance," I said. "You have no idea where we are."

"We're in a gulper. They use them to harvest the air forests in Patagonian Mars. I *told* you all about them last year. Weren't you listening?"

"Well, what's it doing here?" Patagonian Mars was halfway around the planet.

"Gulping us, of course. Come on, Edward. We need to find a way out. Maybe we can take control of the airship."

"Or maybe we can walk around until we fall down a hole and kill ourselves," I said.

She sighed. "Why would anyone build an airship with holes in the floor?"

"Why would anyone build an airship with giant jaws on the front?" I said.

Before Putty could answer, a door opened forty or fifty yards away. Light spilled into the airship's hold. From where we were standing, it looked like we were inside the chest cavity of an enormous beast. Brass ribs curved twenty yards up to the ceiling.

"See?" Putty said happily. "No holes."

The light from the doorway outlined four men carrying long poles with sharp hooks on the end.

"Yeah? Well, how about them?"

"I only said there weren't any holes."

Except the giant, airship-sized hole in our plan to capture Dr. Blood. *Hell!*

"We can see you," one of the men shouted. They were standing on a platform about halfway up the airship wall. The door must lead to the control room or crew's quarters. "Give yourselves up."

"They can't see a thing," I whispered. The light was behind them, and they would be staring into the blackness. There must be a way out. But where? Behind us, the closed metal jaws cut off any escape, and we were at least a hundred feet up in the air. What were we going to do? Jump?

Our cycle-copter bobbed gently at the top of the space, far out of reach. A dozen or more wide brass pipes ran along the ceiling and ended in mouths like horns, pointing down into the hold. Along the curved walls, tall, narrow flaps hinged along one edge, like fish gills stretching almost to the ceiling. Perhaps we could force one of them open. But then where would we go?

Two beams of light stabbed out from the man's face.

"What the . . . ?" I stumbled back. The light was pouring from his eyes. "Death rays!" I whispered. Back in issue thirty-five of *Thrilling Martian Tales*, Captain W. A. Masters had been attacked by Kalian cultists wielding Martian death rays that had looked just like this.

"Photonic goggles," Putty said. "Papa's company started selling them last month."

"Whose great idea was that?" I backed away, pulling Putty with me. "Can they see us?"

"There wouldn't be much point otherwise, would there?"

Light darted from the other men's eyes, pinning us in the crossbeams.

Two of the men clattered down hidden steps, then approached us across the floor, hooked poles raised.

"We surrender!" I called.

"Edward," Putty hissed.

I shook my head. "We can't escape." I laid one hand on her shoulder to make sure she didn't do anything stupid.

"Look," I said, shading my eyes against the light from his goggles. "We didn't mean to get in your way. We were just—"

"Shut up," one of the men shouted. "Get on the ground."

Still holding my arm up against the glare, I knelt, keeping myself between Putty and the men. I might be able to take one of the men by surprise, but that would still leave another three, and there was nowhere for us to run.

"Just let us go," I tried again. "We won't say anything. I promise. We don't even know who you are."

Another set of footsteps approached, slow and light, as though the person was picking his way distastefully across the sticky floor. A pair of small, immaculately polished shoes came to a halt a couple of inches in front of me. I craned my head back to peer up at my captor.

"That does surprise me," Dr. Blood said, looking down from beneath heavy eyebrows. "Because I know exactly who you are. Master Sullivan."

⊰◈⊱

They left us in the hold of the airship, tied hand and foot, in darkness.

"Where do you think they're taking us?" Putty hissed.

I shook my head. "I don't know. Wherever Dr. Blood's been holed up all this time. He must have a base in the desert." I cursed. "We should have told someone where we were going."

"Really?" Putty said. "When? Were we supposed to run back and let everyone know? Maybe we could have asked him to wait around until we got back."

We should never have chased after Dr. Blood. We should have gotten word to the British-Martian ambassador. He could have sent agents after Dr. Blood. And we could have told Captain Kol. He would know people all over Lunae City. They could have tracked Dr. Blood down. Why did I always think I had to do things on my own? Now he knew we were onto him. He'd never let us go.

I couldn't tell how much time was passing here in the

dark. All I could feel was the slow, steady beat of the propellers driving us further and further into the desert. But we must have been lying there at least twenty minutes when I heard a noise from the side of the airship, like metal forcing itself open.

My pulse started to pound in my head.

"How does this thing work?" I whispered to Putty. "This—what did you call it?—this gulper?"

"Oh," Putty said happily. "It's quite clever. They take great gulps of the air forests, then they shoot steam out of the pipes to blast off the leaves and fruits and soften the wood. Then they haul anything they don't want out the gills. It's quite efficient, but I really think they could mechanize the whole process."

"Great," I muttered. A blast of steam to fry us, then out into the night. We'd never be found.

The creak of metal came again, then the sound of something breaking. Cool night air sighed around us. Pale moonlight slipped in through a gap, illuminating a single figure crouching just inside the airship. This was it, then. They were going to toss us out. Last year, we'd only just survived Dr. Blood, and then we'd had Freddie and Captain Kol on our side. This time, it was just me and Putty, and we were helpless.

I pushed myself up. At least I could fight when they came for us. If I got lucky, maybe I could send one of our captors flying back out that hole himself. Maybe he'd even provide a soft landing when they chucked us out after him.

I drew my legs up, waited until the shadowed figure was only a pace away, then kicked out with all my strength.

The figure skipped aside. "Don't do that!"

A dim light flicked on in the figure's hand. I saw long, straight hair. Dark eyes. Suddenly, I could hardly breathe. Every thought of Dr. Blood and horrible death fluttered out of my head.

"Mina?" I gaped at the thief. "What are you doing here?"

She crouched next to me and helped me upright again. "Rescuing you. What does it look like?"

I could scarcely speak. My breath seemed trapped in my throat. "I came to meet you. Honestly. But Lady Harleston—"

"I know. I saw you. And her."

"You did?" I heard the relief in my own voice. I'd been sure when I didn't turn up that she'd think I'd decided not to help.

Putty kicked me. "You told me you just went to the museum! You went on another rendezvous, and you left me behind again!"

"I came looking for you," Mina said. "Afterward. I was going to come to your home again, when it got dark."

"Again?" Putty squawked.

"Then I caught sight of you near the coffee house. I was going to call out, but you went pelting out and stole that cyclecopter before I could get to you."

"I didn't steal it," I said, looking down.

She looked skeptical. "Yeah? I bet that's news to the owner. Anyway, I couldn't let you out of sight again, so I stole another cycle-copter and came after you. Now I'm rescuing you. You know, it wasn't easy to catch you up in this thing."

"You must really want that key cylinder," Putty said.

Putty was right. Coming after us like that when we were so obviously in danger—putting herself into danger—it didn't make sense. Not unless the key cylinder was way, way more important than I realized. Right now, though, I was just grateful she had.

"Let's get out of here, shall we?" Mina said. "Before someone comes to check on you and we all get caught."

— 10 —

Warnings

With Mina's help, we retrieved our floating cycle-copter, then slipped away unseen through the open gill.

We put the cycle-copters down in a field on the edge of Lunae City, not far from the Flame House. I left them hitched to a balloon-palm. Maybe someone would find them and return them to their rightful owners.

"Right," I said awkwardly. "Um. Thanks. You know. For everything." What on Mars were you supposed to say to a girl who'd just saved your life? Particularly when somehow she always made me feel as awkward and flustered as a jellyfish trying to ride a bicycle.

Mina looked away. "Forgive me," she whispered.

I frowned. Had I heard her right? "Forgive you? What for? You saved us."

"For all of this."

"It's not your fault," I said. "Blame the men who kidnapped us. Blame Lady Harleston."

"Yeah," she said, hunching up her shoulders. "The thing is, I thought you were just . . . you know? But you're not. I've seen the way you are with each other. You're . . ." She looked down. "You're good people. Nice people." Her voice dropped so low I could hardly hear her. "I wish I had a family like yours."

I didn't know what to say to that. I wanted to say she wouldn't think that if she lived with us, but her mother was dead and her father had abandoned her and she'd had to become a thief to survive. My family might be irritating, but I was lucky.

So I just said, "I don't have the key with me. I'll bring it to you tomorrow. There's a new gallery opening at the museum. We're going. I'll meet you just before, outside the museum."

She looked up at me with dark eyes. "You promise?"

I nodded. My mouth felt too dry to speak. It must have been from all that dry desert air.

She turned away. I watched her until she faded into the shadows and was gone.

The first faint glow of dawn was just showing over the eastern mesas when we reached home. Even though the hallway clock showed only five in the morning, I went to wake Papa and sent Putty to fetch Olivia. We gathered in the drawing room and I told Papa and Olivia what had happened.

I didn't tell them about Mina or the key, though. I didn't know why. I didn't think Papa would approve. By the light of the old friction lamps, Papa looked haggard and tired. The parlor palm in the corner shed long shadows against the wall.

"I don't know if he knows where we live," I said, "but he'll be able to find out easily enough."

"You should never have gone after him alone," Olivia said. Her voice was tight, and although she was sitting apparently calmly, her hands folded in her lap, I could hear the worry in her voice.

"He wasn't alone," Putty protested. "He was with me."

"That's worse."

Putty's jaw dropped.

"You said he was trying to steal things from the museum, Edward?" Papa said.

I nodded. "I don't know what, though, apart from that fragment of ideograms."

"I looked at them," Putty said. "They're too damaged. They're indecipherable."

Papa ran his fingers through his already messy hair. His hands were shaking. "I will send a letter to the captain of the militia and ask for guards at the house and the museum. I will not let that man endanger this family again. I have some status in this city now, and the council wishes for me to expand my manufactories. They will provide protection."

"And I'll write to the British-Martian Intelligence Service," Olivia said. "They should be able to get a message to

Freddie, although I don't know if he'll be able to get here in time to help." She looked down. "Maybe they'll send someone else."

I hoped it would be enough.

—◆—

The Flame House might have been a disaster of mismatching rooms and confused corridors, but there were a good thirty rooms that could have been used for my lessons. Some had fantastic views over the Martian Nile to the fields and the remains of the dragon temples beyond. Others looked out over the bird's nest of roofs jutting up from Lunae City. A couple of rooms were an education unto themselves, and one would probably kill you if you stepped in the wrong place.

All of them would have been better than the horrible, hot, airless corner Mama had picked out for my lessons. Mr. Davidson was standing before the chalkboard, tapping a length of chalk impatiently on his trousers when I stumbled in. I'd managed to grab a couple of hours of sleep, but that had only made me feel worse.

"There you are, Master Sullivan," he snapped. His small face was pinched in disapproval. "Let us waste no more time! Get out your books. We shall begin!"

By the time I staggered out of the small schoolroom into the burning heat of the Lunae Planum midday, I could hardly remember my own name, let alone conjugate another Latin verb.

The daily airship was lifting off from its tether, heading

back to Ophir City with its load of passengers. A swarm of glass butterflies fluttered around the great balloon like a halo, and as the propellers began to beat, they were swept back in spirals behind it, turning its slipstream into glittering quicksilver.

I stood there for a few minutes staring at it, my mouth opening and closing like a confused frog, saying not much more than "Guh" until my brain slowly came back to life.

Far away, on the southern horizon, a faint smudge of clouds like a line of charcoal showed that the winter rains had reached the hills that bordered the Lunae Planum and in which the Martian Nile began. Soon, the waters would rise and the floodplains on either side of the river would be covered. The Inundation would have arrived, bringing with it the rich, thick silt that would fertilize the fields. For a few brief weeks, the desert would come alive as rain clouds swept over it.

If Captain Kol wanted to travel upriver and reach the network of Martian canals before the current became too strong and the river impassable, he would need to leave soon.

We were running out of time to find Rothan Gal. I shook my head to clear away the last of my Latin verbs, then went looking for Putty.

I finally found her up to her knees in a mole-snake burrow, looking far too pleased with herself. "Do you know what I've been doing all morning?" she said as we made our way through the crowded streets toward the docks.

"Do I want to?" I asked. I was keeping more than half an eye out for Dr. Blood, as well as Lady Harleston and her thugs. I'd only had time to grab a chunk of bread from the kitchen for my lunch on the way past, and I was feeling hungry again already.

"Of course. I've been trying to escape from Miss Wilkins."

"Well, that was a good use of the morning, then."

Putty looked pleased. "I thought so. She's got the eyes of an arrow-hawk and the nose of a tracker-vole. Which pretty much proves she's a spy, otherwise why would she be so good at finding me? She wants to organize every second of my day. Every second! As though I'm not busy enough already! I have things to do, you know!"

"Like hiding from your governess?"

"Exactly! Anyway, it's a shame she's not Papa's governess instead of mine, because then think how well his company would be run. He'd make an absolute fortune. Except she'd steal all his secrets and give them to Napoleon. You wouldn't believe what I had to do to give her the slip."

"I expect I would," I said. "I just don't want to know."

"Well, I wouldn't tell you anyway. So there. Even though I used hover boots and a chameleon cloak."

We turned down a side street, and there at the far end was the forest of masts swaying gently at the dockside.

"There's no such thing as hover boots or a chameleon cloak," I said.

"There might be. Anyway, I expect I'll invent them, then

you'll look silly. You know, the old Martian emperors floated down the river on their dragon barges every single Inundation for thousands of years. I bet some of them sank. I bet they're still there on the bottom of the river. I bet they're covered in gold and full of wonderful artifacts. If we had a submersible, we could go looking for them."

"It's lucky we haven't got a submersible, then," I said.

Putty sighed. "What do you think it would be like to be the emperor of the whole of Mars?"

"Hard work." The noise of the docks was rising as we approached. I could hear the shouts of sailors and the *thump* of cargo being loaded and unloaded. With the Inundation so close, the sounds were even more frantic than normal.

"Honestly, Edward," Putty said. "You're a real misery today. What's wrong with you?"

I pushed a hand across my exhausted face. How did Putty look so fresh and awake? "Forgive me. I've got too much on my mind. There's Lady Harleston, Dr. Blood, Rothan Gal—"

"And Mina."

I blushed. "I wasn't thinking about her."

"Of course you weren't." Putty waved a hand dismissively. "I'm sure we'll sort it out. I'm rather good at things like this. Anyway, I think it'd be great being emperor. I'd be able to do anything I wanted."

"You already do."

"I *used* to," Putty said darkly. "Not since Miss Wilkins turned up, though. What's that?"

We'd stepped out onto the dock. Hundreds of native Martian craft were tied up along the wharfs, but between them was a ship with an enormous metal hull that rose high above the docks.

"I have no idea," I said. I'd never seen anything like it before.

The ship was almost a hundred yards long, and its deck stood higher than the masts of most of the vessels surrounding it. Two large funnels sloped back from the rear half. In front of them, metal walls punctuated with small portholes and iron doors reached sleekly to the front deck. A small upper deck stretched in a U shape around the front half of the ship, jutting out over the lower deck.

"It looks like it's got guns," Putty said. "Dozens of them. And tangleshot and spine shooters, and that's definitely a slingshot cannon." She pointed at a flat cylinder jutting from the side of the ship. "Do you know, a slingshot cannon can fire a cannonball almost ten miles? I bet this is Dr. Blood's ship. I bet he's planning an invasion. We should sneak on board and sabotage it."

"I don't think you invade by tying up at the docks," I said. "And we're not sneaking on board in full view of everyone. We'd be arrested." I'd spent two days in a militia cell with Cousin Freddie; I didn't fancy going through that again.

Putty smiled up at me innocently. "So you think we should do it tonight instead?"

I didn't rise to it. "Dr. Blood had an airship. I can't see him tucking it into the hold of a boat, can you?"

"You could probably make a folding airship," Putty said. "If you could compress the gas in the cells."

"The point is," I said, "Dr. Blood was flying north, out into the desert. He's got a base out there. If he's holding Rothan Gal, that's where he'll be." I thought for a moment. "Maybe Mina will know where it is."

Putty lifted a hand and pretended to wave it like a fan against her face. "Oh, *Mina*," she sighed breathlessly. She fluttered her eyelashes. "You're just like Jane."

I felt my face redden. Again. "All I mean is that she must have contacts. She is a thief, and Dr. Blood has to hire his thugs from somewhere."

Captain Kol's boat was tied up at the wharf, but it had been prepared for sailing. Cargo and supplies were firmly lashed to the decks. Captain Kol came out of the forward hatch and waved us over as we approached.

"You have news?" he asked.

"I think so," I said as I clambered down to the deck. "I hope so. I found where Rothan Gal was captured. You were right. He was in the museum. He was examining an old artifact when he was attacked. Both he and the artifact were taken."

I didn't add that I had no idea if Rothan Gal was still alive. He'd been hit hard enough to bleed, but I hadn't seen any sign of a body being dragged away.

Captain Kol gestured us to low-slung chairs on the deck and poured us bitter green tea. I dropped into my chair.

"Do you know who took him?" Captain Kol.

"You remember Dr. Blood?"

"I remember what you told us of him, and I remember his machines that hunted you."

"I can't prove it," I said, "but I think he's the one who took Rothan Gal, or his men did. He's been trying to persuade the museum's curators to steal something for him. He must have taken it into his own hands when they wouldn't." I grimaced. "He knows we're onto him. We saw him in town and tried to catch him, but he caught us instead. We only just escaped."

"Then I fear I have more bad news," Captain Kol said. "A man was asking about your family along the docks. We told him nothing, of course. He was not of Mars, and we did not know him, but perhaps your Dr. Blood has sent men looking for you."

Already? He must have sent them out the moment he'd discovered we were missing. We wouldn't be hard to track down.

Maybe we could do something about this particular man who was searching for us, though. At least we could give the militia guards his description.

"What did he look like?" I said.

"Tall," Captain Kol said. "For a native of Earth." He held a hand to just below his shoulder. Taller than Freddie, then, and much taller than me. "Broad shoulders. He wore a wide hat to shadow his face. He has dark skin, like those of my people who live on the shores of the Hellas Sea. He has a scar." Captain Kol drew a line across his own face from just below his left eye down across his lips to his chin. "It pulls his lips up into a smile, as though he knows something he will not share."

"We've seen him," I said. But that didn't make any sense. He'd been in the museum and loitering outside our house before we'd ever known Dr. Blood was in town. Did that mean Dr. Blood had been looking for us before? And why? We'd ruined his plans in the past, but if he'd wanted revenge, he'd had plenty of chances.

"Edward," Captain Kol said quietly. "You and Putty must not tackle this man alone. I have known many dangerous men, and I do not fear them. But this one is different. I should not like to anger him."

I got up from the chair. "We've known some dangerous men, too. I'm not afraid." When I said it like that, I almost believed it. But actually I was frightened out of my skin. I'd thought we'd gotten away from all of this last year. I'd thought it was over.

"Did you find anything else?" Captain Kol asked.

"Not much." I pulled out the sheet of paper Dr. Guzman had given me. "This is what Rothan Gal was studying when he was attacked. It was a segment of ideograms. I have no idea if it was what Dr. Blood was after or whether it was just a convenient weapon."

Captain Kol nodded. "Rothan Gal talked of this. He said it disturbed him."

I looked up at him. "Do you know what it says?"

Captain Kol shook his head. "He had not managed to translate it. Just hints, he said. Ideas. As you see, it is damaged, and these old languages . . ." He shook his head. "When we find Rothan Gal, maybe he can tell you what these men wanted with it."

"I'll ask again at the museum," I said. "Someone must have seen something. You can't just kidnap a man unnoticed."

"And I will search for Dr. Blood. We will find him. But, Edward, you have seen the clouds?" He pointed a long hand at the southern horizon.

I nodded.

"The Inundation comes. My boat cannot stay here. It is too dangerous. We must sail in a day, no more than two, or I will lose the boat. It is the home to my crewmen and crewwomen. And yet I cannot abandon Rothan Gal. We do not have much time."

"I know," I said. "I know." We had no time at all.

Attack of the Shark Beetles

T he sun was high overhead as we climbed off Captain
Kol's boat onto the wharf, and even though summer was
gone, the heat pressed down on us like a mountain of sand.
I started sweating within moments.

I'd told Captain Kol that I'd ask at the museum again, but
I'd already interrogated every curator I'd met. I had a horrible
feeling that we'd found all the clues we were going to there,
but I didn't know what else to do. I didn't know how to find
Rothan Gal, I didn't know what Dr. Blood wanted, and I
didn't know how to stop him. All I knew was that we were
in danger again.

Maybe we could get back on Captain Kol's boat and just
sail away. Pick up my family and go. I knew I was being a
coward, but I didn't know if I could go through all this again.
I didn't know if we'd *survive* again.

"Come on!" Putty said, hurrying up to me. "The gallery is going to open any minute. They're going to say how it was all thanks to me that we discovered the dragon tomb, and everyone is going to be terribly impressed."

I shook my head to clear the swirl of bad thoughts.

"I think the rest of us also had something to do with it."

"Oh, I'm sure they'll mention you. Come *on*!"

She disappeared into a side street at a run. I took a deep breath. It would be all right. We would figure this out. The militia would deal with Dr. Blood. All I had to do was make it to the gallery opening, meet Mina to give her the key cylinder, and not lose Putty somewhere in Lunae City on the way. I took off in pursuit.

We were rushing so fast and so determinedly that I didn't notice the men lurking in the shadows near the mouth of a side alley until it was too late.

One moment I had the Museum of Martian Antiquities in my sight, the next an arm had wrapped itself around my neck, choking off my breath, and I was being dragged into the darkness. I saw Putty struggling in another man's grip. Then I was flung to the hard ground and someone kicked me in the ribs.

Pain flared in my chest. I coughed and tried to roll away. A second kick caught me and sent me tumbling into a wall. I tasted dust and blood on my lips. I groaned, and sucked in more dust. My stomach hurt. It really hurt.

"I'm disappointed," a voice said.

Blinking away tears, I rolled onto my back and squinted up.

Lady Harleston stood above me. One of her men held Putty, who still squirmed helplessly in his grip. The other of Lady Harleston's men stood close, ready to kick me again.

"I warned you not to underestimate me, but you did." She peered down at me and shook her head sadly. "I have a problem, you see. When my husband died, he left me with terrible debts. For years, he had lied to me. He said we were rich, but we did not even own the house we lived in. He had wasted every penny we had. Creditors circled me like wolf-vultures."

"What, you want me to feel sorry for you?" I rasped. My mouth was full of dirt from the alley. Being broke was no excuse for what she'd done to us.

She smiled. "No. I'm simply helping you understand how serious I am. I had a choice, you see. I could throw myself on the mercy of my relatives, hang around like a mourning ghost until time and age took me. But I asked myself if that was the only role that a widow on Mars could hope for, and I decided that it was not. I swore that I would not surrender, and that I would not let anyone stop me from doing whatever I chose. Do not imagine that I have reached my position here by allowing people to cheat or underestimate me."

I knew I should keep my mouth shut. I was completely at her mercy, and she hadn't proven very merciful so far. But I'd had enough.

"Oh, please," I spat. "That's the most pathetic excuse I've ever heard, and I've heard some pretty bad ones." Mostly from Putty.

Lady Harleston's face twisted into a snarl. "I gave you the chance to return what you took from me! I would have handed you over to the militia for justice. You wouldn't have liked it, but you would have lived. You gave up that chance." She glanced back at the man holding Putty. "Teach him a lesson. Kill her."

"No!" I screamed. Why hadn't I just stayed quiet?

I surged to my feet. Lady Harleston's man swung his fist into my face. I stumbled into the wall, then pushed myself away again.

Putty was flipping like a landed fish, biting and scratching and kicking, so her captor couldn't get a hand free to reach the knife I saw in his belt.

Lady Harleston's man punched me again in the stomach. I grabbed his arm and held on. He lost his balance and we fell together to the ground, the man on top of me.

"Must I do this myself?" Lady Harleston said. I saw her pull a long, thin blade from inside her jacket and advance on Putty.

"Wait!" I shouted. I slammed my head into my captor's shoulder. He grunted but didn't let go.

Putty kicked out, throwing her own captor off balance. He staggered back.

"Hold her still," Lady Harleston snapped.

I twisted my arm, reaching inside my jacket, and tugged out the key cylinder. I was at an awkward angle, and even if I could have swung it, I couldn't have built up enough force to hurt the man pinning me down.

"Wait!" I called, waving the key cylinder feebly in the air. "I have it. You can take it."

Lady Harleston glanced back and sneered.

"You stole irreplaceable documents. Whole segments of untranslated ideograms. Artifacts that I could have sold for hundreds of pounds. And you offer me that toy?"

I wanted to scream. It was all I had, all I'd ever had. I hadn't broken into her house. I hadn't stolen from her. I had nothing more to give her. She was going to kill Putty, and there was nothing I could do. I couldn't even move.

"It may just be a toy," another voice said. "But it is *my* toy."

I twisted my head. Mina stood at the end of the alley. She was holding something in both hands, but I couldn't make it out from where I lay.

"Who the devil are you?" Lady Harleston demanded. "Another one of their accomplices?"

"Oh, please," Mina said, walking toward us. "If I were looking for accomplices, do you think I'd choose these two idiots? You're welcome to them."

Her glance passed coldly over me, and suddenly I could hardly breathe. She thought I was an idiot? I'd thought she liked me. All she'd wanted was the key cylinder. She'd been using me. She must have been laughing at me all along. I was worse than an idiot. I wondered if anything she'd told me was true.

If I could have, I would have turned my head away, but the man holding me was pressing my cheek into the dirt, so I couldn't even flinch.

"What you're not welcome to is that artifact," Mina said. "It's mine."

Lady Harleston turned away from Putty, her thin dagger catching the sunlight. "And how, my dear, do you propose to take it?"

"Do you know what these are?" Mina asked conversationally. She lifted the object she was carrying. It was a jar, and inside, hundreds of small shapes darted and trembled. "They're shark beetles. They're not from around here, but you're an educated woman. I'm sure you recognize them. When they're hungry, they can tear through a man in seconds. Straight through the flesh and then up into the lungs they go. Down the mouth, up the nose, through your stomach, they don't care. They just want to feed." She cracked the lid of the jar, and one of the shapes darted for freedom. She snapped the lid back down just in time. "Oops."

"You're bluffing," Lady Harleston said, her eyes flicking nervously to the side.

"Do you know the curious thing about shark beetles?" Mina said. "They absolutely hate the smell of mint-vine. They won't go near it. That's why I had mint-vine in my tea this morning." She flashed a smile. "Sorry about the smell. It's pretty vile." She tilted her head curiously. "So, did you have mint-vine in your tea this morning?"

"They'll kill these two as well," Lady Harleston warned, taking a step back. The man on top of me shifted uncomfortably.

"You say that as though I care." Mina's cold gaze slipped past me again. "I'd let you kill them yourself, but really, I'm in a rush. So. Here. Catch!"

She hoisted the glass jar full of shark beetles.

"No!" Lady Harleston leaped back, and her man came up off me in a rush, stumbling away. I saw Putty's captor release her.

Lady Harleston gestured to her men, and they carefully retreated down the alley.

"You're going to regret this," she said. "I'll come after you."

"You could," Mina said. "But you'd have to find me, and I already know where *you* live. I wonder how well you'd sleep knowing that any night these little creatures could come sailing through your bedroom window." She lifted the jar again. "If you look for me, I'll know about it, and they really are very hungry."

With a last look of pure hatred, Lady Harleston turned on her heel and strode away.

I rolled over slowly, clutching my stomach. It still hurt to breathe.

"We should get out of here," Mina said, when they had gone. She held out a hand. I ignored it and pushed myself up against the wall.

"You know," Putty said, "those aren't really shark beetles."

"They're not?"

"Of course not!" Mina said. "What kind of idiot carries shark beetles around the streets? They're deadly."

"They're blister bugs," Putty said. "They look quite similar, but they only feed on sap." She gave me a superior look. "I used to keep shark beetles in my bedroom, but I had to tell Mama they were blister beetles so she wouldn't have convulsions. I'm surprised you didn't know the difference, Edward."

"You . . . saved us," I said, looking at Mina. "Again." I'd thought she'd betrayed us. I wanted to shrivel up inside like a dragonfruit picked too late from a tree.

Mina glanced away. "Yeah. Well."

"I should have trusted you more," I said. Saying it was like chewing on desert sand. It hurt and left my mouth dry.

She still didn't meet my eyes. "You shouldn't trust anyone. Especially not a thief. We're not good people."

I took a step closer to her. "Yes. You are."

"I think," Putty said loudly, "that I'm going to be sick."

I deliberately ignored her.

"You should have this," I said, holding out the key cylinder to Mina. "It's yours."

"You mean I stole it."

I shrugged. "Who does it really belong to? I mean, some-one dug it out of a dragon tomb, but that just means they found it first. It didn't belong to them any more than it be-longs to you. It belonged to the Ancient Martians, and . . ." I glanced awkwardly at her.

Her face clouded. "You mean I'm native Martian, so that makes it mine? You think we're all basically the same person or something?"

"No." I reddened. "I mean it certainly shouldn't belong to Lady Harleston. If it's not in the Museum of Martian Antiquities, it's as much yours as anyone else's."

She looked away again. "You shouldn't be so nice to me. I'm just a thief."

"I'm going to be a thief, too," Putty said. "I'm quite sneaky. I'm always stealing Edward's things, and he never notices."

"I had something to ask you," I said. "Not about the key. I know you don't know what it's for. There's a man we need to find. We thought maybe you'd heard of him. His name is Dr. Blood."

Mina's head jerked around, her eyes widening.

I frowned. That was a . . . weird reaction. "You know him?"

"No. It's just . . . that name. Why would someone call themselves that?"

I peered at her. Okay, it *was* a horrible name, I supposed, if you thought about it. But she looked like someone had stolen her puppy, and she wouldn't meet my eyes. I wondered if there was something she wasn't telling me.

"Are you sure you haven't heard anything?" I pressed. "We really have to find him. He's dangerous. He's already killed lots of people."

"I can ask around." She still wasn't looking at me.

I shook my head. I had no idea why she was acting so strange, but I had more important things to worry about right now.

We left the alley and made our way down the street beyond. A minute later, we came out into the square in front of the museum. The museum's wide doors stood open, and several automatic carriages and mechanized carriers were drawn up nearby. A couple of tough-looking militiamen stood outside the door, holding long cudgels. The gallery opening must already be under way. Papa would be expecting us.

"You should come in," I said suddenly. "See the new gallery. It's impressive."

Mina looked startled. "Me?" She glanced down at her clothes. Unlike mine, they were clean, but they were also cheap and patched.

"Why not?" I said. "Why shouldn't you?" Yes, she would stand out. Most of the guests would be from Lunae City's high society, and I doubted there would be any native Martians there, or even half-native Martians, but Captain Kol was right. The museum contained the history of the Martian people. Mina deserved to be there.

"You should!" Putty said enthusiastically. "I bet you'd know more about the devices in there than most of the guests. I bet you'd know more than Edward."

"Well, if he needs someone to explain it all to him . . ." Mina said with a grin. Her hands had started shaking, though, and she looked absolutely terrified. Somehow that made me feel better. It meant she was actually scared of something. Lady Harleston hadn't bothered her, and neither had rescuing us from the gulper, but facing all those important people at the gallery opening scared her more than a pit of grasp-snakes.

"Good," Putty said, grabbing Mina's hand. "Let's get inside."

I hadn't been in the gallery since it had been finished, but it was spectacular.

The preserved dragon we had found in the tomb filled the center of the room. It was far larger than I'd remembered. Its body was bigger than a whale, and its neck swept up almost to the glass ceiling of the gallery. Arranged around it were the artifacts and devices we'd discovered in the tomb, along with great slabs of wall covered in ideograms and diagrams.

The strange arrangement of delicate brass rods and balls, like an enormous sculpture of a crouching man (or possibly a collapsed clothes dryer), that I'd seen the curators trying to maneuver into the gallery stood by the bottom of the steps.

Not all the artifacts were there. Some had been completely

destroyed when Sir Titus Dane had plunged his excavator into the tomb, and others—the ones considered too dangerous for public display—had been discreetly taken away by the British Martian government for analysis. But even so, looking down the steps into the gallery felt eerily like being back in that tomb.

On the far side of the gallery, Dr. Guzman had cornered Jane. I would have felt guilty, except that Jane had managed to also corner Mr. Davidson, and the three of them stood in an awkward, polite huddle just to the left of the dragon's tail.

"It's . . . incredible," Mina breathed, coming to a halt at the top of the steps. Her eyes were wide, and right now she looked scarcely older than Putty.

"You should have seen it when we discovered it," I said.

She turned to me. "*You* found it?"

I shrugged, trying to look like it was something I did every day.

"Wow."

"I was more interested in saving my family," I said. "They were kidnapped by a man called Sir Titus Dane. He and Dr. Blood would have killed them if I hadn't rescued them."

She glanced away. "All this . . . You didn't want to keep any of it?"

"I found a dragon's egg," Putty said. "I kept that. Except no one knows, so you can't say anything."

Mina stared at Putty. "You did? A dragon's egg?"

"The only one ever."

Mina closed her eyes.

"Are you all right?" I said.

She shook her head. "Your lives . . . I've never met anyone like you. I just . . ." She shook her head. "Your family is incredible."

I cleared my throat awkwardly. "Well. Shall we go in? I think it's about to begin."

Papa and his curators had done a fantastic job of analyzing and repairing the artifacts from the tomb. Although some stood inactive, others were already back in operation. The smooth hum of spring-powered devices filled the room. In one corner, a group of men clustered around some strange, three-dimensional game that consisted of hundreds of different-shaped pieces arranged on half a dozen moving levels. Another machine was building a copy of itself from pieces scattered around it.

"There you are!"

I turned to see Olivia squeezing her way through the crowd toward us.

"Papa's been waiting for you to arrive so he can start his speech." She glanced at Mina. "Hello."

"He really didn't have to. Um. This is Mina. Mina, my sister, Olivia."

Olivia took Mina's hand. "I'm delighted to make your acquaintance. Putty told me all about you." She turned to me, grinning widely. "*All* about you."

I glared at her. "Isn't Papa about to make a speech?"

Olivia waved her free hand carelessly. "Oh, don't worry about that. I'm far more interested in finding out about your friend." She looped Mina's hand through her arm. "I'm sure we have *lots* to talk about." For the first time since I'd met her, Mina looked totally lost. Olivia gave me another grin. "Go and stare at a rock or something."

"This is not going to end well," I muttered to myself as Olivia led Mina off.

Someone cleared their throat behind me. I glanced back to see one of the junior curators hovering a couple of yards away.

"Ah!" he exclaimed. "Master Edward. I had been looking for you."

I frowned. "It's Dr. Tremaine, isn't it?"

"Is it?" he said. "Are we truly our names, or are our names us? Should you better say, Dr. Tremaine is you?"

I closed my eyes for a moment. Now I remembered why I'd avoided Dr. Tremaine. He was probably the most irritating man in the museum, and that was saying something.

"What can I do for you, Dr. Tremaine?"

"An excellent question, young man. Indeed, what can you do for me? I am reminded of a treatise by Professor—"

"You were looking for me," I interrupted.

"Indeed. Indeed. And now I have found you. Should we perhaps conclude that I have achieved my objective and that there is now no more to be said or done? A great accomplishment! A feat worthy of the history books!"

"Are we finished, then?" Putty said, hopping impatiently from foot to foot. "I want to go and look at the exhibits. I'm certain some of the designs could be improved."

Dr. Tremaine's white eyebrows shot up. "Improved? What an astounding idea, young lady. These are not dolls or dresses for you to play with. I'm sure you could, ah-ha-ha, make them pretty, but that is not their function. No, not at all. Baubles and ribbons, and suchlike. I am amused. I laugh."

He reached out a hand, as though to pat her on the head. I quickly inserted myself between them before she could bite it off.

"So what did you want me for, Dr. Tremaine?" I said.

He looked surprised. "Have I not said? No? Well. It has come to my attention that you were inquiring of one of my colleagues about a gentleman of, ah, native persuasion who was to be found perusing the exhibits."

"You saw him?"

"Indeed not. What makes you think such a thing?"

I stared at him.

"My little joke! I did indeed see him, although I thought little of it. No, Dr. Guzman, for it was he who was source of said information, informed me that you were also interested in a fellow who approached him in a coffee house. Not your fellow, another fellow. We must consider them distinct entities for the purposes of this conversation, and indeed, for all other purposes."

Putty groaned loudly.

Dr. Tremaine cleared his throat. "It appears, and it is indeed a fact, that the fellow approached me also. He asked me about the items being considered for display in your father's gallery. He seemed well dressed and reasonably knowledgeable about artifacts, so I humored him. The museum is always looking for donors, you know. Our funds never suffice. It soon became clear that the fellow was interested in one particular artifact, and I must say that I was surprised, because it is not an artifact of significance, nor would its existence be widely known."

That was more than Dr. Guzman had found out from Dr. Blood. Dr. Blood must have tried a different tactic after Dr. Guzman turned him down.

"What was it?" I said, looking around the gallery.

"Nothing you will see here, I assure you. Did I not say it was not of significance? We may be poor fools at the museum, but we are not given to displaying items of little worth." He raised his eyebrows expectantly.

"Very amusing," I said, through gritted teeth, and resisted the urge to punch him.

"Indeed. Indeed. The fellow was interested in a casket made of sandstone. A miniature sarcophagus no longer than my arm."

I felt Putty jerk next to me. "Edward . . ." she hissed.

I laid a hand on her shoulder, quieting her. Putty had found that sarcophagus in the dragon tomb. At first I'd thought it had been for a baby, but it had held the dragon's egg that Putty had kept as a souvenir.

"What was his interest in the casket?" I asked casually.

Dr. Tremaine's lip curled in displeasure. "The fellow asked me to obtain it for him. He wanted to buy it. He would pay the museum a large fee, and he offered me a ridiculous sum to carry out the transaction." He straightened. "The casket may be of little historical value, but it is the property of the Museum of Martian Antiquities, and it is part of the great picture of Martian history. It was not for sale. I informed the fellow as such, and that was an end to it."

"But you didn't tell anyone?"

"I assumed the fellow to be a private collector. It would not be the first time that a collector had attempted to obtain an item from the museum, and I am afraid to say that not all of my colleagues are so, ah, conscientious in their attitudes. I dismissed him from my thoughts, and that should have been the end of the matter. Except that when he approached me in the coffee house, he had been sitting with two other, ah, less salubrious gentlemen. Quite uncouth in their appearance. Dr. Guzman told me he saw them, too. They stuck in my mind, because they did not seem the correct company for a gentleman of means. And then I glimpsed them the next day in the museum. Failing to persuade me to obtain their artifact, it was my assumption that these men intended to steal it themselves."

"You didn't try to stop them?"

Dr. Tremaine lifted his chin. "The artifact in question is locked in a highly secure room in the basement. They could not hope to get it, and indeed it remains in the museum's possession. The fellows have not returned. I believe my course of action was entirely appropriate, that is to say my action took no particular course, and as a result caused no inappropriate actions. I put it from my mind."

"And?" I said.

"Indeed. 'And,' indeed. It was not until I heard of your inquiries about the native personage from Dr. Guzman yesterday that I recalled the coincidence of incidents. Those men had been in the museum on the same day as your Martian. I had seen them heading for the same gallery. It seemed likely to me that the two were connected. It is my conclusion that both your Martian and these rough fellows were in league. Your fellow, I conclude, was a thief. Indeed, there is no other possible conclusion."

I gritted my teeth. That confirmed what I'd already believed: Dr. Blood *had* been the one who'd taken Rothan Gal.

He'd tried to bribe both Dr. Guzman and Dr. Tremaine to steal the sarcophagus, then sent his men after the fragment of ideograms Rothan Gal had been studying. But why? It still didn't make any sense. What did he want with the sarcophagus of all things? It hadn't even been impressive, just a hollowed-out block of stone with a hole in one end and a plain lid, only large enough to hold the single dragon's egg. It was worth no more than the broken tablet of ideograms. I could have understood someone wanting to steal the dragon's egg—it was unique, and probably valuable to a collector—but the egg wasn't even in the sarcophagus anymore and Dr. Blood wasn't a collector.

Why was Dr. Blood trying to steal worthless items when we were in a gallery full of priceless discoveries?

One thing I did know: Dr. Blood would have a reason for all this, and he wouldn't give up. Dr. Tremaine might have confidence in the museum's security, but I didn't. I'd seen Dr. Blood's mechanical crabs bring down an airship. If he wanted to get into that chamber, he would.

I would have to move the sarcophagus. Hide it somewhere Dr. Blood would never think of looking. Stall his plans until Freddie or the British-Martian Intelligence Service could arrive to arrest him and end this forever.

Except the sarcophagus was locked in a secure room behind six inches of steel and the most complicated lock I had ever heard of, one that would only open under Dr. Guzman's hand.

I glanced across the room to where Jane was still cornered by the junior-under-curator, second class.

"Come on," I told Putty, and started through the crowd.

A shadow fell across the gallery, like a cloud crossing the sun.

I looked up.

A shape hung over the glass ceiling. It was a flier, a big one, the size of a small airship, and it was hovering low above the roof. The downdraft from its great copter blades beat against the glass ceiling, making the glass bow and shake in the frames.

"He's too close," Putty said, puzzled, peering up. "What's he doing?"

Long, sinuous metal arms unwound and dropped from the flier, like jellyfish tentacles settling down above us. Claws closed around the ceiling struts.

Then, with a single motion, they ripped the glass roof from the gallery.

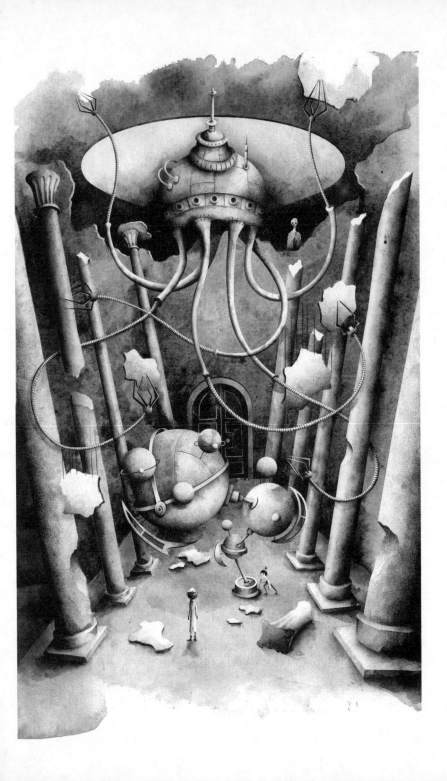

— 12 —

Madness in the Museum

Glass rained down.

Screams sounded around me. I shoved Putty to the floor and threw myself over her. A splinter of shattered glass sliced across my jacket, narrowly missing my face.

With a crash, the glass roof was tossed away. I jumped to my feet. People cowered on the stone floor. Others were already heading in panic for the gallery door. I saw Jane and Papa staring in shock from the far side of the gallery, but I couldn't see Mina or Olivia. Where were they?

"Look at that!" Putty said.

The flier that had torn the roof from the gallery was separating into four parts, each held aloft by twin sets of copter blades.

Figures leaped from the sides of the four fliers, landing with *thumps* into the gallery. At first I thought they were automatons, but then I saw men's faces staring out through thick glass faceplates.

"Clockwork armor!" Putty shouted in excitement.

One of the men turned to us. He held a compressed-air gun in one armored hand. Cogs whirred as he brought it to bear.

I lunged to one side, dragging Putty with me. A *pop* sounded as the bullet whizzed past me.

"This way!" someone yelled.

I spun around and saw Olivia waving wildly from behind a statue near one wall. She and Mina had sheltered there. They were all right! Thank heavens.

There were crashes and shouts everywhere. Glass display cases shattered and artifacts tumbled to the floor. Panicked guests raced past. One by one, the four separated fliers lowered themselves through the gaping roof.

I took advantage of the chaos and gave Putty a shove. "Go and help Olivia!"

"Where are you going?"

"To get Jane."

I sprinted across the room to where Jane, Dr. Guzman, Mr. Davidson, and Papa were pressed against a wall. A fleeing curator slammed into me, knocking me to the floor. I scrambled back up.

"Get out of here!" I yelled, waving wildly. "Get somewhere safe!"

"My artifacts!" Papa wailed. "They're destroying them. They're destroying everything again." He tore at his gray hair.

I reached them, grabbed Papa by the arm, and pulled him toward where Mina, Olivia, and Putty were crouched. "Jane. Come on!"

Jane looked scared, but she wasn't panicking, unlike Mr. Davidson and Dr. Guzman. She glanced around, checking out the positions of the attackers, then grabbed Papa's arm and helped me haul him around the edge of the room. Mr. Davidson and Dr. Guzman scuttled after us.

The first flier leveled out ten feet off the floor. Its snake-like arms flailed around, snatching at artifacts and toppling them, adding to the chaos.

Suddenly, Putty darted away from Olivia. Olivia snatched at her and missed. One of the flier's arms lashed out, but Putty was too fast. She ducked under it and around behind the enormous brass rod-and-ball sculpture.

That would never protect her. A single blow from the flier's arms would crumple it.

"Take Papa," I said to Jane. If I slipped under the dragon's belly, maybe I could reach her.

The flier spun in the air, turning to Putty.

Putty reached for the base of the artifact and pressed something. For a moment, nothing happened. Then the artifact sprang into the air, brass rods spreading like a thousand thin arms, right into the path of the flier. As they collided, the arms clamped tight onto the flier, wrapping around the copter blades. Metal screamed. Cogs jumped.

The flier dropped.

The impact crumpled it. Copter blades plowed into the wall with a shriek.

Then Putty was up and running back to Olivia and Mina. Papa had stopped dead, his mouth hanging open.

"*That's* what it does," he muttered, rubbing at his eyeglasses.

I grabbed his arm again and we raced for shelter.

"We need to get out of the museum," Mina said as we reached them. "Outside we can run. Here we'll be trapped."

"Not out the front," I said. "We'd never make it across the square."

"You think they're after you?" Mina said.

The other fliers spread across the gallery. The armored men herded the last of the crowd out of the door.

"They're Dr. Blood's men," I said. "He'll never let us get away. You should get out of here, though. You'll be safe. We'll find another way out."

She gave me a defiant look. "No. I'm not going to leave you to this."

"You're not?" I said, staring. I'd given her the key cylinder. She'd gotten what she wanted. She could give it to her dad. Maybe he'd even be grateful. She didn't have any reason to stay.

"Edward!" Olivia clapped her hands in front of my face. "Wake up!"

I blinked. Dr. Blood's men were everywhere. In a few moments, we would be completely trapped. My heart was pounding so loud I could barely think. I hadn't expected Dr. Blood to come after us so quickly and so hard. There had only been two militiamen on the door. They wouldn't even slow Dr. Blood's men down. If they'd had any sense, they would have gone for help. If they'd had the chance.

"Get them out the back," I shouted to Olivia. I pointed at the small curators' entrance at the far end of the gallery. "Then through the rear of the museum. You can get to the docks. Find Captain Kol. He'll help you. We'll slow them down." I glanced at Mina. "Any ideas?"

"A few," Mina grunted. "Maybe."

"Edward," Putty warned. "Look."

Balancing on the lip of the roof above us was a single figure. He stood outlined by the bright Lunae Planum sun. Even in the glare, I recognized him, and my heart sank. As if men with clockwork armor and guns weren't enough.

"Apprentice," I whispered.

How were we supposed to fight him, too? Apprentice was Dr. Blood's right-hand man. He wore a cloak covered in hundreds of clockwork bugs that would launch themselves in deadly attack on his command. Where his mouth and nose should have been was a metallic mask, clamped in place by thick staples that dug into the flesh, twisting his face horribly. He absolutely terrified me.

Mina stared at me with shocked eyes. "You *know* him?"

"He's not a friend," I said. "He's a monster. A killer."

"God." She covered her face in her hands.

"It's all right," I murmured. "We've beaten him before." Or Freddie had. But I wasn't about to mention that.

Apprentice took a step forward, off the lip of the roof. His cloak snapped open behind him, stiffening. The hundreds of mechanical bugs attached to it spread their wings, and he lowered through the air as though he were wearing a helichute.

He had changed since I had seen him last. Back then, he'd only had the mask over his mouth and nose, and that had been bad enough. Now he'd added two glittering glass-and-metal half spheres over his eyes. Except they weren't just goggles. They went through his skin and flesh all the way down to the bone. Just seeing them made me feel sick. I couldn't imagine how much they must hurt, but Apprentice didn't show the slightest expression. Maybe he couldn't under all that metal. My stomach turned over again.

"We need to get out of here," I said. "Now."

I ran for the main door, waving my free hand as I ran. Mina and Putty followed. The fliers spun toward us.

Loud clicks sounded from Apprentice's mask. The armored men swung around to form a line between us and the door. Guns swung smoothly up.

"Back the other way," I shouted.

"No," Mina said. She reached into her backpack as she ran, pulling out a cluster of glass balls. They were too small to be photon emission globes, and anyway, something black moved inside them like smoke and water. She threw them just as the first man fired.

The shot snatched at my jacket. I stumbled and almost lost my footing again. We were going to die. They were going to kill us.

The glass balls shattered. Something fine and black sprayed across the men in clockwork armor. Within a second they were slipping and falling in a tangle.

"Micro-oil!" Putty squeaked. "I never thought of using it for that. Papa uses it in his tiniest devices. It has almost no friction."

The armored men were trying to get up, but they couldn't get their footing. They slipped and flailed.

"Jump!" Mina said as we ran toward them.

Jump? That was even worse than one of Putty's plans.

I closed my eyes and jumped.

On Earth, I would never have made it. Even here in Mars's low gravity, I nearly didn't. One of the men snatched for me. His fist closed around my trouser leg, but he was still coated in micro-oil. His hand slid free.

I hit the floor and tumbled forward. Behind us, propellers whined, and the fliers came chasing after.

Mina reached the door. "Quickly!" she shouted.

I scrambled to my feet and lunged. Putty grabbed me and hauled me through. Mina slammed the doors shut behind us and dropped the latch.

Something crashed into the doors, shaking them on their hinges.

The main entrance of the museum stood open at the front of the lobby. Bright sunlight shone in from the square beyond. There was no sign of the militia guards.

The doors shook again. This time, one of them cracked. One more blow, maybe two, and that would be it.

"This way," I said, and headed further into the museum.

Dr. Blood was after the sarcophagus. I had to assume he'd found out where it was kept. Apprentice would head for the storeroom. No matter how thick the door or how strong the lock, he would get through. Dr. Blood would get what he wanted, and then he'd come after us.

"What are we going to do?" Mina yelled.

"We get the sarcophagus before Apprentice does," I said. "We destroy it. Then they won't have any reason to come after us. We'll stop their plan in its tracks." Whatever that plan was.

I hoped.

The doors behind us burst from their hinges. Propellers beat the still museum air. Heavy metal footsteps sounded on stone.

I took a quick left into a hallway that cut behind an exhibit of artifacts from the tomb of the boy emperor Gre-Eb-Tol.

"They're coming," Putty called.

The first flier dipped into the hallway. Its enormous propellers barely cleared the high ceiling. Its sinuous arms trailed across the ancient red rock walls. A second flier followed, and then half a dozen men in automatic armor. Air from the propellers buffeted along the hallway.

"Any more ideas?" I panted.

"Run faster?" Mina said.

"Get to a corner," Putty said. "They'll have to slow down or they'll get stuck."

The hallway stretched ahead. The nearest corner was nearly thirty yards away. "Great."

A whir of cogs sounded behind us. Small portholes opened in the lead flier. Spiny spheres, like metal sea urchins, spun from the portholes. I ducked as one whizzed past. It hit the wall, then ricocheted away, bouncing from the floor and ceiling. Putty flung herself to the side.

The sphere smacked into a wooden statue standing on a plinth just ahead of me. The spines dug in. A moment later, the sphere exploded. The shock wave knocked me from my feet. Splinters sprayed overhead.

I scrambled up, feeling dizzy. My feet didn't want to do what they were told. I stumbled again.

"Keep moving!" Mina said.

More spheres rebounded from side to side. I dodged and ducked. Behind us, the fliers whirred closer.

Mina rolled, reaching into her backpack as she went. She came up with a cylinder in her hand and tossed it into the air. A spray of silvery strips erupted from it, filling the air like gently falling snow, hiding the flier from view.

We dashed around an empty display case pushed against one wall. Sweat was running into my eyes, making them sting. The corridor blurred in front of me. I swiped my sleeve across my eyes and glanced back.

With a whine, the flier emerged from the shower of silvery strips, nosing its way carefully out, but the moment it was free, it sped up. Portholes slid open again.

I darted around the corner, just behind Putty. A sandstone statue of an ancient emperor loomed almost up to the ceiling. The emperor's features had been worn away by time and the scouring winds, leaving a massive, featureless block of stone. Ten yards beyond, a narrow staircase led down to Dr. Guzman's storeroom—and the sarcophagus within.

"Let's tip that into the corridor!" Putty said.

"You're mad," I said. "We'll never move it." I grabbed her shoulder to shove her onward.

She shook free. "It's just mechanics. It'll be easy."

"Easy? It must weigh tons!"

Putty rolled her eyes. "It's just like a lever. Push at the right place and it'll topple."

"And where's the right place?" I said.

Putty looked up. "The head."

I stared at her. *The head?* "That's twenty feet up."

"I'll do it," Mina said.

"But—" I started.

"I'm a better climber than you."

"That's true," Putty said. "Edward's useless at climbing."

She was right. I'd never get up there in time. But Mina could be killed, and none of this had anything to do with her.

I ground my teeth. "Fine."

The first flier appeared at the corner, turning carefully on its axis as it maneuvered in the tight space. Mina leaped for the statue, clambering up like it was a ladder.

Putty and I sprinted for the stairway that led down to the storeroom. As we reached it, I glanced back to see Mina climb onto the statue's shoulders and tie something around it. Beyond, the flier worked free of the corner and started toward us.

Putty grabbed my hand. "Come on."

Then everything happened at once.

The wall opposite Mina exploded in a shower of stonework. She lost her grip and fell. Great metal arms appeared, ripping away at the wall, widening the gaping hole. Black smoke and steam billowed into the hallway as something shouldered its way through.

"Mina!" I shouted.

She hit the ground with a cry of pain. Fragments of stone spun through the air. I ducked as they ricocheted against me, as hard as punches.

Through the gap in the wall, a gigantic, troll-like machine emerged. Its shoulders took up half its squat body, supporting titanic arms. Steam and smoke pumped from twin chimneys where its head should have been.

With a last heave, it ripped away most of the wall. The ceiling creaked and sagged above us.

The machine shuffled back.

I pulled Putty to her feet. My pulse was pounding so loud in my ears I could hardly hear the grinding machinery and shifting stone. The clouds of dust and smoke clogged my throat and nose. I struggled to drag in enough clean air.

I started toward Mina, but Putty pulled me back.

Figures had appeared in the gap left by the troll-machine. Desperately, I rubbed at my streaming eyes.

Apprentice and half a dozen men in clockwork armor stepped through. He stopped beside Mina's sprawled body and stared down at her with his strange, metallic eyes. The thousands of button-sized clockwork beetles on his cloak seethed restlessly.

He would kill her! She couldn't defend herself and she couldn't get away. She was at his mercy.

I scrambled around for a chunk of stone large enough to throw. My hand closed on one.

Then Apprentice stepped around her, and his men followed.

I stared. He'd let her go? Why? Did we bother him so little that he just didn't care?

Putty pulled on my hand again. "Come on, Edward!"

Apprentice and his men swung toward us. A stream of clicks emerged from the mask over Apprentice's mouth, and his men raised their weapons.

Reluctantly, I retreated, backing away from the stairs and the storeroom.

One of the guns spat a bullet in a hiss of compressed air. It smacked into the wall above my head. We stumbled back faster. I pushed Putty behind me.

Without a word, Apprentice turned down the stairs and disappeared from view.

Damnation! I had nothing. No weapons, and no way of stopping him.

The moment Apprentice's men followed him down, Mina scrambled to her feet and limped over to us.

"He let you go," I said.

"He let all of us go," Mina said. She felt her shoulder with long, nimble fingers and winced. "Maybe . . . maybe he's not so bad?"

I stared at her. *Not so bad?* She really must have hit her head too hard.

"I wouldn't be so sure he's let us go," Putty said.

Propellers beat the air. Wearily, I lifted my head. The lead flier dipped down as it accelerated toward us and long, clawed arms reached out.

A Suspicious Savior

I stepped forward, out in front of the flier. I didn't know what I was going to do. I didn't know how to fight something like this. We'd tried everything and it just kept coming. There was nowhere left to run. Maybe if I distracted it, Putty and Mina would be able to get away. I took a deep breath, then tensed to leap.

"Get down!" a voice shouted from behind.

I dived for the floor as a tall figure stepped out at the far end of the hallway and raised a long rifle to his shoulder. I glimpsed broad shoulders, a wide hat, dark brown skin, and a scarred face.

The rifle gave a deafening *crack*.

The bullet smacked into the flier, dead center, and the flier tipped. The propellers whined desperately. The metallic arms whipped back and forth.

The point of the back propeller caught on the wall, and it shattered. Fragments of hardened steel thudded into the sandstone walls and skittered from the marble floor. Mina swore behind me.

The flier lunged forward, driving itself into the floor. Metal crumpled and glass burst. Something inside exploded, making the machine buck like it had been kicked.

I threw myself back, rolling away from the toppling flier.

For a moment, it balanced on its front, jutting like a finger into the air. Then the still-spinning front propeller pulled it forward and the flier came crashing down.

I got to my feet and ran, pushing Putty ahead of me. Mina followed, her harsh breath panting at my shoulder.

With another great crash, the top of the flier hit the ground and it disintegrated. The coiled springs unwound with a fury that tore the machine apart. The museum building groaned as one of the walls took the full force of the eruption.

The tall man was waiting around the corner, back pressed against the wall. His gun was propped, its butt on the floor, the barrel in one of his hands. He spat something into the barrel, then pulled a narrow rod from its clip and plunged it down the barrel.

"You used gunpowder!" Putty said. "I didn't think anyone actually used that."

He glanced up at her. His scar pulled one side of his mouth up into a permanent, lopsided smile. "I like the smell. And I'm a good shot."

He removed the rod, flipped it, and shoved it back into its clip.

"Who the devil are you?" I demanded.

He raised an eyebrow.

"I've seen you," I said. "Spying on us. And you've been asking questions."

"This isn't exactly the time." The man glanced back around the corner. "We need to get going. That won't hold them for long."

I shook my head. "We're not going anywhere with you. Not until I know what the hell you want."

He laughed. "I was told you'd be like this. Your cousin sent me."

I narrowed my eyes. "My cousin Harry, you mean?"

"Freddie," the man said. "You don't have a cousin called Harry. And Freddie's not actually your cousin. You just call him that." He reached into his jacket and pulled out a sealed letter. "He couldn't come, so he asked me to keep an eye on your family. He'd heard some rumors."

I took the letter and unsealed it.

"It's Freddie's handwriting," I said reluctantly.

"What does it say?" he said.

I scanned through the letter. It sounded like Freddie, too. Not the idiot Freddie act he put on to fool people, but Freddie the spy who always knew what to do. "It says we should trust you." I looked up and caught his eye. "What's your name?"

"George Rackham. Is that what it says in the letter?"

Freddie had said he was sending someone to keep an eye on us, but how could I be sure Rackham was Freddie's man?

"Letters can be forged," I said. Jane had forged a letter from Papa so well I'd hardly been able to tell the difference. It would be easy for a professional. This man had been spying on us, following me, watching, asking questions.

"You think you have a choice right now?" George Rackham said. "In two minutes, so much firepower is going to come around that corner you won't even be a memory. I can't defend you. Not here."

I still wasn't ready to trust him. He could be working for Dr. Blood, looking to trick us somehow.

"Why would you risk your life to help us?" I said. "We've never even met before."

"I owe your cousin a favor," Rackham said, his scarred lip twitching up. "And I didn't have anything better to do. Think of it this way: I could have put that bullet through your head as easily as I could into the flier's cogs. Now, we need to get going. Quickly."

I hesitated, glancing back to where Apprentice had gone.

"There are some battles you can't win," Rackham said.

"He's right," Mina said. "Nothing's worth getting killed for. Whatever those people want, let them have it."

Dr. Blood wouldn't let it end here. He wouldn't let us stand in the way of whatever he had planned. We'd stopped him and Sir Titus Dane once before. He wouldn't risk us

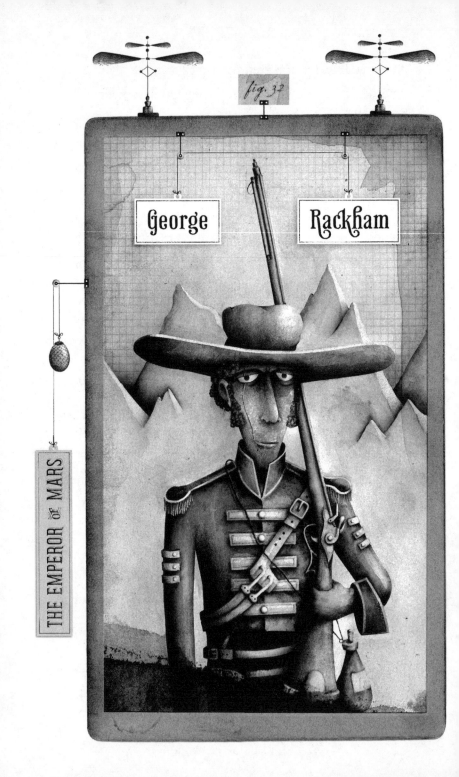

fig. 32

George   Rackham

THE EMPEROR OF MARS

doing it again. He would come after us, and he'd keep coming until we were dead.

Beneath the floor, a great *whoomf* sounded, followed by the clatter of metal. The floor shuddered, and I staggered to one side.

"What . . . ?" Mina said.

"They're into the storeroom," I said. Apprentice was through the steel door.

"I've got a boat," Rackham said. "I can get you out of the city."

"We can't," I said. "Not yet. We have to get Mama. She's still at home. She hasn't got a clue what's going on."

"All my things are there, too!" Putty said. "Dr. Blood can't have my things. I've spent ages on some of them."

Rackham cast one last look around the corner. "Then we move. Now. Keep up and do what I tell you, and we might get out of this."

"Fine," I said.

For now.

⊰◈⊱

There were signs of Dr. Blood's men everywhere. As we hurried through the museum, I saw smashed display cases and glass that had been crunched under the heavy feet of the clockwork armor. Statues and delicate artifacts had been toppled and knocked to the ground. But nothing seemed to have been taken. They really were only after the sarcophagus. Why? It was worthless. Unless there was something hidden in it that we'd missed.

Our pace was painfully slow. At every corner, Rackham paused, listening, before looking around then signaling us forward. Each time he did it, I got more and more jumpy. Any second now, I expected Apprentice or one of his machines to appear behind us, and we'd be caught.

Rackham stopped at another corner and I resisted the urge to scream. Rackham knew what he was doing. It was what Freddie would have done. But if we kept on like this, I would be chewing off my fingers.

Ahead, I knew, the corridor doglegged back, then a door on the right led out to the museum's own wharf and the river. From there, we could cut north toward our house, or south to the main commercial wharfs, where Captain Kol's ship was tied up.

Rackham held up a hand. He glanced back and mouthed, *Someone there.*

I swore under my breath. Of course the exits were guarded. I should have realized.

Rackham raised his rifle. "Stay."

There *had* to be another way out, one that Apprentice didn't know about. Where? I racked my brain, trying to think. A side door. A ground-floor window that could be jacked open.

Rackham took a quick step, swinging his rifle out, aiming down the corridor.

Something flew through the air and caught him on the shoulder. He spun around, dropping to his knee and bringing the rifle back up again.

"Stop!" I shouted, leaping forward.

Rackham was already straightening, pulling his rifle back up. I stumbled out just as a length of wood whistled by, almost taking the top off my head.

"Stop!"

"Edward?"

Olivia stood a yard away, the length of wood raised ready to swing again. It looked like the leg of a display table, and if that caught me across the ear, I'd know it.

"He's a friend," I said. "Probably."

Rackham rolled his shoulder. "You're fast."

Olivia gave him a suspicious look but lowered the wood.

"What are you doing here?" I demanded.

"We can't get out this way," Olivia said. "I was about to look for another when your friend snuck up on me."

"Freddie sent him," I said. "He says."

Olivia's hand fluttered to her throat. "You know Freddie?"

"We spent some time together. Once."

"What have you done with Papa and Jane?" I said.

"I put them in a closet with Mr. Davidson," Olivia answered. "It seemed like the best idea." She pointed along the corridor, past a statue of some minor emperor.

"You said there were guards," Rackham said. "How many?"

"Just one," Olivia said. "But he's armored, and he's carrying weapons." She swung her length of wood. "We're not exactly equipped for that."

"Keep an eye behind us," Rackham told me, "and follow me."

While Olivia let Papa, Jane, and Mr. Davidson out of their closet, Rackham led us to where the corridor cut back. Up ahead, daylight shone through the open door, outlining the bulky shape of one of Dr. Blood's armored men. He was so large in his clockwork armor that he almost blocked the doorway completely.

"Keep back," Rackham said. He strode out into the middle of the corridor. "You!" he called.

Cogs whirred as the armored man turned. His compressed-air gun swung up more smoothly than any man could have managed. A targeting light flicked on, settling on Rackham's chest.

Rackham snapped his rifle to his shoulder. There was a crack, like a stick breaking, then a puff of smoke. The rifle kicked back and up.

The armored man jerked. Gears screamed. His gun spun wildly. I dropped to the floor, pulling Putty with me.

"Get off!" she said. "I want to see."

The armored man seemed to leap, almost crashing into the ceiling. Then he toppled back and lay motionless.

I scrambled up and ran over to him. He was lying on his back, unmoving.

"You killed him," I said.

"Just disabled his armor." Rackham squatted over the fallen figure and rapped on the thick glass faceplate. Angry eyes stared back. "If he wants to get up again, he's going to have to move half a ton of armor all by himself."

Somewhere behind I heard a crash as something was flung aside.

"And that's our cue to get out of here," I said. "Before his friends come along to help."

There was a small open area between the back of the museum and the wharf. Thousands of years ago, when the temple that once stood here had been built, the Martian Nile had flowed almost half a mile further to the west. The temple grounds and buildings had stretched gently down to the river. Now all that was left was this narrow stretch of ground before the wharf. The remains of worn statues and pillars jutted through the flagstones.

To the north and south, native Martian buildings crowded to within fifty feet of the museum, then stopped abruptly, as though not daring to get any closer to the ancient temple.

I took Mina by the arm as the rest of our party spilled out into the sunlight.

"You could still get away," I said. "They don't know who you are. You could disappear. They would never find you."

"What about you?"

I shook my head. "It's not your problem. You don't have to be involved." She had nothing to do with Dr. Blood. If something happened to her, I would never forgive myself. "You've got your key cylinder."

She stared at me as though I'd slapped her.

"How can you say that?" she whispered. "You think I'd just walk away and let you get killed? Is that what you really think of me?"

"No!" I protested. That wasn't what I'd meant at all. Why couldn't she see that? "I was just . . . I mean . . . Why are you helping us?"

"Because you're good people, and I don't want to see you get killed. I thought by now we were friends."

"But—"

"Edward!" Olivia called. "We have to get going. Now."

I tried to catch Mina's gaze, but she wouldn't look at me.

Rackham came up behind me and laid a big hand on my shoulder. "I'm not coming with you."

"You're not?" He'd gone to all this trouble to rescue us and now he was abandoning us?

"You'll never make it to the docks if you go to your house first," he said. "Your friend back there is going to be coming after you with everything he's got. You're going to be trapped."

"So you're going to run," I said. "Some friend of Freddie's you are."

Rackham's eyes hardened, and I had to force myself not to retreat.

"I told you. I owe your cousin. I made him a promise and I keep my promises. I'll bring my boat around and meet you at the edge of your estate, where it abuts the water. Be there. We might not have much time."

With that, he turned and ran to the buildings to the south, his rifle held loosely in his hand.

I helped Olivia round up the rest. Papa was white-faced but grimly determined as he clutched his hat to his loose hair. Mr. Davidson, though, looked as though he could collapse at any moment, while Jane was surprisingly calm. We headed in the opposite direction to Rackham.

Mina still wouldn't meet my eyes.

A detachment of militiamen ran past as we made it to the shelter of the northern buildings, and only just in time. We'd scarcely made another dozen yards when the back of the museum exploded. The giant troll-like automaton smashed its way through the wall, followed by a dozen men in clockwork armor. Behind them came the two remaining fliers and Apprentice. Except now he wasn't walking like his men were. He was hovering in the air.

"Great," I muttered. "Now he can fly, too."

Several of the militiamen raised guns, but most were only armed with cudgels.

"The militia are going to get themselves killed," Mina said.

"They won't fight," Olivia said. "Not when they see what they're up against. They're not soldiers."

There are some battles you can't win, Rackham had said. This was one of them. Gritting my teeth, I turned away.

"We run," I said. It was all we could do.

So why did I feel like such a coward?

— 14 —

In Which We Bravely Run Away

The Flame House stood on the northern edge of Lunae City, where the Martian Nile, which had been traveling almost directly north until then, swung to the northeast to make its long way to the sea. We were almost a mile from the museum, but even as we approached our small estate, I could still hear shouts and explosions from the city. The militiamen were making a fight of it, but they weren't going to win.

"We need to be quick," I said. "Five minutes, no longer. Putty, you go and find your governess. The rest of us need to find Mama."

Putty gave me an appalled look. "I'm not getting my governess! She's a spy and she deserves to be left behind. I'm going to get my stuff." Without waiting for an answer, she turned on her heel and dashed into the house.

"Let her go," Olivia said. "Miss Wilkins is probably with Mama anyway."

"We should split up," I said. "Papa, you and Olivia search the ground floor. Jane, if there's anything important you need, find it. I'll—"

"Go with Mina?" Olivia said, raising an eyebrow.

I blushed furiously and glared at Olivia. "Shall we just get on with this?"

—◆—

Searching the Flame House was *not* the easiest job in the world. There were places in which even I could get lost or stuck or possibly eaten by a stray, hungry corridor. Luckily, Mama kept very strictly to only a few reasonably respectable rooms. Mina and I searched for Mama in her bedroom and dressing room without luck and were heading for the nursery when I heard Papa calling. His voice sounded urgent.

"Something's up," Mina said.

"Something's always up with this family," I said as we hurried along a hallway. "You get used to it."

"Do you always get attacked by armed men and deadly machines?" Mina asked.

"More often than you'd think." I sighed. "You're right. Let's find out what's going on."

Papa was in his study when we finally made it through the maze of the Flame House.

"What is it?" I called as I burst in. "Is it Mama?"

Papa glanced back at me, a distracted expression on his face. "What? No. She's in her drawing room with Miss

Wilkins. This is far more important! I've been burgled. Look!"

I peered past him. His study was in chaos. Papers were scattered everywhere. Books lay open in piles on the floor and chairs and desk.

"I thought it always looked like this," I said.

Papa drew himself up. "I know exactly where every single piece of paper is in the study. Someone has been in here and moved everything."

"Putty?" I suggested.

"Parthenia is a more careful burglar than that. She knows to put things back where she found them. In any case, nothing has been taken from here." He crossed to the back of the room, stepping around the slumped stacks of paper. "It is my safe." He pushed aside a portrait and swung open the safe door. "See? The lock has been burned out. It would take a powerful acid to eat through the metal. My papers have been taken." He rubbed a tired hand across his eyes. "My most important work. The plans for my improved water abacus. My theories on photonic storage. My thesis on the history of spring power in the Third Age. All of it is gone."

"I'm sorry, Papa," I said, "but we have rather more important things to worry about right now."

Papa's forehead furrowed. "You don't understand, Edward. The plans for my water abacus have been stolen. The Emperor Napoleon *will* get hold of them now, one way or another. This is bad, Edward."

I glanced toward the window. Dr. Blood's men and machines weren't in sight yet, but they would be soon.

"How long?" I said.

"I beg your pardon?"

"How long until Napoleon can make use of the designs?"

Papa rubbed at his eyeglasses. "A month to get the designs to Earth along the dragon paths. Six months to install water abacuses in his machines of war if his mechanicians are good, and they are good. The emperor has always understood the potential of Martian technology, which is why he has been able to conquer most of Earth. Another month for an invading force to travel back to Mars, if he holds the dragon path terminals by then. Eight months. Less than a year, certainly."

"Eight months." I shook my head. "Then we can worry about it another time. Right now we don't have eight *minutes* before Apprentice gets here." I took Papa's elbow. "I really am sorry, Papa, but we have to get Mama and we have to leave. Now."

<hr/>

Mama was waiting in her drawing room with Olivia, Jane, Mr. Davidson, and Miss Wilkins. She was sitting so straight and stiff it looked like someone had glued a board to her back. Jane had an oddly shaped bag between her feet. I'd assumed she would want to bring half a dozen gowns, but this was something else.

"What is the meaning of this, Edward?" Mama snapped. "Hugo? Olivia tells me we must leave the house. It is absurd. I have no intention of leaving my home." She turned her eye on Mina. "And who, pray, is this? Is she here begging?"

I closed my eyes. *Why?* Why did Mama have to be like this? I'd never introduced a girl to her before—not that this really counted, what with Apprentice trying to blow us to atoms—and when I did, she acted like this? All I wanted to do was stick my head in a bucket.

"That is hardly fair, madam," Mina said. "I am not a beggar." She smiled sweetly. "I am a thief."

Mama's jaw dropped. *Serves you right,* I thought and had to stop myself from grinning.

"Olivia's telling the truth," I said. "The house is about to be attacked. We need to leave. Right now."

"I have never heard such a thing!" Mama said. "Where do you propose we go? I will not stay in a *hotel.*"

"We've got a boat." I glanced around the room. "Has anyone seen Putty?"

"Behind you." She darted into the drawing room, carrying a heavy-looking bag. "Why are we all still here?"

"The children are right, Caroline," Papa said. "We must leave immediately. There can be no discussion." At Mama's rebellious expression, he added, "I insist."

Mama rose hesitantly. "I will not leave without my valuables."

"I have taken the liberty," Papa said, indicating a valise by the door.

"And I have Parthenia's bag packed," Miss Wilkins said.

Putty looked startled. "You do?"

"You may find it hard to believe, Parthenia," Miss Wilkins said, "but it is my job to keep you safe and under control, and I am very good at my job. Do not imagine that I did not fully understand the history of this family when I accepted your mother's offer. I am *always* prepared."

Putty shot me a wounded look as we headed for the door as though to say, *You see what I have to deal with?*

We followed Papa and Mama out of the house, across the terrace, toward the lawns that led down to the Martian Nile.

"I'm not suitably dressed for this," I heard Mama complain.

I pulled Putty to one side. "What have you got in there?" I demanded, pointing at her bag.

"My dragon's egg," she said defiantly.

I stared at her. "We're running for our lives, and you bring a stone egg?"

"I'm not letting Apprentice and Dr. Blood have it."

"Leave it," Mina said urgently. "You won't be able to run with it. It'll slow you down." She looked around. "Put it here." She pointed to a table on the edge of the terrace. "It'll be out of harm's way and you can get it when you come back."

Putty's jaw tightened. "I'm not leaving it! It's mine. And I can still run faster than the rest of you." She jogged a couple of paces forward. "See?"

"Fine," I said. "Then prove it by running to the river door and seeing if Rackham is there yet."

"This isn't a good idea," Mina murmured as Putty ran off, the bag banging awkwardly against her hip.

"There's no point arguing with Putty," I said. "Not unless you want to waste your whole day." I looked back toward the high roofs of Lunae City. The shouting and explosions had ended. In the still, hot, desert air, clouds of dust slowly rose, becoming thin and tattered and finally drifting away.

"They're on their way," Mina said. "I'll go and look out for Rackham, too." She took off at a trot, heading after Putty.

"Your friend seems nice," Jane said from behind me. She'd come up while I was talking to Mina. I gave her a hard look. Jane considered everyone nice, but I thought I detected a touch of sarcasm. Or maybe I was being too sensitive.

Jane had been walking with Mr. Davidson, but he'd hurried forward to talk to Papa.

"It's a long story," I said. I glanced at the bag she was carrying. "And what have *you* got in *your* bag? I hope it's more useful than Putty's dragon's egg."

Jane looked around nervously. "Books," she said quietly.

I stared. "More books?" What had happened to Jane? "What is it this time? More history?"

She shook her head. "Sir Isaac Newton's *Principia* and Sidney Smith's *Ancient Martian Calculus*." She snuck a look at Mr. Davidson.

Ah. *That* was it?

"You're doing this to impress *him*?"

"No! Mr. Davidson has nothing to do with this." She winced. "You can't tell Mama. You really can't."

I nodded, mystified.

She sighed. "Mama always told me that if I wanted to attract the best husband, I must have more admirers than any other lady. I must be more charming, more beautiful, and more talented, and I must never make a young man think that I am more intelligent than him. But I am tired of it, Edward. I am tired of being held up as some bauble to every eligible young man on Mars, of being part of a game for young men who are no more constant in their affections than I have been in mine. I fear . . . I fear that I have never been in love."

I blinked. "You?" Jane fell in love three times a week. Didn't she?

"Not truly. I have felt but it was always . . . it was always that game, Edward. Now I have seen Olivia and Freddie in love, and I have never felt anything like that, not with any of those young men. Mr. Davidson is different. He is a scholar."

I shook my head. "So now you're in love with him."

"No. You're not listening, Edward. I believe Mr. Davidson

is someone I could talk to about more substantive things. I am not in love with him, but when I do fall in love, I would like it to be with someone who would be more interested in discussing natural philosophy than in showering me with empty compliments."

I peered at her. "You're serious, aren't you?"

She straightened, and I saw a glimpse of that same stubborn determination I so often saw in Putty's eyes. For some reason, it gave me a chill. I looked back over my shoulder toward the city.

"Come on," I said. "We need to hurry it up."

⊰◈⊱

Putty and Mina were waiting on the other side of the river door as we reached the end of our garden.

"Any sign of him?" I called.

Mina shook her head. "Nothing."

I cursed.

I'd hoped there would be a lot of boats on the river so we could slip away, but it was empty. The water had risen noticeably since this morning, creeping up the bank, over the lower of the steps that led down to the river. The Inundation must be closer than I'd thought.

I wondered if we'd be able to hide down here by the river when Apprentice came. If we crouched down on the riverbank in the shadow of the wall, maybe they wouldn't spot us.

Papa led Mama through the door. I pulled it closed,

cutting off the view of the Flame House, and locked it with the heavy iron key.

"We're out of time," Mina whispered. The feeling of her breath on my ear made me shiver. She nodded toward Lunae City. There, rising above the rooftops, came the fliers.

"They won't see us," I said. "Yet." But the moment they reached the estate we'd be exposed. A couple of balloon-palms hung over the bank, their air-filled leaves drooping toward the rising river. Maybe one or two of us could hide beneath them.

The fliers would aim for the house. Apprentice's men would search it first. That would take time. The Flame House was a maze, as well as a hazard. If we were lucky, Apprentice would break his neck in there.

But eventually they would spread out. We couldn't stay here.

The fliers were growing in the deep blue of the desert sky. The thrum of their copter blades sounded like the rapid heartbeats of some great monster from the Martian wilderness.

I dropped down, my back pressed against the sandstone wall, and scanned the river. A couple of small boats had appeared on the river, but they were heading the wrong way and neither was paying any attention to us.

Rackham had lied. He'd tricked us, or he'd gotten cold feet and fled. I reached out and gripped Mina's hand. She looked startled, then squeezed back. At least she hadn't abandoned us.

Between Mina, Putty, Olivia, and me, perhaps we could think of something. Anything.

The sound of copter blades reached a crescendo behind us. Then, with a roar, one of the fliers swept out over the river, curving around. The downdraft sent patterns skittering across the surface.

"They've seen us!" Mina shouted.

The flier swooped around again, passing over us, then coming to a halt, hovering over the river, fifty yards away. It turned slowly until it was pointing directly at us.

"Move!" I shouted, hauling at Mama and Papa. We'd never all get out of here before it could fire. We'd never get through the door, and even if we did, the other flier would be waiting.

Portholes slid open in the flier's front.

An enormous metal boat came sliding around the bend in the river, moving fast with scarcely a ripple on the water. It was the gigantic ironclad that Putty and I had seen tied up at the docks when we'd gone looking for Captain Kol. It was as tall as a house, with twin funnels sloping back from the rear half. Powerful engines drove it smoothly through the river.

Black lines sprang from its side, like a hundred spears shot from giant bows.

The hovering flier was snatched from the air and thrown

back with the force of a hurricane, splintering as it tumbled. Fragments of shattered metal rained down into the river over a hundred yards away.

Putty let out a whoop. "Did you see that? Did you see that?"

"We could hardly miss it," Mina said. She sounded like she'd lost her breath.

The ship turned and slid close to the bank. The sound of the other flier had gone, but there were shouts from behind the wall.

A metal gangplank emerged from the side of the ship with a whir of cogs.

A door opened on the deck, and Rackham emerged. "Hurry!" he called. "You're not safe yet."

I pushed Putty at the gangplank. She skipped her way on board, and Jane and Olivia followed. Mr. Davidson wobbled his way across on legs that seemed to be made of wet noodles. I was certain he was going to topple into the Martian Nile, but Jane reached out a hand and pulled him to safety.

"I will not go on that *thing*," Mama exclaimed. "This is ridiculous, Hugo. It is undignified."

Something smashed against the river door. Planks shattered and bowed outward. One of the hinges snapped. Mama shrieked.

An armored face appeared at the gap. I snatched up a stone and flung it at the man. Despite the thick glass protecting his face, he flinched away, and I shoved the door back into position.

Another blow and it would be destroyed.

Mama, Papa, and Miss Wilkins were all on the gangplank now, creeping slowly across.

"Got anything left?" I asked, nodding at Mina's bag.

She shook her head. "I'm out of tricks."

A whine started behind the wall, like a flywheel spinning up.

I met Mina's eyes. She took my hand again. Together we leaped from the riverbank.

Behind us, the wall exploded.

The force of the explosion threw us through the air. A fragment of stone punched into my back, kicking the air from my chest. If I hadn't already been jumping, it might have shattered my ribs. Instead I hit the river still gasping for air. Water swirled into my throat, but I had no air in me to cough it out. My lungs shrieked.

Mina's arm curled around me, pulling me up. I burst from the surface, gasped in air, and coughed out water. I could hardly see.

"You're all right," Mina shouted into my ear. "You're all right."

A rope smacked the river beside us, and Mina grasped it.

I blinked water from my eyes as the rope tugged us from the river and up the high metal side of the ship. My back was in agony.

The gangplank was rolling back in. Mama, Papa, and Miss Wilkins had reached the safety of the deck. On the shore, a line of men in clockwork armor stood watching, Apprentice in their center. They made no move to raise weapons.

A hand reached down and hauled me on board.

"I told you I had a boat," Rackham said.

Danger from the Deep

Rackham settled us into cabins below deck. Above deck were a grand ballroom, a large dining room, and a couple of well-appointed lounges. The furniture in them was covered in heavy white sheets, dusted with the fine red sand of the desert.

"Used to be a cruise ship on the Valles Marineris," Rackham said. "I had it refitted." He banged a fist against the thick iron plating that covered the ship.

My cabin was decorated in fine paneled wormwood and fitted with a bed and wardrobe. The wardrobe was empty. A porthole showed the banks of the Martian Nile slipping by. I could scarcely feel the engines, but we were moving fast.

I toweled myself down, grimacing at the pain in my back. My jacket looked like a cleaning rag that had gotten caught in an automatic servant's cogs, and my shirt wasn't much better. It hung off me limply and dripped onto the floor.

I pulled off my jacket, bundled it up, and threw it into the corner, then made another futile attempt to dry my shirt. I was just wondering if I could turn the bedsheet into an outfit when the door opened. I turned to see Mina step in.

"Don't you ever knock?" I said, stepping past her and shutting the door.

"Thieves don't tend to. It's against our code. Are you feeling better? You looked dreadful when I pulled you out of the river."

I gestured down at my ruined outfit. "I think it's how I dress that makes all the difference."

I should have been shocked by the impropriety of her entering my bedroom, but I just didn't care anymore. I was tired and bruised and wetter than a deep-sea sponge.

"You look fine to me. Just . . ."

"Wet?" I said.

She grinned. "Very."

I narrowed my eyes at her. "So why aren't you dripping as well?"

"I've been up on deck. Come on. Everyone's gathering."

I gave my arms another shake and sighed. It was no good. I wasn't getting dry.

My family, along with Miss Wilkins, Mr. Davidson, and George Rackham, was sitting in the forward lounge. Wide metal doors had been rolled back on both sides to allow a flow of cool air.

"There you are, Edward!" Mama said. "What is the meaning of this? Why are you dressed like a vagrant?"

"I apologize, Mama," I said. "I was too busy being blown up to dress properly." I looked around the room. "Who's steering the boat?"

"It has the brain of an automatic servant," Rackham said, "modified and integrated with the controls. Based on your own father's invention." He nodded to Papa.

"You are a mechanician, sir?" Papa said.

"An amateur," Rackham replied. "It's a hobby. I daresay you would make many improvements to my design."

"I would be happy to take a look."

"What I want to know," Olivia said, from where she stood by the open doors, peering out, "is why Apprentice didn't follow us. He just let us go."

"He didn't need to follow us," Rackham said. "Where else could we go? We're nearly eight hundred miles from the sea. We can't turn back without passing Lunae City and being seen, and this boat is too large to navigate any of the tributaries or to enter the canals. It's not something we can hide. We can travel only one way. He knows where we are."

He'd only have to follow the course of the river and he'd find us.

"Then we're not safe?" Jane said.

"We are for now," Rackham said. "We're well armed. But

if the man who's after you is truly determined and has sufficient resources, he might cause us trouble."

Mr. Davidson cleared his throat. "If we were to reach the sea—"

"Dr. Blood is no fool," I said. "He won't let us reach the sea. If he really wants us, he'll find a way to stop us." Which just left the question, *did* he want us? Or did he just want us out of the way?

"I shall be in my cabin," Mama said. "I think . . . I think I must lie down. It is too much." She raised a hand to her forehead. "I shall not think of it. Miss Wilkins . . ."

Putty's governess hurried over to take Mama's arm. I headed out onto the deck with Putty and Mina. We had already left Lunae City far behind as the great engines of the boat drove ceaselessly through the water. On either bank, fields stretched away to where the mesas rose on both sides of the valley and the desert began. The fields had been harvested and lay bare, waiting for the floodwaters to rise and spread rich soil across the land. Here and there, on higher ground, stood the remnants of ancient buildings and statues. Once, this whole area must have been covered in temples and palaces.

Why would any emperor need so many palaces? The Ancient Martian civilization must have been vast. Far greater than any empire on Earth. Yet it had fallen into dust and ruin, and nothing had risen in its place. Perhaps when you fell that far, it was hard to rise back up again.

"What will you do?" Mina said. "If you can't stop him, I mean. If he keeps coming after you."

I shrugged. "Run. Keep running. Hope he gives up. He *should* pay for all the people he's killed or hurt, but that's not my job. All I want is for him to leave us alone." Although that wasn't completely true. If I got the chance, I *would* capture him and turn him over.

"How about Rothan Gal?" Putty demanded. "How are we going to rescue him if we're running away?"

"I don't know," I said, slumping onto the guardrail. "I don't know any of it."

A shoal of hover-fish, floating twenty feet in the air, their long gills dangling down into the river, parted in front of the boat as it powered remorselessly along the river.

"This is all my fault," Mina said.

I turned to stare at her. "What?"

Her shoulders hunched. "If I hadn't gotten you into my mess, none of this would have happened. You wouldn't be in danger. None of you would be."

"I like danger," Putty protested.

"This isn't your fault," I said. "This is about Dr. Blood, not Lady Harleston. You were the one who saved Putty and me from both of them. You're not to blame."

Mina looked away. "I don't know why you're so nice to me. I don't know why you still like me." Her voice dropped to a whisper, and I wasn't sure I caught the last few words correctly. "You won't," I thought she said. "Not in the end."

I didn't know what to say. How could she not know why I liked her? She was the most amazing person I'd ever met. What I really didn't understand was why *she* seemed to like *me*.

Metal doors closed behind us, and Rackham joined us on deck. He leaned next to me on the railing at the front of the ship, peering down at the water below. The water looked darker and heavier than normal.

"Your family is resting," Rackham said. "You could, too. This has been a hard day."

"Why do you carry a rifle that uses gunpowder?" Putty said. "It takes you ages to reload it, and I'm sure it's not very accurate. A compressed-air gun would be much better."

Rackham blinked. "My rifle?"

"You know," Putty said. "The long gun. Shoots bits of lead."

He laughed. "Maybe I think it makes me look dashing."

"I don't think so," Putty said seriously. "It all looks a bit messy. And awkward."

"I was a soldier once," Rackham said. "A rifleman. We were skirmishers in Spain and Portugal against Napoleon's great machines of war. When you need to travel light and fast and you've got no easy way to get supplies, you'll go a lot further and faster with a horn of powder and pouch of musket balls. A compressed-air gun is heavy and bulky, and you can't carry enough ammunition." He sighed. "Not that it would have made much difference. Even a cannon wouldn't have slowed those machines down much."

"Were you very brave?" Putty said.

"Very."

"I expect I would have been, too. Except I wouldn't have lost the war." She smiled up at him. "I think I shall be a soldier if Napoleon ever invades Mars. Maybe even a general. We could use your ship to destroy all his machines of war."

"If Napoleon ever comes to Mars," Rackham said, "I'll be heading in the opposite direction as fast as possible. The emperor isn't much of an admirer of mine."

Putty's jaw fell open. "Did you meet him?"

"No. But I stole his money, and that really didn't make him happy."

"You stole his money?"

"Long story. I'll tell you about it one day. Now, I'd suggest you all get some rest. This could get rough before we're through."

He was right. Now that the terror of being chased through the museum and blown up had faded, I felt almost ready to fall over.

"Come on," I told Putty.

"But I want to hear his stories."

"Later," Rackham said, with a laugh. "I've got work to do. This boat might run itself most of the time, but I still have to prod the odd lever."

At least my clothes had dried in the heat of the desert.

I took one last look over the edge of the boat at the mud-brown river flowing by.

And there, in the water below, a face stared back at me.

It was as though I was looking into some weird, distorted mirror. The face was enormous. It had two round, black eyes and an almost flat snout. Its mouth was wider than I was long, and I saw row upon row of sharp, curved teeth.

I threw myself back, shouting, just as the face erupted from the water. It lunged up, higher and higher, rising above the rail. The ship rocked violently, as though we'd hit a rock, and I stumbled, falling onto the deck. Water cascaded over me as whatever it was kept climbing up and up into the air.

Someone grabbed my arm and yanked me away. I blinked water from my eyes.

The creature towering above us was enormous, as wide as a cart, but far longer—almost as long as the ship. Its scaled skin was black and lined with sharp, spiked fringes. Giant fins, each larger than a man, protruded from its body. A head the size of a bull stared down at us. A frill of scaled skin, stretched between long spikes, made a halo around the creature's face. Water cascaded from its gills, down the length of the creature, making it glisten in the late sunlight.

"Sea serpent!" Rackham bellowed.

For a second, the serpent peered at us. Then its body came crashing down, falling like a tower on the boat.

I threw myself aside, hitting the wet deck, and skittered

across it like a stone on an icy pond. The ship juddered. The railing came up at me and I thumped into it. Gasping for breath, I flipped onto my back. Rackham was herding Putty and Mina toward a door that led below deck.

The serpent's body lifted off the deck. Its head turned toward me. I pushed myself up, my back against the rail. Black eyes stared down at me. Then the sea serpent was coming again, snaking toward me, faster than a falling stone.

I shoved myself off the rail, springing forward. If I lost my footing again, I was finished.

The sea serpent's head hit where I had just been standing. With a shriek of protesting metal, a section of rail ripped away from the ship.

For a moment, the sea serpent's body arched over me like a bridge, cutting out the evening sunlight. If it fell, I would be squashed.

Then, with a screech, the sea serpent bucked upward. The metal rail had become wrapped around its head. It shook wildly, trying to throw off the rail. The ship pitched from side to side. I dived past. Behind me, the rail splashed down into the river.

"Inside!" Rackham said, pushing me through the open doorway.

Putty and Mina were waiting at the bottom of the flight of stairs beyond the door, peering up. I scrambled after them.

The sea serpent hit the boat again with enough force to

make it leap sideways in the water. I almost fell. I grabbed for the handrail and caught myself.

I reached the floor just as the door at the far end of the hallway opened and Papa looked through. The rest of my family and Mr. Davidson crowded behind him.

"What's going on?"

Rackham jumped down the steps, landing beside me and rising.

"Sea serpent. We need to drive it off. Get back to your cabins. You'll be safe there."

"A sea serpent in the river?" Olivia said, squeezing past Papa.

Rackham was already hurrying down the hallway in the opposite direction. I turned to follow.

"They come upriver during the Inundation," Papa said, "but not usually this far, and I have never heard of one attacking a boat."

"Can you shoot a gun?" Rackham called back to me.

"No," I said. I'd never liked guns, and Papa wouldn't have them in the house.

"I'll shoot a gun," Putty said.

"You will do no such thing, Parthenia!" Mama said, grabbing hold of Putty. "You will stay in your cabin and let your father kill the thing."

Papa blinked in surprise. I didn't blame him. Papa would have had trouble hunting down a moth. But he straightened

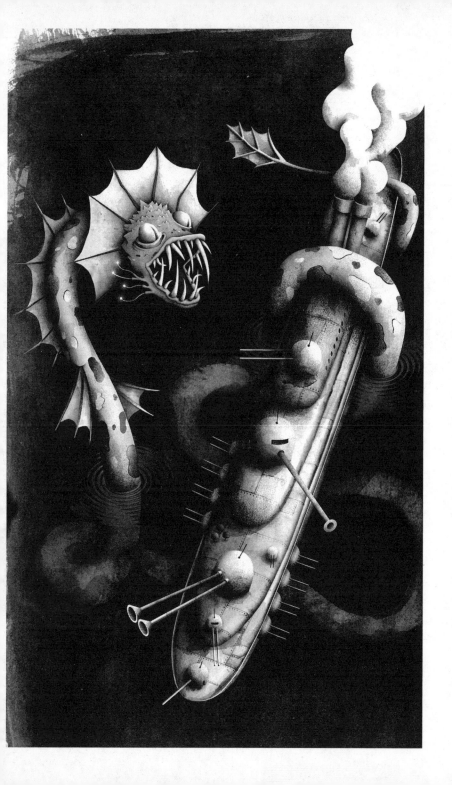

minutely. "I may be of some help. I have studied the creatures."

"Good," Rackham said. "You, me, and Edward."

"And me," Mina said.

Rackham shrugged. "The more the merrier. Now follow me."

Another crash sounded, and we all lurched to our left. "Are you sure the ship can take this?" I said.

"Not forever. But she's tough."

The sea serpent hit the side of the boat again, shaking it. I staggered against the wall. Rackham took off down the hallway. I pushed myself upright and grabbed Papa to steady him, then we followed.

"We must watch out for its spines," Papa panted as we ran along the hallway. "They are highly venomous. A single spine is enough to stun an attacking plesiosaur."

Rackham reached the end of the hallway and pulled out a key. He fitted it into a metal door. We caught up just as he got the door open. Inside was a small armory. The far wall was covered in a rack of guns. Shelves covered the other walls, stacked with boxes.

Papa wobbled as we came to a halt. His face was red and his breath was coming hard. He leaned against the doorway.

"I am not . . . accustomed . . . to such . . . haste."

"What else can you tell us?" Rackham said, strapping a long, straight sword around his waist. He pulled his rifle from the rack, then dropped its butt to the ground and pulled a small paper packet from a pouch at his waist.

"Their eyes are sensitive," Papa said, between breaths. "They are used to hunting in the deep oceans. They do not like bright light."

Rackham tore open the packet and poured a dark powder into the barrel of his rifle, keeping a pinch between his fingers.

"Didn't seem to bother that one."

A *thump* shook the boat again, then a great scraping began at the bow, working its way along the boat, as though we'd run up against a rock.

"It has membranes to protect its eyes against sunlight, but a bright enough light will cause it pain."

"We could use photon-emission globes again," Putty said from the doorway.

"What are you doing here, Parthenia?" Papa said. "I distinctly heard your mother instruct you to stay in your cabin."

"Oh, don't worry," Putty said. "She doesn't know I've gone, and Miss Wilkins wasn't around. I expect she was making tea when all this happened. She drinks a lot of tea."

"No photon emission globes here," Rackham said. "We're a bit more primitive." He dropped a small, leather-covered ball into the end of the rifle and rammed it down. "Give those a go." He nodded to a box on one of the shelves next to him.

Mina pulled them down and opened them. "Flares."

"Throw them at the beast. They might drive it off." He clipped the ramrod back on his rifle and hoisted it again. "I'll try to get a lucky shot. Now let's move."

A ladder led up to a hatch near the end of the hallway. Rackham swarmed up and peered out.

"Clear!"

Bright evening sunlight poured down from above. I squinted against it and started up the ladder after him.

I'd only made it halfway when the sea serpent crashed against the side of the ship. It tilted and I lost my grip.

Rackham reached down and grabbed my shoulder. "Hold on tight!"

The sea serpent smashed into the ship again and again. The creature was working itself into a frenzy. Banging its head into hundreds of tons of iron probably wasn't helping it keep calm. I heard glass smash somewhere in the ship. Metal protested loudly. The battering almost tore my arms from my shoulders as I clung on to the ladder.

At last the pounding stopped. My hands felt numb, but I forced myself up and out onto the deck. Rackham crouched beside the hatch, his rifle raised, watching for the sea serpent.

"Why don't we use the ship's weapons?" Putty said as she scrambled up.

"It's not staying still long enough, and I can't get the elevation down low enough to fire into the water," Rackham said. "Unless it comes up in front of one of the guns, we're on our own."

Mina joined us and passed Putty and me flares. "Your father's taking a rest."

Probably for the best. Papa had a great mind, but he hadn't exactly been a man of action, even when he was young.

The river had gone quiet. Rackham's ship was still powering downstream. On either side of the river, beyond the reeds and the balloon-palms, the water was beginning to creep over the sides of the banks. Flocks of birds sprang from the reeds as we passed, wheeling up and around to settle again behind us. Apart from the nearly inaudible sounds of the ship's spring-powered engines and the hush of the water against the hull, everything was silent.

"Do you think it's gone?" I whispered. My hands were sweating where I clutched the flare. I realized I didn't even know how the flares worked.

With an explosion of water, the sea serpent rocketed out of the river. Its vast head rose up high. Its spines and frills were spread wide.

"Now!" Rackham yelled.

Putty tore the top off one of her flares and flung it into the air. It tumbled over and over toward the sea serpent, then burst into furious light. The sea serpent's head whipped back, away from the flare. I copied Putty and threw my own flare. It arced up, right next to Mina's, and the burning glare of the two made the serpent flinch back again, waving its head from side to side as it tried to avoid the painful intensity of the light.

"Again," Rackham called. "It's working." The end of his rifle followed the beast as unerringly as if they were connected by a string.

Putty flung another flare right at the sea serpent's nose. That was enough for the beast. It plunged back into the river. The wave rocked the boat.

A moment later, the serpent burst from the river again. This time it wasn't the head that rose up, but the tail. Water rushed over the deck.

I pulled the end off my last flare and threw it as the sea serpent's head lifted again, but it was sodden and it didn't light.

The sea serpent rose, higher and higher. Then the length of its body plunged forward, right across the boat, and dropped.

Metal bent. Glass exploded in a porthole to my left.

"It's wrapping itself around the boat!" Papa called from where he'd emerged in the hatch. The water had soaked him, too. I wondered how much had washed into the boat. "That's how they hunt whales."

"The boat's metal," Rackham grunted. He helped Putty to her feet and retreated toward the rest of us. The sea serpent's coils slid over the top of the boat, and metal complained and twisted.

"Metal bends," Papa said. "Its coils will be more than strong enough to rupture the hull. It will drag us down."

The head emerged again, back around our side of the boat. The whole boat was wrapped in a gigantic, scaly coil.

With a squeal of metal, the coil began to tighten.

— 16 —

My Really Terrible Plan

The sea serpent's head stared down at us where we crouched under the shelter of the protruding upper deck.

This wasn't the way I wanted to go, killed by a sea serpent and dragged to the bottom of the Martian Nile. I hadn't done *anything* with my life yet. I hadn't even figured out what I *wanted* to do.

The serpent's coils constricted slowly on the ship. Metal creaked, and the whole ship let out a moan.

I wasn't going to give in without a fight. I wasn't going to let this be the end.

"Can you distract it?" I asked Rackham.

He looked up at the slowly swaying head. "For a minute, maybe. Why?"

"I need your sword," I said.

"You'll never cut through its hide. It's too tough."

"That's not the idea," I said. I couldn't kill the sea serpent. I couldn't even injure it. I had to be cleverer than that.

Rackham dragged his sword free of its scabbard and passed it over. "Think you can handle this?"

The sword was much heavier than I'd expected. It took both hands to lift. "I'll manage."

"Don't lose it," Rackham said. "That's my favorite sword."

"I'm coming with you," Putty said. "I'm much quicker than you, and smarter."

"You're not," I said. "Mina. Hold her. Don't let her get free. She's slippery."

"Edward!" Putty shrieked, but Mina had her, and Mina was strong.

The sea serpent's long body reached up over the rail, then arced across the top of the ship, before curving around and under, then back up. The only place I would get close enough was by the rail. Right underneath the sea serpent's head.

"I need you to get it looking the other way," I said. "Not for long."

Rackham nodded. "Be quick. If it catches sight of you, I won't be able to stop it."

Without waiting for a reply, Rackham pushed himself off and ran out onto the deck.

"Here! This way!" He waved his rifle above his head.

The sea serpent turned to watch him, its head swaying gently, and tightened its coil.

Move! I silently urged it. *Move!* Why wasn't it moving? I bit my lip.

But why would it? Rackham was just a flea scampering around the deck. In a few more minutes it would have the whole boat.

Rackham must have thought the same thing, because he knelt and took aim. "Now!" he shouted, and fired.

The shot hit the serpent's snout. Its head whipped up. A hiss of spittle erupted from its mouth. Then it lunged at Rackham. Its head crashed into the deck where he'd been kneeling, but Rackham had already moved, rolling backward and away.

I hefted the sword and sprinted onto the deck. The entire boat shook under the sea serpent's fury. It reared up and darted at Rackham again. This time he barely dodged. Planks splintered. The serpent's body writhed in fury. Spines and frills stood straight out from its body. Venom glistened at the end of the spines.

If only it would stay still.

The serpent's body twitched sideways as the top deck buckled. Spines came at me like spears. I fell and rolled back as the gigantic body crunched the deck where I'd been standing. One long, venomous spine, almost the length of my body, twitched a hand's breadth above my face.

I'd dropped the sword. As I'd fallen, it had spilled from my hands. It was lying there, only two or three feet away, but it was underneath the trembling spines.

The boat groaned again. It wasn't running so smoothly in the water anymore. It felt like it was bumping over waves.

I didn't know how much longer it could hold out.

The sword was just out of my reach. I'd have to squeeze beneath the spines. A single twitch at the wrong time, and it would impale me.

If only I had a stick or something to hook the sword. But if I went back for one, I'd miss my chance.

I wasn't even wearing my jacket as armor.

"Oh, God," I groaned.

The muscles beneath the sea serpent's hard, black scales contracted ever tighter, squeezing the ship, as though it could choke the life out of it.

I drew in a deep breath, then pushed myself beneath the spines.

The creature squeezed again, and the spine above me came down. It tapped the back of my shoulders so gently it almost felt like a feather. I froze.

Why exactly had I volunteered for this?

The sword was almost within reach. Another foot and I'd get it. Then I could pull it out and be free.

I wriggled another few inches, and the spine caught on my shirt. Even my slight movement pulled the spine further down. All the creature had to do was shiver and the spine would go through my skin and deliver its load of venom. If this could knock out a plesiosaur, I'd be dead before I could cry out.

I stretched my fingers for the sword. It was still too far. I groaned. I was going to have to go back, then try again, and all the time hope the sea serpent didn't move.

I couldn't do this.

But if I didn't, we were all finished. Me, Putty, Mina, Olivia, Jane, Mama, and Papa, not to mention Miss Wilkins, Mr. Davidson, and George Rackham.

The sea serpent prepared for another mighty contraction and its spines lifted no more than an inch. It was enough. I thrust forward.

My fingers closed around the sword just as the serpent crunched down again. Spines jarred against the deck. I scrambled back against the bulk of its body. The spines made a tight cage in front of me. I was pressed against its side, feeling the creature's blood thrumming under its scales.

"Ah, hell," I muttered.

Translucent skin stretched between the spines, like a tight leather umbrella. It lifted and fell with the creature's exertions and breaths.

The sea serpent wasn't going to like this.

I pulled the sword back as far as I could, then thrust it into the skin between the spines and tugged down. The sword sliced through like cutting through a ship's sail. The creature twitched, as though it had been stung by a mosquito. Then the skin was hanging loose in a flap. I pushed myself between the spines, and stumbled out onto the deck and into the sunlight.

I shaded my eyes and looked up.

The creature stared back down at me. Either it had gotten Rackham or it had lost interest in him.

It hadn't lost interest in me.

Its head drew back. Its mouth spread, showing the rows and rows of long, curved teeth.

I swung Rackham's sword as hard as I could. I wasn't aiming for the sea serpent's body. Even as sharp and as heavy as the sword was, it would just have bounced off the scales. I slammed it into one of the spines a hand's breadth from where it joined the body. There was a *crack*, like a branch snapping. The impact jarred every bone in my arm. My hands went numb.

The sea serpent flinched. The movement was enough to rip the sword from my hands. It went tumbling end over end to land with a splash in river.

I'd severed one of the sea serpent's spines. It hung from a flap of torn skin, like an insect caught in a spider's web. I grabbed hold of it.

The sea serpent's head rushed down at me. I tugged, throwing myself backward. For a moment I thought the skin was too thick and I wouldn't be able to pull it free. Then the skin tore and I tumbled away, clutching the severed spine.

The sea serpent smashed into the deck not a foot from me. Hardened ironwood planks shattered. Helplessly, I toppled toward the jutting spines.

Then someone grabbed my shirt and heaved me back.

"You lost my sword," Rackham said in my ear as he pulled me to my feet.

"I got this, though," I said, waving the spine.

"At some point you can tell me why that's a good exchange."

He dragged me away from the serpent.

Behind us, near the stern of the ship, something ripped into the air with a rush of sound like torn cloth. I jerked around in time to see a small object, the size of my head, rising toward the blue sky as fast as a cannonball. At about a hundred feet, the object leveled, hung in the air for a moment, then raced off southwest, in the direction of Lunae City.

"What on Mars is that?" I said.

"Nothing to do with me," Rackham said as we stumbled back into the shelter of the overhanging upper deck. The sea serpent seemed to have lost interest in us again as it watched the object streaking away.

"It's an inertially-guided automatic courier," Papa said. "I am quite envious of the design. It can be turned on and carried, and it will always return to its place of origin, no matter where it is taken."

"Napoleon's agents use them to send messages back to their headquarters," Putty said. "They're almost impossible to intercept and they're very fast. I told you Miss Wilkins was a spy."

I watched the ball fade to a dot in the sky. "Great." I slumped back down on the deck.

Mina crouched beside me. "What were you thinking?" she hissed. "You could have been killed."

"This is what I was thinking," I said, holding out the spine. "Papa said the venom in this could knock out a plesiosaur. I figured the sea serpent wouldn't much like a taste of its own medicine."

"Edward is right," Papa said. "The sea serpent is not immune to its own venom. But its scales are far too thick for the spine to penetrate."

Mina peered out at the enormous creature. Its coils were still tightening slowly on Rackham's ship.

"What if we could get the serpent to swallow it?" she said.

Papa shook his head. "The venom must enter the bloodstream to work."

"The mouth," I said, "or the eyes."

Mina looked at me like I was crazy. "You want to get that close to its face?"

"I don't *want* to. I don't have a choice."

"Yes, you do," Rackham said. "You can give it to me. I'll do it."

I stared at him.

"I told you I owed your cousin a debt. I don't like owing debts." He grinned his lopsided grin that tugged at his long scar. "I've faced worse."

Reluctantly, I handed the spine over.

Rackham darted out onto the deck and ran right in front of the sea serpent. Its head whipped around furiously. In less than a second it was on him, rushing up behind as he sprinted across the deck. Its jaws spread wide.

Rackham spun on his foot and thrust, just as the jaws loomed over him. His arm disappeared inside the creature's mouth, and I was sure it would snap shut, cutting off his arm as cleanly as Mama might cut off a thread of cotton. Then his arm reemerged, without the spine.

But he couldn't escape the creature's momentum. Its lower jaw smashed into him, throwing him back. He rolled, bouncing like a ball. I thought that he was going to go over the side, into the river. But at the last moment, he grabbed what was left of the rail and hung on. He dangled over the side, his feet banging against the metal hull.

The sea serpent let out a screech that nearly deafened me. Its body convulsed. I heard something snap in the ship. The serpent's head thrashed back and forth. It shook its mouth, trying to dislodge the spine. Then, slowly, it toppled, falling across the deck with a *thump* that shook the ship from end to end, and was still.

I ran past it to where Rackham hung from his ship, and helped him pull himself up.

"Your . . . plans . . . leave . . . something . . . to be . . . desired," he panted.

"We're alive, aren't we?"

"Speak for yourself." He staggered toward the fallen sea serpent. "We need to get it off before it wakes up. We want to leave it far behind. We'll tip it into the river."

Now that it was lying unconscious across the deck, its coil loosely looped around the ship, the sea serpent didn't look as big as I'd thought. It was still enormous, but I could have climbed onto its back without a ladder.

"Won't it drown?" Mina said. She was peering at the sea serpent's eyes. The lids had closed, but the eyes were twitching behind them.

"No," Papa said. "It is a sea creature. It often rests for weeks on the bottom of the ocean after a large meal. Mr. Rackham is right. We should dispose of it before it wakes."

"I'm going to fetch the lifting gear," Rackham said.

He returned a minute later, just as Jane and Mr. Davidson emerged from below.

Mr. Davidson looked pale. "Is it dead?"

I shook my head. "But it's safe now."

Rackham swung a long metal arm with a pulley, steel rope, and straps dangling from it out over the sea serpent. "This should do it." He clambered onto the serpent's back.

Papa had been examining the creature, and just as Rackham looped the first of the straps around its body, Papa called, "Wait." He peered behind the head frills. "Look at this."

I scrambled up next to him. A brass box had been attached to the sea serpent's head, just out of sight behind the frills. Papa pulled a screwdriver out of his jacket and levered off the casing. Inside was a complex arrangement of cogs, levers, and rods.

"See here," Papa said, pointing to a set of dozens of rods that seemed to protrude into the sea serpent's skull. He disengaged a lever and carefully drew out a long brass needle. "I've seen something like this before."

"That must go into its brain," Putty said.

"You are right, Parthenia," Papa said. "The needles penetrate the creature's brain at carefully selected points."

"I don't understand," I said. "Why would anyone do that?"

"I wondered why the creature would attack a ship, when it is not normal behavior for a sea serpent. This is why. When a needle is inserted into the creature's brain, that changes its behavior. With enough needles being inserted and withdrawn in the right places, you can gain some rudimentary control over a creature's actions. The sea serpent didn't attack us by choice. It was forced to."

"You said you'd seen this before?" Rackham said. "I've never heard of anything like it."

"When I was studying for my doctorate at Tharsis University, I shared a laboratory with another student called Archibald Simmons. He was an unpleasant fellow and he was expelled for stealing ideas from other students, but he had a strange fascination with the idea of controlling creatures by manipulating their living brains in a manner similar to this. He was never successful, but it is possible that Dr. Blood came across Archibald's ideas and has perfected them."

Rackham looked grim. "You know, it would be really

useful if we knew what your Dr. Blood was planning. Then we might be able to figure out what he's going to do next."

Everyone turned to look at me. Great. Now they all expected me to know what was going on, and I didn't have any more of a clue than I had two days ago.

"I don't know," I said. "He's got a fragment of unreadable ideograms from the museum, the stone sarcophagus from our dragon tomb, and he seems to have kidnapped Rothan Gal. Maybe he's just crazy. Maybe he hit his head and he thinks he's a crannybug building its palace."

Putty sighed. "Clearly, he wants Rothan Gal to translate the ideograms for him."

"You said they were impossible to translate." I frowned as an idea came to me. "What if he had another fragment of the same ideograms?"

Putty shook her head. "That's not how ideograms work. Really, Edward, I don't have time to explain right now if you still don't understand them."

I hid my annoyance. It wasn't *my* fault I wasn't a genius like Putty. "So you're saying Rothan Gal can't read them no matter what?"

"He really can't."

"May I see them?" Papa asked.

I pulled out the copy that Dr. Guzman had given me. I'd kept it wrapped in waxed cloth to protect it, and the water hadn't penetrated. If anyone understood ideograms better than Putty, it was Papa.

He wiped his eyeglasses on his sleeve, smudging them even more, and squinted down at the paper. He traced a finger across the marks, then sighed. "I fear Parthenia is right. The ideograms are too badly damaged. Too many are missing. They cannot be translated."

"But it has a key," I said, pointing to a symbol above the rest of the ideograms. "Last time we had ideograms to translate, you said you needed a key. It's here."

Papa nodded. "Even so. Ancient Martian ideograms are an odd form of language. Every individual ideogram changes the meaning of the surrounding ones. If too many are missing, there simply isn't enough information to interpret what was written. Much of the ideographic writing we recover is like this. You must remember that they are thousands of years old, and even in the desert, time erodes. I am sorry, Edward."

I slumped. "So why does he want it?" I said. "Why did he go to such an effort to steal it?"

Papa straightened, wiping his glasses. "I cannot say. Perhaps he does not understand ideograms well enough to realize the impossibility of the task. But this fragment will not help us. We must find another way to understand his plans."

"Wonderful." I turned away.

"Perhaps we might try?" Jane said tentatively. "Mr. Davidson is a scholar, and I might be of some help."

"Why not?" I said, and handed the paper over. She wanted to find a way to talk to Mr. Davidson, and this was as good a way as any. Maybe when he failed it would convince her he wasn't such a wonderful intellectual. I had a sudden, horrifying vision of Mr. Davidson translating them, impressing Jane so much that she married him, and me never being able to escape his lists of Greek and Latin verbs. I almost snatched the paper back.

Thank God it was impossible.

I watched the pair of them disappear back into the boat and felt the weight of the day settle over me like a mountain of rock.

"Maybe if we knew what other artifacts Dr. Blood has," Putty said conversationally, "we could figure out his plan."

I blinked. "What?"

Putty gave me a look. "Just because we know about the sarcophagus and the ideograms, Edward, that doesn't mean he hasn't got a hundred other artifacts we don't know about. What do you think he's been doing for the last eight months? You can't see a whole painting when all you've got is a scrap torn off one corner."

I groaned. "So we don't know anything."

Putty sniffed. "I know lots of things. A lot more than Dr. Blood. I'm sure I'll work it out."

Great. This was really great. "Whenever you're ready, then," I said, turning away.

"Come, Parthenia," Papa said. "We must remove the device from the sea serpent. When it awakes, it will no longer feel the urge to attack. It will return to its natural state, and no one will be able to control it again. And I should like to examine the device."

Within a couple of minutes, Rackham had finished securing the straps to the sea serpent. He jumped down to the deck.

"We should get to work," he told me. "We need to be ready for whatever Dr. Blood tries next. As soon as we get the sea serpent off, I need to check over my ship. She's pretty badly damaged."

"And I want to make sure the others are all right," I said. "Then I want to find out where that automatic courier ball came from." Because someone on this boat was sending messages back to Lunae City, and that was not good news.

Mina let out a huff of breath. "Yeah, I don't think we're going to have time for that."

I turned to her. "What? Why not?"

She pointed down the river, where the Martian Nile curved around a large sandbank. Three long arrowheads of water were cutting upstream, against the current, beneath the surface.

"We've got more company."

— 17 —

Disaster

"Three?" I said. *"Three sea serpents?"*

This was a bad joke. One had been almost more than we could deal with.

Rackham grabbed my arm. "Get everyone. Your sisters, your mother, everyone. I want them armed."

"That's not going to do any good. Bullets only made that one angry."

"You got a better idea?"

I shook my head.

"Then go. Hurry."

I turned and dashed for the hatch, followed by Putty and Mina.

The cabins were at the other end of the ship, past a small below-deck drawing room. Jane had set up there. She was leaning over the table, an intent expression on her face.

Mr. Davidson hovered ineffectually at her shoulder. They had only been down here for a few minutes, but the table was already covered in books and papers. Jane's bag lay empty beside the table. It looked like she'd had more books in there than she'd let on to me.

"We need you," I panted, coming to a halt.

Jane waved a dismissive hand. "I'm busy, Edward."

"It's going to have to wait," I said. "We've got trouble. Where's Mama?"

"Her cabin." Jane looked up. "What's going on?"

"Sea serpents. Lots of them. We're going to have to fight."

Whirring started up in the depths of the ship, growing louder with every second, until the whole boat was shaking.

"What's that?" Mr. Davidson shouted, cringing back.

"The slingshot cannon," Putty said. "It could knock a sea serpent's head clean off. Come on. Let's go and get some weapons."

The ship rocked violently as the cannon discharged. Mr. Davidson hugged a book to his chest.

I left Mina and Putty to shepherd Jane and Mr. Davidson to the armory and went looking for the others.

Mama, as Jane had said, was in her cabin, being comforted by Olivia and Miss Wilkins.

"We need you," I called. "There are more sea serpents. We have to drive them off or we'll be sunk."

The fight with the first sea serpent had wrecked the cabin.

There was broken glass on the floor, and a wardrobe had been overturned, scattering clothes and splintered wood.

Olivia untangled herself from Mama. "I'll come."

"Olivia!" Mama snapped, her fingers digging so tight into the material of her dress that it looked like it might tear. "That is hardly proper!"

"I'd rather be improper than drowned, Mama," Olivia said.

"We need the rest of you as well," I said.

Mama wafted a hand to her forehead. "I feel faint. . . ."

"Oh, forget it," I said. I grabbed Olivia's hand. "Come on."

❧

We reached the hatch leading up to the deck just as one of the sea serpents hit the side of the boat. The impact sent me sprawling to the floor. I picked myself up. I'd bitten the inside of my cheek and I could taste blood.

I pushed Olivia up the ladder, then scrambled after her. Putty, Papa, Mina, and Mr. Davidson were already on deck, crouched near the rail, guns raised. Jane stood behind them, flares held in both hands. The water in front of the boat was still.

"Where are they?" I demanded.

"They dived," Papa said. "Rackham's shot bounced off the river."

"I could have told him it would," Putty said. "It's like skipping a stone."

"So they're going to sink us without even emerging?" I said.

Papa cleared his throat. "No. The nature of the sea serpent is such that it wraps itself around its prey and constricts it."

"Because being crushed to death is so much better," I said.

"There are worse ways to go," Rackham said, emerging from a doorway.

"And I'm sure you'll tell us all about them," Mina said, flashing him a smile that immediately made me feel furious. Why was she smiling at *him*?

"Maybe another time," Rackham said.

Mina laughed as he pushed past and peered down into the silt-laden water. I glared at his back. Why was that supposed to be funny?

"Something's happening," Rackham called. "Get ready."

I grabbed a flare from the box beside Jane and joined Rackham.

A patch of water ten feet from the boat had turned smooth. Even the ripples on the river from the light breeze had gone. It was as though water was welling up from a deep underwater spring and flattening on the surface. I gripped the flare tightly in my fingers. If I could fling it right in the creature's eye as it surfaced, I might blind it or hurt it enough to drive it away.

Yeah, and while I was at it, I might defeat Dr. Blood and stop the Emperor Napoleon from invading. All with one puny little flare.

Assuming the sweat from my hand hadn't soaked it through.

I was going to be eaten whole by some miserable sea serpent with a stupid clockwork control box plugged into its brain. What a way to go.

The flat patch of river sucked down, as though something vast had opened its mouth and *swallowed*. Then the water rushed back, rising up and up and up, like a hill, bulging higher and higher until it seemed impossible that it wouldn't burst or collapse back on itself. Water shouldn't be able to hold a shape like that. Gravity shouldn't allow it.

Something came up inside the column of water. Like a preserved creature in a vast, liquid specimen jar, the sea serpent seemed to stare up at us.

Then the water did burst, and the creature was rushing out of the river as fast as an arrow.

I threw my flare. It blazed into bright life as it tumbled through the air toward the creature. Then the water swept over it and it was gone into the river. Around me, I heard the *pop* of compressed-air guns. The sea serpent didn't even flinch.

A second flare curved up from behind me. Olivia had waited until the water subsided before she'd thrown hers.

The sea serpent arched back, its head instinctively pulling away from the burning light, and its body splashed back into the water like a falling tree. I cheered. *One down.*

Something hit the back of the boat with enough force to

make it jump in the water. The drive screws screamed in protest, and the boat lurched wildly.

"It hit the rudder," Rackham snarled. He pushed away from the rail and raced along the walkway, toward the stern. Snatching another flare, I followed him.

The attack had broken something in the steering mechanism. The boat slewed back and forth as it fought its way downstream. The bulk of the first, unconscious sea serpent that was still wrapped around the ship wasn't helping, either.

"Don't you have anything you can use underwater?" I shouted as I pounded after Rackham. The creatures were only showing themselves to launch attacks. There was no time to bring any of the ship's heavy weapons to bear.

"Never thought I'd need it," Rackham called back.

The boat rocked, and a volley of shots sounded behind us. Metal crunched, and I staggered again.

Rackham reached the stern ahead of me.

"Damnation!"

I joined him and peered down.

The rudder was jolting awkwardly in the water. One of the couplings holding it in place had burst, and the rudder itself was bent.

"One more blow and we'll lose it completely," Rackham said.

"And then what?"

"Then we're helpless," he growled.

As opposed to now, when we were doing so well.

The water behind the boat swirled.

"It's coming back," Rackham said. He dropped his rifle from his shoulder and knelt. "I need you to get the creature to turn aside."

Turn aside? How on Mars was I supposed to do that?

The sea serpent surged out of the water above the stern. The fringes and spines jutted erect around its head and along its thick body. Its mouth was wide, showing needle-sharp teeth as long as my hand. I shuddered.

I waited until the wash of water had subsided, then tossed the flare.

The serpent's head whipped away from the burst of light, and for a moment I saw the metal control box clamped to the back of its skull. Then Rackham fired.

The control box exploded. It looked like it had been hit by a giant, invisible hammer. Cogs, springs, levers, and brass plates spun through the air, like a firework made of metal.

The sea serpent convulsed, as though hit by an electric shock. Its coils jerked and slashed through the water, throwing up rainbow sprays in the sunlight.

Its tail swept around, coming out of the water and toward us. I shouted, but there was nothing I could do. It was like a clockwork express train bearing down on us, and we were trapped on the rails.

Then, at the last moment, its tail fell. It crunched down full on the rudder. With a screech of tearing metal, the rudder ripped away.

Another of the sea serpents crashed into the boat, shaking the iron hull. Without the rudder to straighten it, the boat lurched to the side. The powerful current caught the port side and swung the boat further around. The ship tipped, and I lost my footing on the wet deck. I grabbed the guard-rail and hung on fiercely.

"Cut the power!" Rackham roared.

The ship's enormous screws were still turning, driving the ship at an angle across the river. Up ahead, another rattle of shots and a bone-shuddering *thump* announced that the others had more serious things to worry about. Light flared behind the forward chimney, and a sea serpent shrieked. I didn't know how much more battering the boat could take.

The deck at the front of the boat was smashed and torn, as though it had been pummeled by falling rocks. Papa lay at the rear of the deck with Jane bent over him. At least he was moving. Putty, Mina, Olivia, and Mr. Davidson crowded behind the remains of the guardrail, watching the river. I hurried up and crouched with them, grabbing a flare.

"We took out one of them," I said.

"Just leaving two then," Olivia said grimly.

"We lost the rudder."

"We guessed," Mina said. She nodded toward the loom-ing riverbank. "Unless Rackham's steering is really bad."

Behind us, with a rush, the body of the unconscious sea serpent slipped off the ship into the water. The ship bounced up, released from the great serpent's weight, and surged forward. The sudden motion threw us all to the deck.

Then the engines cut out.

Too late. The front of the ship plowed into a hidden sandbank beneath the water. The impact bowled us forward. Iron groaned and bent beneath us. The deck smashed into my back, tossing me up again. It was like being kicked by a firebull. I hit a stanchion jutting up from the deck and clung on. Mina thumped into me. I wrapped an arm around her.

Water and wet sand rained down on us. The ship seemed to tremble. Slowly, the current caught the stern and swung it around. For a second, I thought we might pull free to be thrown helpless out into the river's clutches again. Then the ship scraped over sand and settled. It tipped to the port side, threatening to tumble us all into the river.

I hugged Mina tight against me and hoped my sisters had found somewhere to hold on.

"You can probably let go now," Mina said breathlessly. "I mean, unless you're planning to do what the serpents couldn't and crush me to death."

I suddenly realized just how tight and close I was holding her. Where we were touching felt like I'd brushed up against one of Putty's scientific experiments: tingly, like an electric charge, and hot. I let go with a jerk.

"Thanks," she said. "For all of it, I mean. Catching me and all."

"Yeah," I said, red-faced. My ribs ached like I'd been shot, and I was too scared to touch them in case they'd broken.

Putty and Olivia stood further along the railing, while the bedraggled figure of Mr. Davidson struggled up just beyond them.

"Edward! Olivia!" Jane called. "Watch out!"

Two arrowheads of water were slicing across the river toward us.

"Ah, blast," I muttered.

The remaining sea serpents were coming back, and we were stuck.

— ◆ —

Something whirred beneath my feet, just above the water-line. Bent metal complained, then gave. Something clunked loudly.

"What's going on?" I said, backing away. Were we sinking? God only knew what damage the serpents had done to the ship.

Of course, we wouldn't be around to worry about it, because those sea serpents would have us for dinner long before we could sink beneath the Martian Nile's slowly rising waters.

I could see the serpents now, not twenty yards distant, their long, sleek bodies outlined in the silty water.

The ship leaped back. A cluster of iron spears as long as two men erupted from its side, spreading through the air almost faster than I could follow. They plunged into the water just ahead of the serpents, turning the water to foam. Blood bloomed like spilled ink, and then the bodies of the sea serpents were gone and the water ran calm and flat.

"Why the hell didn't you do that before?" I demanded as Rackham emerged from the interior of the boat. "We were almost all killed fighting those things off, and you just . . ." I waved my hand helplessly at the river.

Rackham shrugged. "Couldn't get the weapons low enough until the boat tilted over. Now get everyone ashore. We don't know if there are any more serpents. Your father and I will inspect the damage." He glanced back at where Papa sat slumped against the wall. "That is, if you are well, sir?"

"I'm well enough," Papa said, struggling up with Jane's help. "A knock, that's all."

"Good." Rackham turned to the rest of us. "Hurry. Take only what you need."

⬤

We set up a small camp on the sand a hundred yards from the river, far out of reach of any sea serpent. Putty insisted on bringing her fossilized dragon egg in its canvas bag, and Jane lugged the bag full of books and papers, but otherwise we brought only a few supplies.

The sun was already sinking onto the distant mesa far to the west, and the heat of the desert day was slipping away. If we were stuck out here, it was going to be a cold night.

Jane settled herself on the sands with her books and papers around her, studying them in the fading light and occasionally scribbling in a notebook, while Mr. Davidson stood resignedly behind her, not contributing at all. I didn't know if Jane had even noticed. I'd never seen her in such a mess. Her hair had been tied back in a loose knot, but strands had come free to dangle around her face. Her cheeks and forehead were streaked with ink.

I slumped next to Putty, Mina, and Olivia, while Mama and Miss Wilkins sat primly on a spread-out blanket. I felt battered and so drained that my bones wanted to fall out of my body and leave me as a limp bag of skin on the cooling sands. Someone could have rolled me up and stuffed me into a sack for all the strength I had left in me. At least my ribs didn't actually seem to be broken. Just horribly bruised. Which was almost like a victory for today.

"I thought that was quite fun," said Putty.

Luckily for her, before I could summon the energy to strangle her, Rackham and Papa clambered down from the boat and trudged across the sands toward us.

"What's the damage?" Mina called as they approached.

Papa looked exhausted. He wasn't a big man, but with his shoulders slumped and next to Rackham's enormous frame, he looked like he was sinking away into the desert sand. His eyeglasses were askew, and he hadn't bothered to straighten them.

"Do you want the good news or the bad?" Rackham said.

"Good," I said, just as Putty said, "Bad."

"The good news is that the hull is intact," Rackham said. "A few dents and some sections I wouldn't want to trust in an ocean storm, but she's tough. She'll float."

"And the bad?"

"The rudder," Rackham said. "Without it, there's no way we can risk this river. In any case, the engines took a battering. I'm surprised they kept going so long."

"And the springs are unsettled in their casings," Papa put in. "I would not run them. They could unwind catastrophically. They would tear the boat apart. We might run the engines on coal, but it would be slow, and we cannot rely on the engines not to fail."

"So we're stuck," Olivia said.

"Until we can get a crew from Lunae City," Rackham said.

I frowned, trying to figure out how far we'd come. "That must be twenty miles away."

"More like thirty."

Too far to hike. We'd walked through the desert before, me, Putty, Olivia, and Freddie. We hadn't walked anywhere near that far, and it had been too much. There was no way we could make it.

"I have a small land-crawler," Rackham said. "We might get three, maybe four, of us back to Lunae City, except . . ."

"Yeah." The realization hit me before he finished speaking.

I looked down at the sand between my feet. "Except that Lunae City is exactly where we're fleeing from."

We might go back and look for help. But Dr. Blood's men would be waiting. We'd lead them right to us.

"In other words," I said. "We're not going anywhere."

— 18 —

Betrayed!

"Well I, for one, do not intend to spend the night here," Mama said. "Hugo, you must do something about it." She lifted her chin and glared at Papa.

Papa rubbed at his eyeglasses. "Ah. I am not sure what you expect, my dear."

"Make this man take us home. Pay him or something."

"Also," Putty said, "we might be eaten by sandfish."

"Parthenia!" Miss Wilkins barked, rising from the sand like a sea serpent coming out of the Martian Nile.

Mama's eyes widened. "Hugo! I refuse to be eaten by sandfish. It would be a quite improper way to end one's days."

"And how exactly would you like to go, Mama?" Olivia said sweetly. "I do not believe you have informed us, and we would hate to be improper."

Mama gave her a suspicious stare. "I wish to end my days in my bed, with my loving family around me, having finished my tea. As any proper lady would. Not eaten by . . . *sandfish*."

"Sandfish don't eat people," I said wearily. After everything that had happened to us these last few days—with everything that *might* happen to us over the next few hours—I wasn't in the mood for my family's squabbling. It just didn't seem worth it.

"As far as we know," Mina said with a grin. "I don't know if anyone's actually *tested* it. Maybe we should try. In the interest of scientific investigation, of course."

I gave her a baleful look.

Shadows spread across the red sand as the sun finally slumped behind the western mesa. I rubbed my arms against the chill. Maybe we should go back to the boat and get blankets and warmer clothes for the night. But I was too exhausted to get up. I wondered if Dr. Blood was done with us. We were out of his way, stranded in the desert and unable to interfere with his plans.

That depends on what he wants us for, I thought.

If all he wanted was to get us out of the way, he'd succeeded. We couldn't rescue Rothan Gal. We couldn't stop whatever he was planning. He might leave us alone.

But if he wanted something else, something more, we were sitting ducks. I had no proof that he did, but something felt wrong. It felt off. He'd put too much into chasing us down and wrecking Rackham's boat.

Maybe I was just tired.

"I've got it!" Jane leaped up, scattering papers around her. My heart jumped almost as high as it tried to escape out my mouth. Why was she trying to frighten me to death?

"Ah . . . Got what, my dear?" Papa asked.

"The answer!" She waved a piece of paper in the air.

"Jane!" Mama snapped. "Control yourself. What will people think?"

Jane looked confused. "What people, Mama? We're in the middle of the desert."

Mama drew herself up. "It does not matter. A true lady acts as a lady whether there are people to see her or not. How can you expect to attract a suitable husband if you let your . . . passions . . . get the better of you?"

Jane shot her a mulish look. "I am not seeking a husband, Mama."

Papa stepped between them. "Answer to what, my dear?"

"Edward's ideograms. You know, the Ancient Martian writing? The ones Edward wanted translated. I worked out what they say."

Papa smiled gently at her. "I am sorry, my dear, but that is impossible. You see, each ideogram influences the meaning of those on either side of it. When ideograms are missing or badly damaged, the meaning is lost. It is not like English or French or German, where a missing word can be guessed at. The whole sentence changes with the change of a single ideogram."

"I know that, Papa," Jane said, cutting him off with one hand. "But you are mistaken."

Papa frowned at her over his glasses.

"You're right that each ideogram influences the meaning of its neighbor," she said. "But it's also true that the neighbor therefore passes on a secondary influence to *its* neighbor, so it's possible to infer through a suitable regression which ideogram is missing. With a given key, there are only a limited number of options that make any sense, and within the context of the text, we can in fact narrow down the possibilities to a tiny selection." She brushed back her loose hair unconsciously. "I *have* picked up some things over the years, Papa."

"I have no idea what she just said," I commented to Mina.

"It's simple, Edward," Jane said. "Either this text is a commentary on the ball gowns worn by young gentlemen while burrowing for worms, or . . ."

"Or what?" I said.

"Or it says something like this: 'The dragon's egg may only be awoken when the casket is activated in the dust of a dragon.'"

There is a particular kind of exhaustion that comes over you when you realize that every one of your siblings is a genius and you are not. Especially when the sister you'd always thought was empty-headed and silly solves a problem that has stumped generations of scholars.

Papa was frowning and blinking furiously as his super-brain whirred away. Mr. Davidson was gazing at Jane, mouth hanging open, as though he'd just been hit over the head with a large stick.

Jane noticed and started toward him, her hand rising from her side as though to reach for him.

"Mr. Davidson . . ."

His body twitched, like he'd trodden on a glass scorpion. "I have much to think about. Much." Then he strode away, his movement, as jerky and sudden as a rusty automatic servant.

Jane stared after him, her hand frozen in midair and her face reddening in the falling light.

"Mama was right," she whispered. "I should never have let him know I was cleverer than him."

"No," I said. "She wasn't. If he doesn't want to know you because you're cleverer, he's not worth knowing at all."

Jane didn't answer. She just kept staring after him.

"Are they talking about my dragon's egg?" Putty demanded. "Edward, do they mean *my* dragon's egg?"

"And what's all that about 'the dust of a dragon'?" Olivia said.

"The last part of the puzzle," Mina murmured.

My head snapped around to stare at her. "What?"

She shook her head. "Forgive me."

"For what?"

"Everything. All of it."

"I don't understand," I said.

Mina rubbed a hand across her face. She looked completely exhausted. "I wish your sister had failed. I really do."

I didn't know what to say. Why did she want Jane to fail? Why was she sorry?

Around us, the desert sands began to shake. Grains of sand danced like tiny balls on a drum skin.

"What's happening?" Mama cried, clutching at her chest. "What's going on?"

I twisted around, all tiredness forgotten, and scanned the darkening sands. From here, I could see hundreds of yards in every direction. There was only the desert and the rising Martian Nile. There weren't even any boats on the river, except Rackham's grounded ship.

But the ground was shaking like a giant land-crawler was about to run over me. For one wild moment I wondered if Dr. Blood had figured out how to make his machines invisible. Then Putty shouted, "It's under us!"

The next moment, the sand was rising in a hump, cascading back like water, as something pushed its way through the dunes. Whatever was beneath the sand was the size of a whale, but it was moving as fast as I could run, and it was coming toward us.

"Back," I shouted, reaching Mama and pulling her to her

feet. Miss Wilkins stumbled after us, losing her reticule as she fell and scrambled up again.

I racked my brains trying to think what kind of creatures lived beneath the sands of the Lunae Planum and what on Mars you could do about them, but all I could think of were the monsters that Captain W. A. Masters had battled in *Thrilling Martian Tales*. In issue eighty-five, *The Riddle of the Ant Queen*, Captain Masters had been chased by a giant sandworm. He'd only escaped by scrambling up its side and riding it to attack the ant queen's fortress. But I was pretty certain giant sandworms were made up.

Sea serpents couldn't swim in sand, could they?

Rackham loaded his rifle as we retreated, but whatever was coming was far too big to be hurt by a bullet.

The vibrations coming up through the sand were turning it liquid beneath my feet. It was becoming quicksand. I sank to my ankles and there was nothing to get purchase on. Mama slipped, and as I tried to pull her up, I only sank deeper.

What was it you were supposed to do in quicksand? I'd read it somewhere. Were you supposed to lie flat and swim, or was that what you were meant *not* to do? Would it even work without actual water in the quicksand?

And where was I going to swim to? The whole of the desert around me seemed to be liquefying. Ten yards away, Olivia, Mina, and Putty were wading through the heavy sand, but they weren't making any progress. Even Rackham was struggling.

Maybe I could make some kind of balloon out of my shirt and float on it, or . . .

The sand exploded in front of us.

A giant metal screw burst into sight, still spinning. Like a sleepy animal hauling itself from its burrow, a colossal machine lurched out to lie vibrating on the surface of the desert.

"Get behind me!" Rackham yelled, waving us back.

Slowly, the screw stopped turning. A crack of light ten yards long appeared along the top of the machine, spreading down as a ramp levered out and thumped onto the sand. The moment it hit, a dozen figures in clockwork armor leaped out.

I threw myself down, dragging Mama with me.

We were too far from Rackham's boat, even if the machine hadn't come up between us and it. The armored men would be on us before we were even halfway. That was if they didn't just shoot us down; every one of them was armed. Rackham had his rifle trained on them, but no matter how good his aim, he would only get one shot.

We would have to surrender. We didn't have any choice.

I hoped surrender was an option.

"Who are these people, Edward?" Mama demanded. "What do they want?"

"That's who," I said grimly as Dr. Blood and Apprentice followed their men out of the machine.

"Dr. Blood," I said. "He's been behind everything that—"

I didn't get to finish my sentence. Papa was striding toward the men, and he was furious.

"You!" he shouted, jabbing his finger at Dr. Blood. "I should have known from the shoddy nature of your mechanisms! You, sir, are a fraud. A scoundrel. A thief. An *amateur*!"

Dr. Blood's face turned as red as a wind turtle. "Amateur? I? I am the greatest mechanician that Mars has ever seen!"

"Ha!" Papa shouted. "You are no mechanician! You never had a single idea of your own." He swept his arm out to encompass the rest of us. "This . . . man . . . was a student at Tharsis University at the same time as me. Every idea he had he stole from me or from some other student."

"I perfected them!" Dr. Blood shouted. He was almost bouncing on the balls of his feet, he was so angry.

Papa slapped his head. "Perfected? Your ham-fisted attempts—"

"Enough!" Dr. Blood shrieked. "Shoot him!"

Rackham's rifle snapped up. "You'll be dead before your men can move."

Dr. Blood sneered. "You have only one shot. My men will kill every one of you."

"And you will still be dead," Rackham said calmly. "I never miss."

No one moved on the sand. The men in automatic armor stood motionless, their weapons fixed on us. Rackham's rifle didn't waver. Apprentice gazed at us through his metallic eyes.

Dr. Blood took a deep, shuddering breath. "Hold your fire."

"You were always a coward, sir," Papa said.

"Papa!" I hissed. Carefully, I made my way toward him, hand outstretched, slowly so as not to spook the armed men. "Don't agitate him. We're still outgunned."

Slowly, I took Papa by the arm and pulled him back.

"He's a fraud, Edward!" Papa objected loudly.

"A fraud with lots of guns."

"Do you know this man, Hugo?" Mama demanded.

Papa nodded grimly. "This," he announced, "is Archibald Simmons."

"That was my old name," Dr. Blood spat. "My *Earth* name. I have taken a new name. A Mars name." He lifted his chin. "I am Dr. Octavius Blood."

"You're not even a doctor," Papa said. "You were thrown out of Tharsis University long before you could obtain a doctorate, if ever you could have, which I dispute."

Dr. Blood didn't seem to hear him. "We are Martians now. Mars is our mother, and she names us anew. We are reborn. All former things have passed away."

"You're mad," Papa said.

"Am I?" Dr. Blood stepped between two of the armored

men. Apprentice followed him, his heavy cloak seething restlessly. "Let me tell you something. When you had me expelled from Tharsis University, when I was still Archibald Simmons, I was forced to obtain employ as an engineer on a harvester platform in the air forests of Patagonian Mars. After all, my scholarship had been taken away and I had not yet obtained funds to set up as a mechanician. I was forced to labor, repairing and improving their machinery. Not a job for a great man, but it was a blessing, because there, in the high mountains, beneath the drifting air forests, I came across a great secret written on the bones of our mother. The truth was carved into the ancient rocks. I was transformed, and I became a Martian in truth. I became Dr. Blood."

"I have no idea what you're talking about," Papa said.

"No. You wouldn't. You never looked up from your machines. Do you know, in the days of old, during the Inundation, the Ancient Martian emperors would float down the Martian Nile on great barges, their dragons at their feet, and the populace would bow to them? They would prostrate themselves to the emperors, and all Mars was one."

"I told them that!" Putty protested. "Edward, I told you first!"

"Is that your plan?" I demanded. "To awaken a dragon's egg and proclaim yourself emperor? To float down the Martian Nile and expect everyone to bow to you? It's not going to work, you know. No one is going to bow."

Dr. Blood smiled. "Who better to be emperor? And I have

something a bit more impressive than a barge in mind." He shook his head. "How can you live on Mars and not see this? The Ancient Martian civilization was far greater than anything that Earth has produced. Compared to them, Alexander the Great was an infant squalling in his crib! The Ancient Martians ruled a world, and flew between worlds on the backs of dragons. Their technology made Earth's greatest achievements look like toys. And yet Mars is reduced to this! A patchwork of colonies, subservient to the decaying kingdoms of Earth. Now, once again, another Earth upstart threatens to sweep across Mars and ravage its treasures. This so-called Emperor Napoleon. I will swat him like a child. Mother Mars will rise again."

"Except that you need the dragon's egg," Rackham said. "To get that, you'd have to cross the sand. And you can't do that before I put a bullet in your head."

As if in response, Apprentice's cloak rose and fell.

"Do you have the key?" Dr. Blood shouted.

Rackham's forehead creased in confusion. But Dr. Blood wasn't looking at Rackham or Papa or me anymore. He was looking over my shoulder to someone behind us. I turned.

Mina was staring at Dr. Blood. Her face was pale, as though every drop of blood had drained from it. Slowly, she nodded.

"Mina?" I demanded. "What's going on?"

She wouldn't meet my eyes. She just kept staring down, as though there was something fascinating on the dry sand and she couldn't tear her gaze away.

"And the dragon's egg?" Dr. Blood called.

Mina glanced across at Putty, who was clutching the heavy canvas bag to her chest.

"Take it," Dr. Blood said. "Bring it to me."

Mina hesitated.

"You don't have to," I hissed urgently. "Dr. Blood won't dare do anything. Rackham would kill him."

"Now!" Dr. Blood barked.

I could scarcely look at Mina's face. She looked like she was being ripped in two. Her eyes looked like bruises. She didn't even seem to be breathing.

Then she shuddered, and took a single step toward Putty. Her arm came up, reaching for the bag, except it didn't look like her arm. It looked like a clumsy puppet's arm, being lifted by a string.

"No!" Putty said fiercely, hugging the bag tighter. "It's mine."

"Let her," I said. My voice sounded hollow. There were too many guns pointed at us, and once someone started shooting, no one would stop.

The look Putty gave me was wounded.

Mina pulled the bag free and started across the sand. As she passed me, I said again, "You don't have to do this."

Her expression was haunted. "I do." She sounded like she'd swallowed stones. "He's my father." Her voice fell to a whisper. "I said you shouldn't trust me."

Then she was gone, trudging toward Dr. Blood, Apprentice, and the armored men.

I didn't move. I couldn't. I felt like she'd punched me so hard something had come loose inside me. I'd been so *stupid*. I should have known. I should have figured it out. Her turning up at the same time as Dr. Blood, wanting to get to know me, saving me. She'd been working for Dr. Blood all along, and all she'd wanted was the key cylinder and Putty's dragon egg.

She was a thief. Why did I ever think I could believe her or trust her? I was an idiot. Just because she had a pretty face, that didn't make her a good person. She'd manipulated me, made me think I was her friend, just so she could get what she wanted.

When she'd "rescued" Putty and me from Dr. Blood's airship, she must have been laughing at me. She'd gained my trust, and I'd just *given* her the key.

I'd believed her. I'd even thought she'd liked me. Then she'd betrayed me.

"No!" Putty said, starting across the sand. "They can't have it!" She looked furious.

I grabbed hold of her and held her. "Let them go."

She stared up at me. I could see the same betrayal and shock in her eyes that must have been in mine.

"Edward?"

"They'll kill you," I said.

"Very wise," Dr. Blood called.

I looked back over my shoulder at him. He, Mina, and Apprentice had climbed the ramp into the tunneling machine. Mina wasn't looking back. She stood there, as stiff as a statue. Then Apprentice's cloak rose like a shield, and I couldn't see her anymore.

One by one, Dr. Blood's men retreated into the machine. With a whir, the ramp rose and closed. The screw began to spin. The machine tilted forward. The screw bit into the desert sand.

In less than a minute, the machine was gone, the sand had stilled, and we were left there, alone, as the last of the daylight fell into shadow and night came down over the desert.

PART THREE

The Emperor
of Mars

— 19 —

The Spy

We looked a pretty sorry bunch as we trudged back to Rackham's boat.

Dr. Blood had the egg. He had the sarcophagus. He had the key. Jane had even translated the ideograms for him. We were nothing to him anymore. He hadn't even bothered to kill us.

Now we were stuck out in the desert, and all the strange creatures that hid from the burning heat of the day would soon be emerging. According to Putty, half of them could kill us with a single bite, sting, or lunatic diving assault into our eyes.

I should have been angry that Mina had betrayed me. I should have been hurt. But I wasn't. Not anymore. Finally, I could see clearly.

I had been obsessed with getting the key to Mina when

I should have been trying to work out why Dr. Blood had kidnapped Rothan Gal and where he'd taken him. I'd let Rothan Gal and Captain Kol down.

I'd known from the first moment Putty and I had followed him that Dr. Blood must have a base somewhere out here in the desert. I should have been searching for it rather than helping Mina steal things for him.

"We can't just let him get away!" Putty protested as we lowered ourselves wearily into chairs in the below-deck drawing room of Rackham's boat. Mama and Jane had retired already to bed.

"It's over," Rackham said. "Take the victory. Walk away."

"What victory?" Putty demanded. "They stole my egg."

"And left all of you alive. *That's* your victory. They could have killed every one of us." He sighed. "We can't fight him. He has a small army and deadly machines, and he intends to conquer Mars. I don't know if he can do that, but I do know that *we* are not capable of stopping him. We need to inform the British Martian government of the threat. Let them deal with it."

"What about Rothan Gal?" I said. "Do we just let him die?"

Rackham shrugged. "You can't save everyone. I've fought in a lot of battles. This is not a game. It is a war, and we cannot win."

"How about your promise to Freddie?" I said. "You said you owed him. Was that just a lie?"

"I said I would keep you safe, and I will. But I won't do that by taking you into a war. This isn't a negotiation. Tomorrow, I will take the crawler back to Lunae City." His mouth lifted in its one-sided smile. "We don't need to hide anymore. We can get help. In the meantime, we should rest. We've had a hard day."

I looked away. He was right. I hated it, but he was right.

Putty shot me a bitter look. "This is all your fault, Edward. *You* gave him my egg. I *trusted* you."

I didn't answer. The waves were lapping gently against the metal hull of the boat, sounding like leaves brushing against a window. I wondered how long it would take for the water level to rise enough to lift the boat and send it drifting off downstream again. Papa and Rackham didn't seem to be worried, though, and they ought to know. My eyes started to drift shut. Maybe I'd just sleep here. For a moment. Not too long. A week or two.

I stood. "I'm going to bed."

Tomorrow, we would get word to Captain Kol. Maybe he could figure out how to rescue Rothan Gal. *We* couldn't do it alone.

I pushed open the door to my cabin, dropped onto my bed, and kicked off my shoes. The cool air felt wonderful on my feet. My eyes drifted shut and sleep closed over me.

My door clicked open. I sat up, my head suddenly pounding. What was it now? Had Dr. Blood come back?

Putty crept in and shut the door behind her. I fell back on the bed.

"What are you doing here?"

Putty rolled her eyes. "Looking for you. Obviously."

I rubbed my hand across my eyes. They stung with tiredness. "Go to bed, Putty."

"What are we going to do about the spy?" she said.

"What spy?"

"The one who broke into Papa's office and stole his papers. The one who sent up the message in the inertially-guided automatic courier. It had to be Miss Wilkins."

"Don't start that again," I said. "Your governess is not a spy, and for all we know, one of Dr. Blood's agents planted the automatic courier on the boat."

"That's absurd, Edward."

I had to admit it didn't sound very likely. How would Dr. Blood know we'd be on the boat at all? But I just didn't see Miss Wilkins as a spy.

"It wasn't Miss Wilkins," I said. Maybe it had been Mina. I could certainly believe it of her. I could believe *anything* of her.

"Well, I've got proof," Putty said stubbornly. "Probably." She pulled a sheaf of letters from under her shirt. "I stole these from her cabin."

I sat up. "You did what? Tell me you haven't read them."

"Not yet."

"Then put them back. You've got no right to read some-one else's letters. They're private."

She looked stubborn. "Are you *so* sure she isn't the spy? Are you so sure she hasn't been stealing from Papa or work-ing with Dr. Blood? They were in the same coffee house at the same time. Is that coincidence?"

I was too tired for this. All I wanted was to get to sleep. "If I read the letters, will you promise to give up on this non-sense about Miss Wilkins?"

"Of course," she said. "But I'm right, you'll see. The letters will prove it."

I took them from her reluctantly. How would *I* feel if someone was going through my personal letters, finding out all my secrets? Not that I had any letters, or any secrets with Putty around. I unfolded the first letter and read the tiny writing.

By the time I'd finished, I wished I'd never agreed to this. I put the letters down softly on the bed.

"She's not a spy," I said.

Putty's jaw dropped. "What? She's got to be. You saw what she was up to." She snatched the letters.

"She's married," I said. Each word seemed heavy as I said it.

Putty's eyes widened. Then she leaped off the bed. "Yes! We've got her. I've won!"

Mama would never employ a married governess. No one

would. It would be completely inappropriate. Miss Wilkins must have known that, so she'd kept it a secret. Living with us in the Flame House, the only chance she'd had to meet her husband was on her evenings off. She'd snuck away to the coffee house to spend a few hours with him. And what was worse, it was clear from the letters that her husband was a native Martian. Mama would think that a complete scandal.

"We should take these to Mama right away," Putty said. She was so excited her eyes were almost glowing in the dim cabin.

"Then what?" I said. "Miss Wilkins will lose her job. No one else will ever employ her when this gets out. She'll be ruined. I know she's awful, but she's only doing what Mama wanted her to and she's still a person. We can't just throw her out on the streets to starve. I couldn't live with that. And nor could you."

Putty's face twisted in anguish. "I *can't* let her stay. I can't! She never lets me do anything."

That was true as well. Whatever she said, Putty did need someone to look after her. But not Miss Wilkins. Miss Wilkins was too strict. She would either crush Putty, or Putty would explode. Putty needed someone who could rescue her from her worst scrapes but not get in the way of her ideas and schemes.

"We'll talk about it back in Lunae City," I said, taking the letters from her.

Putty glared at me. "You're supposed to be on my side, Edward. First you give Dr. Blood my dragon's egg, then this. You're supposed to be my brother. You're supposed to *care*."

"I do," I said.

"No, you don't. You haven't since we got to Lunae City. You haven't cared about anything I do. If you don't want to be my brother, then fine. Don't. I don't care. I don't *need* you."

She threw open my door and stamped out into the corridor. I followed her.

"Leave me alone," she hissed. "You don't even care about Rothan Gal or you'd be out there right now finding him."

I winced. She was right. I was failing Rothan Gal after I'd promised to help save him. But what else could I do? I felt like it was tearing me in two.

But all I said was, "You need to get back to your cabin before Miss Wilkins catches you."

Putty crossed the corridor, then turned to give me an angry glower, before throwing herself into her cabin and slamming the door behind her. There was still a key in the lock. I slipped across, turned the key, and dropped it into my pocket.

It would keep her out of trouble until the morning. Maybe then, when we'd all had some sleep, we could figure something out.

◈

I must have been even more exhausted than I'd thought, because I only woke when the bright sun through my porthole worked its way across the cabin to fall on my face. Peering out, I saw the waters of the Martian Nile glittering in the light. The river had risen noticeably overnight, but the ship was still stuck fast on the sandbank.

Yawning, I pulled on my shoes and ripped jacket, stretched, and wandered out into the corridor. Putty's door was still locked. I fumbled in my pocket for the key. Putty was going to be furious with me. I just hoped she hadn't spent the night constructing some awful trap to pay me back when I opened the door. I'd ended up with more than one bucket of water tipped over my head in the past, and once a whole tank full of eel-worms had been dumped down the back of my shirt when I'd burst into her room too quickly.

Cautiously, I unlocked the door and swung it open.

The room was empty. I checked behind the door, then under the bed and in the wardrobe.

Hellfire! Where was she? There was nowhere else she could hide. The porthole was latched from the inside. The door had been locked all night. But she just wasn't here.

I groaned. I was an idiot! How long had I known my sister? And I'd thought a locked door would slow her down?

I don't need you, she'd said. I had been leaving her out of everything I'd been doing since we'd come to Lunae City. I'd been so determined to find something I actually wanted to do for myself that I hadn't thought what Putty would think.

I'd just assumed she would come to me before she did anything stupid.

Not this time. This time she'd decided to go off on her own, just like I'd been doing.

She must have gone after Dr. Blood to get her dragon's egg back. She was going to get herself killed. It was madness, and it was my fault.

She would have set out as soon as she knew everyone else was in bed. She could have six or seven hours' lead. There wasn't a moment to waste.

I dashed out of her room. And ran straight into Mr. Davidson.

"Edward!" my tutor said, grabbing me by the arms. "There you are! I haven't slept all night."

His small, pinched face looked frantic and his cravat hung loose from his neck.

"Sorry to hear it," I said, trying to free my arms. "But this isn't a good time."

"It can't wait! Have you enjoyed your lessons?"

I stared at him. Enjoyed? Was he mad? Survived, just about, but enjoyed? I'd rather be eaten by a flock of Xanthean cockroach bats.

"Er . . . Well . . ." I managed to get one arm loose. I gestured toward the drawing room. "I have to—"

"I fear they are about to come to an end," Mr. Davidson said.

"What are?"

"Tell me, Edward, if you were going to get married—"

"I'm not getting married." Why was he talking about this? I didn't have *time*.

"But if you were—indulge me—would you believe that you had to be honest—completely honest—with the woman you intended to ask to marry you, or do you think that some lies are the better choice if they might turn your intended against you, that some secrets should be kept forever because they are so terrible?"

I peered past him. Every minute we wasted, Putty was getting further away. "Um . . . Be honest, I suppose? Is this a test?"

Mr. Davidson let out a long breath, as though he'd been holding it inside all night. "I . . . I think you are right. We must be honest, no matter the consequences, or a marriage cannot be true."

"Well, I'm glad we cleared that one up. Now, I'm kind of in a hurry."

He spun and headed for the drawing room. I scurried along behind him, trying to squeeze past. The ship was still leaning to port, where it was jammed up on the sandbank, and getting past Mr. Davidson, who had his arms out for balance, was impossible.

"Wait!" I said, but he wasn't listening. He was mumbling under his breath, fidgeting agitatedly as he hurried along.

"Come on," I muttered. "Come *on*!"

No. I didn't have time for this. *Putty* didn't have time. I shoved past. Mr. Davidson lost his footing on the sloping floor. His hand shot out and grabbed my jacket. We both collapsed in a tangle against the wall. Mr. Davidson gave me an astonished look, and then he was off again before I regained my balance.

I swore and raced after him. I didn't know what he was up to, but Mr. Davidson could waste time like no one I'd ever met. I caught up with him just as he swung the drawing room door open and strode in.

Everyone else was already there. Everyone except Putty. Papa and Rackham were bent over schematics of the ship, while Mama, Jane, and Miss Wilkins were whispering together in one corner. Olivia was reading a book, but she looked up with the rest as we burst in almost together.

"Something's happened—" I started, but Mr. Davidson rode straight over me.

"I can wait no longer!" he said.

Everyone stared at him.

Papa removed his glasses and polished them on one sleeve. "Whatever is the matter, Mr. Davidson?"

"It is your daughter, sir."

Papa frowned. "Parthenia? What has she done now?"

"Parthenia?" Mr. Davidson said, temporarily stumped. He glanced around the room. "No, sir. Your oldest daughter."

He hurried across the drawing room and dropped to his knees before Jane. Her eyes widened in shock.

"No! Mr. Davidson . . ."

"Please. Allow me."

"Please don't."

"I have adored you since I first set eyes upon you, Miss Sullivan! You are the most beautiful young lady I have ever encountered, but I told myself—I *forced* myself—not to act. You could never feel the same for me, and it would be a terrible betrayal of the trust your worthy father put in me. And the scandal, the shame, to be brought upon your family. It was not to be borne."

"Oh, for heaven's sake," Olivia muttered.

"But now . . ." He leaped to his feet again. "Now I see the only thing that matches your beauty is your intelligence. You have astonished me, and I can hold it back no longer. I know you cannot share my feelings, and I know that I can only bring you embarrassment, but there is nothing I can do. You have overwhelmed all my self-restraint and propriety."

"The *tutor*?" Mama demanded. "Jane!"

Jane was already out of her seat. Her face was as red as a Lunae Planum sunset.

"Mr. Davidson. I do not—"

Mr. Davidson raised a hand. "Miss Sullivan. You *must* allow me. I am not yet done. Edward has convinced me that I must tell you everything."

"I really didn't," I said, but no one was paying any attention.

"There is something I wish to ask you," Mr. Davidson continued. "But first, the truth. You will hate me, all of you, but Edward is right. Without the truth, there can be nothing."

"Maybe later," I interrupted. "I've actually got something important to tell everyone."

"Be quiet, Edward!" Mama barked. "What is this truth, Mr. Davidson?" Her eyes widened. "Are you perhaps not what you seemed? Are you a viscount in disguise, fled from Napoleon's vicious hordes?"

"And I thought it was Jane who read all those terrible novels," Olivia said.

Mr. Davidson's face twisted into pain. "No, madam, I am not. I am the son of a clerk. But I am a man whose ability has been unrecognized for too long. *I* was the one with the talent, but it was others who ascended to wealth and fame." His voice rose and his face reddened. "All because they had the right connections. I was ignored! Overlooked because my family was poor." He cleared his throat. "I fear . . . I fear that my resentment led me to make choices that I wish now—I wish with all my heart—that I had not made." He turned to me. "Are you absolutely sure about this, Edward?"

"No," I said. "Absolutely not. Whatever it is. No."

He wasn't listening. He closed his eyes and straightened further. "I . . . I am a spy."

"For . . . the British-Martian Intelligence Service?" Papa said. He looked as confused as I did when he tried to explain his inventions to me.

"No, sir. I . . ." Mr. Davidson licked his lips. "I am in the pay of Emperor Napoleon."

— 20 —

Chasing Putty

The room erupted into noise. Mr. Davidson stood there, as unmoving as a statue. Papa leaped from his chair to face my tutor.

"It was you!" I said, starting toward him. "You were the one who broke into Papa's study. You were the one who sent up that automatic courier when we were fighting the sea serpent."

He nodded mutely.

Papa's voice was cold. "And what did you steal from me, sir?"

"The plans for your water abacus," Mr. Davidson whispered. "I took them from your safe and put them in the automatic courier." His voice sounded scratchy, as though he'd been drinking sand. "Napoleon's agent in Lunae City will have received them by now. They will be on their way back to Earth."

"And there's nothing we can do to stop them," Rackham ground out. "I should shoot you where you stand."

"Napoleon will integrate the water abacus into his machines of war," Papa said. "It is a hundred times more potent than the brain of any automatic servant. He has turned his gaze upon Mars, and you, sir, may have given him the means to invade."

I pushed to the front. "Papa," I said loudly. "This doesn't matter right now."

Finally they noticed me. Papa's eyebrows shot up. "It doesn't?"

"No. Eight months, you said, until Napoleon could even try to invade. That's something to worry about another day." And, hopefully, for someone else to worry about. "We have a problem *right now.*"

"We do?"

"I've been trying to tell you," I said. "Putty is missing!"

Papa shook his head. "What do you mean, Edward?"

"She's not in her room. I shut her in last night because I knew she was going to do something stupid, but she got out. She's gone."

"I don't understand," Mama said. "Where would Parthenia go? We are in the middle of the desert."

"She's gone after Dr. Blood," I said. "She's gone to get her dragon's egg back."

I waited until Rackham had locked Mr. Davidson in his brig before I shared the whole story. It wasn't fun. No one said anything, but I knew what they were thinking: This was my fault.

And they weren't wrong.

I had put my little sister into danger. My voice was grim as I told of how I'd trusted Mina. How I'd let her rob Lady Harleston and keep the key cylinder, and how Putty and I had chased after Dr. Blood. At every single stage, I'd made the wrong decision, and now Putty was gone, and Dr. Blood would kill her.

There was a horrible silence when I finished.

"Well, how far can she have gone?" Mama said, her voice brittle with forced cheer. "She is a child. You must get out there and search for her."

"She took the crawler," Rackham said. "I checked. She could be miles away. There's no point just searching the desert."

Mama drew herself up. "Do you mean to abandon her, sir?"

"Of course not. But we can't simply plunge off into the desert and hope to find her. Even if the crawler has left tracks, there will be patches of rock and scree and we'll lose the trail. We have to know where she has gone."

Everyone turned to look at me.

"How should I know?" I said.

"Think, Edward," Papa said. "You've been with Parthenia throughout this. Where would she go?"

She would go wherever Dr. Blood was, of course. But where was that? Putty would figure it out. She was far cleverer than I was. But I had exactly the same information she did. I should be able to figure it out, too. *Think!*

"We followed Dr. Blood north from Lunae City," I said slowly, "across the Martian Nile toward the desert. Do you have a map?"

Rackham retrieved one and laid it out on the table. The Martian Nile ran almost due north until it reached Lunae City, where it swung northeast and finally east to the ocean. I traced my finger from Lunae City, cutting across the river at an oblique angle then past the rich fields, and finally to the fragmented mesas beyond. The map showed a tangle of small valleys.

"He's got a lot of equipment," I said slowly. "His airship, and the tunneling machine, and he must have somewhere for his men to stay." I shook my head. "This is too close to Lunae City. The Imperial Martian airship flies into Lunae City every day. He couldn't risk being seen, and these valleys are too small."

I ran my finger further up the map. "Here." The mesas lifted higher, fracturing into true mountains above the desert. A line of them ran parallel to the Martian Nile for several miles before breaking away north. I looked up.

"This is where he would hide. No one would come across

him by chance, and it's not too far from the city or the Martian Nile."

Rackham peered at the map. "We could search for a month and not find your sister there. It would take us weeks just to find Dr. Blood's encampment."

It wasn't good enough. *I* wasn't good enough. I wasn't *smart* enough. I lowered my head into my hands.

"Putty wouldn't just launch herself into the desert," Olivia said. "Not if she really wanted something. She knows exactly where Dr. Blood is."

"Of course she does," I said. "She's a genius, just like the rest of you. Me?" I spread my hands. "I'm lost."

"Then try to think like her." Olivia's fingers were tight on the edge of the table. "Come on, Edward. You know Putty better than any of us. How would she work it out?"

I stared down at the map. It was a mess. Valleys and broken rock everywhere. She could have gone anywhere. How was anyone supposed to know where Dr. Blood had gone? He'd been in a little flier when we'd chased him, and he'd been picked up by his airship. It was an airship designed to harvest the air forests of Patagonian Mars. The mountains there were higher than anything on Lunae Planum. It could go anywhere.

I stared at the map, despairing.

Whatever Putty had seen, I wasn't smart enough to follow.

Except . . .

Dr. Blood might have been in an airship when we chased him from Lunae City, but when he'd come to pick up Mina and the dragon's egg, he'd been in a tunneling machine. I'd seen it come up out of the sand and lie there on the desert. Out in the open, it had been ungainly and slow. There was no way it could crawl over rocks or up the sides of mountains.

I squinted closer at the map, trying to make sense of the markings.

"Where are we?" I said.

Rackham pointed to the bank of the Martian Nile about thirty miles from Lunae City. I peered closer. The desert stretched several miles in great, sweeping dunes, all the way to the mesas. The sand would be easy for the tunneling machine, but then it would have to stop. Unless it had a way through. Quickly, I scanned the map, picking out the valleys that cut into the high rocks.

Only half a dozen were large enough and deep enough to have filled with desert sand.

And only one zigzagged its way to the great mountains.

"There." I jabbed my finger onto the map. "She's gone that way."

Rackham followed where I was pointing. "That's got to be ten or twelve miles. The crawler can manage it, but on foot?" He shook his head. "It would be murder."

"We've done it before," I said, although that had been less—more like seven or eight miles—and over broken stone, not sand.

"Then we'll go tonight, when the heat's lessened," Rackham said. "Only those of us who are fit and strong. The rest will wait here."

"No," I said. By tonight, Putty would have reached Dr. Blood's camp. "We go now."

"We can't walk into the desert in the heat of the day," Rackham said.

"Watch me. If you don't want to come, stay behind."

He looked at me coolly, then nodded. "Very well. Until you're all safe, I haven't kept my promise to your cousin nor paid my debt to him."

"I am coming, too," Papa said. "Do not argue, sir. Parthenia is my daughter, and I have a score to settle with Archibald Simmons."

"Then let's gather weapons and supplies," Rackham said. "We leave in twenty minutes. And God help us, for I fear no one else can."

⬥

At home, back at Valles Marineris, with a good path or road and a hard hike, we could have made twelve miles in four hours, even allowing for Papa having to stop for rests. Out here on the Lunae Planum it was a different matter. Although it was early autumn, the heat burned down like a furnace. Within seconds I was sweating, and every step felt like I was carrying a basket of rocks on my back. I hadn't realized how much I relied on the shade from buildings, the thin cloths stretched between them, and the cooling breeze from the river to make the day manageable in Lunae City. Here there was only the red desert radiating the heat back up at us.

Soft sand slipped away beneath our feet. Saber-toothed spiders lunged at our shoes from their little sand lairs, their fangs leaving sharp holes in the leather. Up above, shark kites slowly circled, looking for prey on the desert below. I was almost certain we were too big for them. Almost.

The only thing that kept me placing one foot in front of another was the knowledge that Putty was out there somewhere, in danger, and it was my fault.

Even so, by two o'clock Papa was stumbling and weaving and we were making less and less progress. In the last half hour, we'd scarcely made a hundred yards.

Rackham dropped down in the shade of a high dune.

"We rest," he said, pulling off his backpack. "We'll be no use to your sister if we collapse out here."

I bit my lip in frustration, but he was right. The day was only going to get hotter, and we weren't going to make it. Using a couple of backpacks and Rackham's rifle, we turned a sheet into a shelter against the sun and waited for the heat to fade.

Dr. Blood had only let us live because he thought we were no threat to him. Next time we might not be so lucky. But he already had Rothan Gal, and by now he could have Putty, too.

Lying there in the desert, hiding from the sun, was one of the hardest things I'd ever done. Every minute we lay there, unmoving, was a minute we weren't rescuing her.

I wondered if Mina would do anything to protect Putty, then cursed myself for being so stupid. Mina hadn't cared for Putty or me, no matter how much she'd pretended to. She was a thief, and she'd only stuck around long enough to get hold of the cylinder key and the dragon's egg, then she'd left us out in the desert. She was Dr. Blood's daughter, and all she cared about was helping him with his lunatic plan. She was as much the enemy as he was. The fact that I'd fallen for her didn't change that.

By four o'clock the sun had begun to sink lower in the sky and the edge had bled from the heat.

"We need to get going," I said, pushing myself upright. "I don't want to do this in the night."

Papa looked pale, but he nodded as he struggled to rise. "We still have a long way to go."

We pressed on, nobody saying much. It was hard enough to walk without wasting energy on talking, and I had nothing to say.

Before dusk, the mountains were rising before us and we had entered the deep, sandy valley slicing through the mesa. If I was right, it should lead us to Blood's base and Putty. Although none of us spoke, we picked up our pace. I could see Papa was struggling, but he didn't protest. He just put his head down and kept going.

Shadows sank into the valley, like ink filling a well, thick and cool and deepening with every passing minute. Up above, the sky was still bright from the evening sun, but the first of the stars were appearing, and I could just make out Earth as a tiny bright point above the valley wall.

Ahead, the valley narrowed and turned to the north as the first of the mountains jutted up above the mesa.

"The valley goes on another two miles," Rackham said. "After that, it becomes too narrow for Blood's machines."

"The map might not be completely accurate," Papa said. "The valleys this far from Lunae City haven't been well charted. Not many airships fly over the mountains."

"Which is why Blood chose it," I said. "We have to believe the map's right. Otherwise we've got nothing."

"The point is that your sister must have consulted the same map," Rackham said. "This is the only route she could have found. She'll have come this way. It doesn't matter whether Blood is there or not. In fact, it's probably better if he isn't."

We followed the winding valley another mile, and by then the darkness had thickened so much that I could scarcely see a dozen yards in front of me. The mountains still formed jagged, high silhouettes against the sky.

I hurried around a fallen boulder, and there the valley widened again, briefly, before high cliff walls rose and rose again to become the shoulder of a great mountain.

There was nothing on the sand. Not even a tent.

I'd been wrong.

I leaned against the boulder, exhausted. This wasn't where

Dr. Blood was hiding, and, worse, there was no sign of Putty. I slid down onto the sand and held my head in my hands. I had failed. Again. Putty had figured out something I hadn't. I just wasn't clever enough.

Slowly, I became aware of a sound in the night air. I hadn't heard it at first over the pounding of the pulse in my ears. It was low and deep like the beating of hundreds of giant wings above me. It echoed heavily from the cliff walls.

I tipped my head back, looking higher and higher.

There. Above and ahead of me, high in the valley, were faint lights, but they weren't stars. They were too evenly spaced, and the color of the light was wrong.

There was something up there. Something vast. It was far bigger than any airship, bigger than some towns. It blotted out the sky.

"What on Mars is that?" I breathed.

Papa came limping up behind me. He'd pulled out a small spyglass and squinted through it, adjusting a dial on the top.

"Ah! You can see it clearly in the infrared. It is still radiating the heat of the day."

I put the spyglass to my eye.

"It's a harvesting platform," Papa said. "In the mountains of Patagonian Mars, where they harvest the air forests, there is nowhere flat enough or accessible enough for the gulpers to land and disgorge their cargo, so they use harvesting platforms. Each platform has a fleet of gulpers that delivers the harvest every day."

The platform must have been half a mile wide. Hundreds of giant propellers beat above it, and as many enormous balloons floated above them, suspending the enormous platform.

"You see how it's been modified?" Papa said. "A harvester platform is usually just a giant storage container."

"It's been fortified," Rackham said. He had his own spyglass out and was examining the platform. "There are gun emplacements around the sides and underneath it, and it's been hardened against attack." He looked uneasy. "If I had to guess, I'd say that the platform has been modified for war. I don't know what weapons British Mars could deploy to bring that thing down. Lunae City certainly couldn't. You'd have to land a force on it and take it yard by yard. I've fought in battles like that. I wouldn't choose to do it again."

"That's what Dr. Blood meant when he said he had something more spectacular in mind than floating up the Martian Nile on a boat," I said. "He's going to hatch Putty's dragon and then come flying in on that thing."

He'd declare himself the Emperor of Mars, and anyone who put up a fight would have to deal with that flying fortress. One way or another, there was going to be a bloodbath.

"What do you think you're doing?" a voice hissed from the darkness.

I spun. Putty was peering out from behind a boulder.

It was like someone had splashed clean, cold water over my sweating face. I rushed over and grabbed her up in a hug.

"Putty! Thank God you're all right."

She wriggled free. "Not for long. Do you think you're the only ones who have infrared spyglasses? Why are you just standing out there?"

I met Rackham's eyes. *Hellfire!* We'd been staring up at the platform, and none of us had thought that someone might be staring back down at us.

I grabbed Papa and dragged him into the shelter. Putty's stolen crawler was folded up neatly against the rock wall.

"I've been figuring out how to get up there," Putty said. "I'm going to wait until it's completely dark, then I'll float up there in a balloon. I'll have to wait until the sand's cooled, though, so the balloon won't show up against the heat of the sand. The timing's going to be critical."

"Do you even have a balloon?" I said.

She stared at me. "Who *doesn't* have a balloon?"

I shook my head. "It doesn't matter. You can't sneak on board that thing. It's too dangerous. We're taking you home. The government can deal with this." Somehow. It was too big for us.

"Rothan Gal is up there," Putty said stubbornly. "Don't you even care about him? And they've got my egg. I'm not going without it."

"I don't think we're going anywhere," Rackham said. He was staring up at the platform through his spyglass again. "We've been seen. They're coming for us."

— 21 —

Captured!

I snatched the spyglass back from Papa. Through the infrared view, I saw small, warm specks dropping from the platform like hail, falling into the night air. They were people. Soldiers.

Giant black wings snapped open above them, and they swooped down like shark kites spotting their prey. There were ten, then twenty of them, and they were heading right for us.

"What do we do?" I demanded.

Rackham was gripping his rifle. "What do we do? We surrender."

"We can't surrender!" Putty protested. "Not to them. They stole my egg."

"We can't fight them." He laid his rifle on the ground and stepped out onto the sand, hands carefully raised.

"You're a coward!" Putty said.

"I'm alive," Rackham said. "Because I know when to fight, when to flee, and when to surrender. This is a time to surrender." He turned his one-sided smile on Putty. "At least you'll be getting onto the platform."

She turned to me. "Edward?"

My chest felt so heavy, I could scarcely get enough breath to speak.

"He's right," I said. "We can't fight this. We've lost."

⋅◈⋅

They took us up onto the platform in a couple of small fliers. We were surrounded by armed men in clockwork armor, and we didn't stand a chance.

Up here, the scale of the platform was even more intimidating. It was as though someone had made a fortress entirely from metal and then lifted it into the sky. Metal towers ran on rails around the edge of the platform, with enormous guns jutting from them. In the center, reaching above the deep bulk of the platform itself, was what looked like a palace built of steel. It must have been a hundred feet tall. A great dome made of glass panels rose above it.

The interior of the platform had been transformed as well. Inside the giant storage tanks that had once held the harvested forests, a city had been built. I glimpsed corridors and open squares and hundreds of doors, but apart from the guards who were shepherding us along, I didn't see anyone.

"This place is crazy," I muttered. Dr. Blood had built

himself a capital city in the air but he hadn't populated it with anyone. Who would want to live somewhere like this? Everything was bare metal. Only once or twice did I catch sight of anything decorated. It was like the whole place was an iron dungeon. Gas lamps burned along the walls of the hallways, but most of the metal city was in shadow.

Dr. Blood wanted to be the new Emperor of Mars, but this palace of his wasn't anything like the incredible Ancient Martian palaces that had once lined the banks of the Martian Nile and hung from the slopes of Tharsis Mons.

Eventually, the guards took us down to a line of cells deep in the platform. The metal walls here were vibrating as the gigantic springs that turned the propellers above the platform slowly unwound. Somewhere down here, a furnace would be burning, producing steam to wind more springs. It was certainly hot enough, and I could smell oil and smoke in the stuffy air.

The guards pushed Putty and me into one cell and slammed the iron door behind us, cutting off the light from the corridor. I slumped against the wall. Only a faint glow-panel spilled weak green light across the cell, but it was so run-down, I could hardly see my own hands.

"Can you get us out of here?" I asked Putty, without much hope.

"I'm not talking to you," she said. "You ruined everything. I was going to get my egg back and rescue Rothan Gal *and* stop Dr. Blood, but you ruined it. You got us caught. You're not even my brother anymore."

She turned her back on me. Her shoulders hunched and her head ducked down.

"Are you crying?" I asked.

"Shut up."

I levered myself up, went over to her, and put a hand on her shoulder.

"I was trying to rescue you. I didn't want you to get hurt. I didn't mean for any of this to happen."

She pulled away. "You should have thought about that earlier. You should have *helped* me. That's what brothers do. They don't pretend you don't exist. They don't leave you out of everything fun."

"I didn't mean to," I muttered again, but she didn't answer.

With a sigh, I crossed to the door. It was made of solid steel and fixed so tightly into its frame that I couldn't have slid a sheet of paper into the gap. There wasn't even a lock on this side of the door.

"There are bolts on the other side," Putty said. Her voice was so flat I hardly recognized it. "There's no way out." She hadn't even turned to look at me.

I dropped to the floor and rested my head on my knees. I'd ruined everything, and it couldn't be fixed. There was no one to rescue us this time. I had failed.

The light didn't change in the cell, nor did the slow vibration of the colossal machinery in the heart of the platform. We could have been in there for hours, or even most of a day. Neither Putty nor I said a thing. I didn't know what Putty was thinking, but I couldn't stop myself going over and over everything in my mind and wincing at every mistake I'd made. There were a lot of them.

I had drifted into half sleep when the sound of the bolts shooting back jerked me awake. I was so confused, I didn't know where I was. The sounds of the bolts had been gunshots in my dream, and I flinched back so hard, I banged my head into the metal wall.

When I could see again, Mina was kneeling in front of me.

"What do you want?" I growled. "Come to tell us some more lies?"

She looked away, her dark hair falling across her face, hiding her expression. "That's not fair."

"Really? Because the way I see it, I can't think of a single thing that you told me that was the truth."

"It wasn't all lies."

I pushed myself up. I couldn't tell whether the floor was thrumming from the gigantic engines deep in the platform or whether I was just shivering with fury.

"You betrayed us! You pretended to be my friend. You pretended you *liked* me, but all you wanted was to steal from us. We trusted you."

Her hands were clenched into fists. "You don't understand. My father was going to have Apprentice kill you. I couldn't let that happen. I told him I'd get what he needed instead." She looked up at me with those deep, brown eyes.

"So it was all for our sake, was it? That's fantastic. We're so grateful." I shook my head. "You really think I'm going to believe that?"

"Not just yours. His."

I blinked. "Whose?"

"Apprentice's," she said.

"What?" I wasn't keeping up with this. Talking to Mina was sometimes like talking to Putty. "He's a monster. Why on Mars would you care about him?"

She looked away again. "Because he's my brother. I couldn't let him do . . . something like that."

I stared at her. Her *brother*? Apprentice had tried to kill us over and over again.

"Wow. You really have a lovely family, don't you?" I sneered. "You fit right in."

She raised her chin. "I told you the truth, you know. We were both orphans. He was my big brother, and he looked after me. He was brilliant. You should have seen him. He was an apprentice mechanician in Lunae City, and he could build anything, even when he was no older than you. He made wonderful things, but he couldn't make enough money to support us. No one would give him a real job, not a half-breed orphan like him. That was why I became a thief, to help us get by. Then he got a job on a harvesting platform as an assistant engineer, and he met our dad. But when he came back, he'd . . . changed. You've got to understand. All we ever wanted after our mother died was to find our dad. We wanted to be a family, so when Nicholas found him—"

"That's your brother?"

"Yeah. That's his name. Nicholas. Not 'Apprentice.' When he found our father . . . You know. We just wanted our father."

"You wanted to please him?"

She nodded. "We had to. You wouldn't get it. You've always had a family. We didn't have anything or anyone. Orphans out here, most of them don't survive at all."

"And how about now?" I said. "How about now that you know your father is a murderer? Now that you know he's mad?"

Her shoulders hunched and she stared down at the floor.

"I don't know. But I have to look after my brother, the same way he looked after me. I have to." She took a deep breath. "I'm letting you go. You can get your dad and Rackham and rescue Rothan Gal. You can get away. I know where the airships are. Father's distracted with that dragon's egg. He won't chase you. You'll be all right, all of you."

The cell door was open. The corridor beyond was empty. We could be away, back to Mama, Jane, and Olivia. We could go back to Lunae City or Valles Marineris. She was giving us back our lives.

"No," I said. "That *was* what I wanted"—it still was—"but now I've seen this place." I shook my head. "This is too

305

much. It's not just about rescuing Rothan Gal anymore, or Putty's egg, or escaping from your father. If we don't stop him now, if he uses this platform, a lot of people are going to die. He could destroy Lunae City. He could probably threaten large parts of Mars before anyone could get together enough of a force to defeat him. They wouldn't see him coming. This is our only chance to stop him. This is down to *us* now."

"And I'm getting my egg back," Putty said from behind me. "So are you going to help us or not?"

—◆—

Papa and Rackham were being kept in separate cells. Papa looked dazed when we let him out, but Rackham came within an inch of taking my head off with a right hook as I swung his door open.

"You got out," he grunted, lowering his fists.

My heart had leaped out of my throat and done a double somersault. I finally managed to swallow it again.

"Yep," I croaked.

Rackham caught sight of Mina behind us in the corridor. "Want to lock her up?"

I shook my head. "She's helping us."

He raised an eyebrow. "Your choice."

"She's going to show us where Dr. Blood is. He's been preparing to wake Putty's egg."

"You trust her?"

I looked at Mina standing there at the other side of the

corridor, hunched up as though she wanted to disappear into the metal wall.

"Yes," I said reluctantly. "I do." I wondered if I was making another big mistake.

"Then let's move out." He turned a hard gaze on Mina. "If you try anything, anything at all, I *will* kill you."

There was one more cell in this block with its door barred. "Who's in this one?" I asked Mina. "Is it Rothan Gal?"

"It's been locked as long as I've been here," she said. "I haven't seen inside."

I pulled back the bolts and peered in.

"Careful," Rackham warned.

The glow-panel had failed completely in this cell, and it took a moment for my eyes to adjust to the darkness, but when they did, I saw a shape lying motionless against the far wall.

I crossed and knelt down by the man. At first, I thought he was dead he was so motionless, but then he groaned and shifted, as though the light from the doorway was hurting him. He had an arm across his face, and his ragged robes obscured his features, but I could tell from his height that he was a native Martian.

"Help me get him up."

Rackham took one arm while I took the other, and together we propped him against the wall. His head lolled loosely and his hair fell across his face, hiding him. Even sitting slumped he was almost as tall as me. Standing, he would have towered over even Rackham.

"Is this your friend?" Rackham said.

I shook my head. "I don't know."

I should have recognized him. We'd spent a week together on Captain Kol's boat, and Gal had often stopped by to tell us stories of Ancient Mars, but it was dark in the cell, his face was bruised, and I just wasn't sure.

"Of course it is," Putty said.

At the sound of her voice, the man looked up.

"We've been searching for you everywhere," Putty said. "Edward said he'd find you, but I was the one who figured it all out first." She shot me a dirty glance.

"We need to get out of here," Rackham said. "Can you walk?"

Rothan Gal nodded. "I believe so. With help."

Rackham put an arm under his shoulder and lifted the bigger man up. "We need to get you to an airship. Someone can go back with you while the rest stop Blood." He turned to Papa. "Mr. Sullivan . . ."

Rothan Gal shook his head. "No. I must help. This is important to my people. This thing he attempts, it is something we have sworn to prevent."

"Then let's all get going," I said. "Before we're discovered."

We made a pathetic sight as we limped our way along the hallways, following Mina. Papa still looked dazed, and I suspected I didn't look much better. My feet were covered in blisters from the hike across the desert, and I ached all over. Dr. Blood's men hadn't been gentle when they'd captured us. I'd been thrown to the floor and one of the armored men—a big man the others called Flood—had knelt on my back. I'd thought my spine might crack. Rackham was almost having to carry Rothan Gal, and the native Martian was heavier than he looked.

Only Putty seemed to have any energy. She darted back and forth impatiently, her hands twitching as though she were preparing to snatch her egg back from Dr. Blood.

At last, the hallway we were walking down changed. The plain steel walls became more elaborate, with carved pillars holding up the ever-rising ceiling, and ornate doors inset with gold and silver. Up ahead, a heavy door was decorated like the Ancient Martian temples, with twisting, slipping figures of dragons and men and strange beasts. The widely spaced gas lamps that lit much of the interior of the platform had been replaced by photon emission devices set into the ceiling.

"This is where Father . . . It's his . . ." Mina said.

"It's his palace," I said. "He's built himself a palace."

"Yeah," she said. She nodded toward the great door. "We can't go through there. It leads to the entrance hall. There'll be guards. Lots of them. He doesn't trust them enough to let them into the main hall beyond, but they're outside." She produced a key and opened a small door in one wall. "In here. I stole the key from Father. In case."

It was dark inside. But in the light coming from the hallway, I saw a narrow metal staircase leading up into the blackness. It looked old and rusty. It must have been something left over from the platform's original use. There were even traces of the fine pollen I'd seen when we'd been captured by Dr. Blood's gulper.

"The palace is built where the gulpers used to come in to land," Mina whispered. "Nicholas showed me the original plans. This staircase used to go up to where the controllers sat to guide in the gulpers."

"So where does it go now?" I said.

"Above the main hall. There's a balcony. No one goes up there, except for maintenance or cleaning. We'll be able to look down and see what's happening."

The narrow, steep stairs ended in a small door. It was locked, but Mina scarcely took a minute to pick it. We came out on a long balcony under the enormous glass dome. In the day, sunlight must have poured in through the glass, but at night the blazing light from the hall below turned the glass as black as oil.

"We're about thirty feet above the hall," Mina whispered.

I nodded and slowly lifted my head above the parapet to take a look.

The hall was two hundred feet long. At the far end, a dais so large it looked like a small pyramid rose almost as high as the balcony, and on top there was an enormous seat.

"This isn't a hall," I said. "It's a throne room."

Control panels covered in dials and switches surrounded the throne. Above the throne, levered arms held a selection of lenses and small mechanical devices.

Pillars ran the length of the throne room, reaching up to the glass dome. They were carved with twisted shapes that seemed to evade the eye. At one moment I thought I was seeing a dragon curled around the pillar, the next a convoy of boats on a river, the next a thousand men kneeling before a temple. I couldn't focus on any part of the carvings for long enough to tell exactly what they were.

Behind the pillars, gigantic banks of machinery—glass tubes larger than a man, bronze wheels, giant cogs, wires, metal cabinets, and enormous steel tanks—ran the length of both walls and along the back wall behind the dais. In front of the machinery stood lines of unmoving automatic servants, but every single one of them had had their left hands and forearms replaced with long blades. Other unfathomable contraptions hung below the ceiling on chains that stretched across the hall.

In front of the dais, on a workbench, was the stone sarcophagus Apprentice had stolen from the Museum of Martian Antiquities. Dr. Blood and Apprentice were working over it. Dozens of rubber tubes snaked across the floor to end six inches above the sarcophagus. Optical cables trailed from photon emission devices, and each illuminated the sarcophagus in different-colored light. Levers and mechanical arms stretched in from every direction. It looked like a dozen giant metal spiders were all reaching toward the sarcophagus.

"That's my egg!" Putty hissed.

It was nestled in the middle of the sarcophagus, almost hidden by everything around it.

"What's all the machinery?" I asked.

Mina shrugged. "Not my field. Nicholas is the one who understands machines, not me."

Papa squinted through his dirty eyeglasses at the banks of machinery that lined the walls. "I saw something similar before at the University of Tharsis when Archibald and I were students. It was used as a means of storing electrostatic energy and discharging it quickly. But it was no more than a curiosity. It was far easier to generate the energy when we needed it than to store it."

"So what does he want it for?" I said.

"Ah." Papa rubbed his eyeglasses on his jacket. "The device at Tharsis University was no larger than a plate. If Archibald has succeeded in scaling it up, the energy it contains could be catastrophic. Release it in one place, and it could rip apart a city."

"Use a weapon like that once and no one will dare stand against you again," Rackham said. "He means to make an example of someone."

"We cannot allow it," Rothan Gal said. The native Martian was still weak, and he had only taken a peek over the edge of the balcony before slumping back, but he was more alert than he'd been when we'd pulled him out of his cell. "The Martian emperors must never return." He coughed, muffling it with his elbow. I glanced back at the throne room below, but Blood and Apprentice didn't seem to have noticed. They were still working at the sarcophagus.

"They were a scourge on the land," Rothan Gal said. "With their great machines, they were too powerful. No one could resist them. They enslaved the people and ruled over them for thousands of years. We have only fragments of knowledge from the time of the emperors, but it is enough. Native Martians—most of us, anyway—swore long ago never to let the emperors rise again. Why do you think we have never made use of the technology hidden in the dragon tombs? Why do you think we never opened those tombs ourselves?"

"I thought—" I started.

"You thought we were incapable," Gal said. He raised a hand before I could protest. "You are not alone. We are primitives, your people think. Yet who built the devices that you have based your own inventions on? We were not incapable. We were unwilling. We would not take the risk. We have seen what happens when too much power is granted to men. Never again. That is why your Dr. Blood cannot be allowed to succeed."

"How do we stop him?" I said. "We haven't got any weapons, and I don't like the look of those automatic servants."

"I think I have an idea," Papa said. "But first we must get down there and get close."

"There are armed men outside the hall doors," Mina said. "We'll never get past them."

"And if we try to climb down, we'll be spotted," I said. I shook my head. "I don't see how we're going to manage it."

"I do," Rackham said with a tight smile.

Before I could move, Rackham had leaped to his feet and was waving. "Up here!" he shouted. "Up here!"

— 22 —

Murderous Machines

I stared at Rackham. "What are you doing? Are you crazy?" I tasted something bitter in my mouth. "You're betraying us!"

He glanced down at me. "Don't be foolish. I'm getting us down there as quickly and easily as I can. Hey! Up here!"

Dr. Blood and Apprentice had stopped working on the sarcophagus and were staring at us. Then Apprentice spoke. A series of clicks came from the metal mask clamped across his face.

Half a dozen automatic servants turned and clanked their way to the doors beneath the balcony. Apprentice's cloak rose around him, spreading like wings. The tiny metal beetles that covered the cloak whirred. Apprentice lifted into the air and sped toward us. Metal footsteps sounded on the narrow stairs leading up to the balcony.

"You'd better know what you're doing," I said.

"No idea," Rackham said cheerfully. "But if your father has a plan, I trust it."

"Ah . . . I wouldn't quite say it's a plan," Papa said. "More, ah, an idea. Of sorts."

"That's wonderful," I muttered.

Apprentice landed on the balcony next to us. His metal eyes glittered soullessly at us. Mina met his gaze with a nervous expression, but Apprentice's face didn't change. I didn't even know if it could under all that metal. The mechanical beetles shifted restlessly on his cloak. At the other end of the balcony, the first of the automatic servants appeared, the blade where its left arm should have been raised.

"I guess we're going down." I smiled at Apprentice. "You win. We surrender."

Dr. Blood was waiting for us by the sarcophagus. Each of us was shepherded by one of the automatic servants. Rackham warranted two, and their blades didn't waver an inch from his skin. Others watched impassively from in front of the banks of machinery.

I stayed as still as I could. I recognized these types of automatic servants. Despite the blades instead of arms, they were Papa's finest model. They could react instantly to commands, and they were fast. I didn't give myself more than a fifty–fifty chance of getting clear of the blade behind me before I was skewered.

"You helped them," Dr. Blood said coldly as Mina was brought up beside me. "You betrayed me."

She didn't answer. She just stared at the floor.

"No matter. I have you all now." He turned to Papa. "I'm delighted, Hugo, that you can see what I've built. You always claimed I would achieve nothing, yet look at this." He waved his hand around the throne room. "Nothing you have made is comparable. I have surpassed you, and while all that you do is for your own profit, I have worked only for the greater glory of Mars, our mother. I can have a hundred platforms armed like this within the year. If Napoleon or any other Earth usurper tries to invade, I will annihilate their forces before they can even land. Mars will stand triumphant."

"Then arm the Martian governments," Rackham said. "Give them the help they need to defend this planet."

Dr. Blood sneered. "The Martian governments have always been subservient to Earth. British Mars! Chinese Mars! Turkish Mars! Patagonian Mars! Just listen to the names. Earth lays claim to Mars. No more! It is time for all true Martians to reclaim their destiny, to throw off the shackles of Earth and free their mother again."

Rothan Gal stared away over Blood's head. Like all Native Martians, he wouldn't meet the eyes of someone he did not know. "We will never allow the Martian emperors to rise again. Mars does not need emperors."

"Peasant!" Dr. Blood spat. He looked at the rest of us.

fig. 43

Dr.

Blood

THE EMPEROR OF MARS

"Today you will witness something that has not been seen for almost two thousand years. You will see a dragon awaken."

"From *my* egg," Putty growled. "I didn't say you could have it." She glared. "You'd better not break it."

Blood ignored her. "Come. Let us begin."

He gestured to Apprentice, who crossed to a small table near the sarcophagus and brought back a small, sealed bottle.

"This," said Dr. Blood, "is the dust of a dragon. Until you translated the ideograms, I didn't even know I needed it."

I frowned. "What's the dust of a dragon?"

"When the resin that protects the body of a preserved dragon is cut open, the body inside decays into dust. The chemical composition of the dust is extremely complex, and the process takes several weeks. Fortunately, it is a superstition among the ignorant natives that the dust of a dragon can cure certain diseases. I was able to obtain this." He unsealed the bottle and poured the dust over the egg in the sarcophagus. It was so fine it flowed like water. "And so we are ready."

He picked up the key cylinder Mina had stolen from Lady Harleston. My heart dropped at the sight of it. If I hadn't told Mina I'd found the key cylinder, none of this would have happened. Dr. Blood would have been helpless. But I'd wanted to impress her. I'd wanted to see her again.

I should have thrown it in the Martian Nile.

Dr. Blood inserted the cylinder carefully into the hole at the end of the sarcophagus, then adjusted a couple of dials.

The rubber tubes above the sarcophagus began to vibrate, and a thin white gas drifted down over the egg.

"You're wasting your time," I said. "That egg turned to stone hundreds of years ago. It's dead."

Dr. Blood twisted the key cylinder. I heard cogs whir and tiny levers snap out. Something inside the stone sarcophagus began to hum.

I watched, unable to take my eyes off the egg. I wasn't the only one. Dr. Blood and Apprentice hovered over it, peering intently at the dials that surrounded it and at the egg itself.

Something brushed my ear. I flinched, then realized that Papa had leaned in close.

"I will need a minute," Papa whispered. "A distraction."

I closed my eyes. The automatic servant's blade was only inches from my back. What would it do if I moved? It might just stand there, or it might react by plunging the blade straight through me. I could almost feel the metal cutting into me.

We had to stop Blood, though. We had to. It wasn't just about me or my family. It was about the whole of Mars.

I took a breath, then threw myself to the side, clattering into the automatic servant guarding Putty.

Even though I'd moved as fast as I ever had, the automatic servant behind me reacted just as quickly. Its blade snapped forward, tracing an agonizing line along the side of my ribs. I shouted in pain as I knocked Putty's automatic servant flying.

Rackham twisted as I moved, turning inside one of his

automatic servants and slamming into it. It tottered, then overbalanced with a crash.

I scrambled to my feet and darted away as my automatic servant came after me. It was fast on its feet. Why on Mars had Papa worked so hard to improve this model? Why couldn't he have left it as slow and clunky as the earlier ones?

It swung for me again. I dived behind a pillar. The blade glanced off it. The other automatic servants came lurching from in front of the machinery. There must have been twenty of them. I was going to be sliced like an onion.

I darted out from the pillar and took off across the floor, automatic servants in pursuit. Rackham was dancing in and out of the rest of them, pushing them at each other, but he wasn't doing any damage.

I hoped Papa had a good plan, because those automatic servants could keep going for hours. I risked a glance at him. He'd pulled out his pen and a piece of card and seemed to be jotting something on it.

"Really not a good time for that!" I shouted as another automatic servant loomed up in front of me. Its blade thrust straight for my chest, but before it could hit, Putty crashed into it, spinning it around.

"Thanks!" I puffed, then ducked away from another.

This was a nightmare. In fact, I'd had nightmares like this, chased around and around while maniac machines tried to chop me into ribbons. We were doing so badly, Apprentice and Dr. Blood had gone back to work on the sarcophagus.

"Edward!" Papa called. "Over here!"

He waved his piece of card in the air.

"Seriously?" I muttered. There were only about a dozen mad killing machines between me and him, all slashing the air with long blades that made swords look like butter knives. Putty, Rackham, Rothan Gal, and Mina couldn't help, either. They had enough of their own automatic servants to deal with.

I gritted my teeth and raced toward the murderous mechanicals, pulling off my jacket as I went. A dozen blades lifted toward me.

I tossed my jacket up, just as I let myself fall to the floor and roll.

I heard the horrible sound of ripping as my jacket was neatly shredded to rags. Then I was tumbling among their metal feet. A blade skidded off the floor beside me. I kept on tumbling, as the automatic servants slashed at me, getting in each other's way and tangling together.

I jumped up and kept on running.

"You know," I panted as I reached Papa, "you should think about some changes to their programming for the next model."

Papa peered at them over his glasses. "There do appear to be some flaws. . . ."

He pushed the card at me. He had poked holes in it with his pen, leaving smears of ink.

"What am I supposed to do with this?" I demanded.

"Put it in one of the servants' command slots."

I stared at him. "Are you insane?"

"I would do it quite quickly," he said, backing away.

The automatic servants were advancing again, spread out in a line, blades held before them. Putty, Mina, and Rackham were being backed into a corner by another group of the servants.

The command slots were in the front of the automatic servants' chests, just below the shoulder line. It had always seemed a convenient place to feed them the punch cards that held their commands, but now I was seeing another design flaw. I couldn't get anywhere near without being skewered.

"Hey! You! Metal face!" I shouted at the nearest servant. "Yeah, you. Come and get me."

I pulled off a shoe and flung it at the servant. It bounced off the servant's chest with a *clang*. They kept advancing, in line. Well. That hadn't worked. And now I only had one shoe.

I hobbled back. I needed to get one of the automatic servants away from the others, just for a minute.

"Hurry up, Edward!" Papa called. A couple of automatic servants had noticed him and were now pursuing him back across the hall.

I turned and ran parallel to the line of automatic servants. They followed, getting closer with every step.

When I reached the end of the line, I was only a couple of feet clear. I dashed around another pillar, and the automatic servants followed.

They were a fantastic invention, brilliant even by the

standards of Martian technology, but they were still machines. They weren't intelligent. They had been instructed to attack us, and so they were following mindlessly. They wouldn't stop. They'd just keep on following. They trailed after me in a line, like homicidal ducklings trying to catch up with their mother.

My foot went from under me on the polished marble. I just had time to curse myself for throwing my shoe away before my head bounced off the floor and everything went black for a moment. When my eyes popped open, an automatic servant was looming over me. Its left arm went back, then the blade shot forward. I twisted to the side and the blade shrieked across the marble, throwing up sparks. I grabbed hold of the arm above the blade. With a sigh of pistons, the automatic servant straightened, and I came up with it.

I shoved the piece of card at its chest, too hard. It caught on the edge of the command slot and crumpled.

I tugged it back and pushed again. This time, the card slipped into the slot. The mechanism took over and pulled the card in. I gritted my teeth, waiting for it to jam.

A second automatic servant came up behind. I let go and fell back to the floor. More blades rose.

Then the first automatic servant let out a series of high-pitched clicks and froze as solid as a statue. Around me, the other automatic servants stopped moving, too.

I was lying there on the floor, surrounded by a forest of

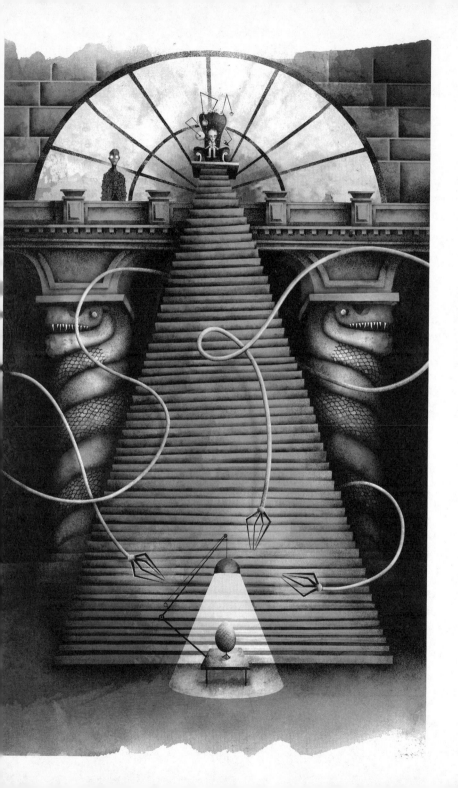

blades, and none of them were stabbing me. I wriggled my way out, holding my breath every inch of the way.

"What have you done?" Dr. Blood shrieked. He'd abandoned his work on the egg and was staring at Papa.

"These servants are my invention, Archibald," Papa said, advancing on Dr. Blood. "Did you think I wouldn't have some way of shutting them down?"

"How about a big red button somewhere easy to reach next time?" I panted, clambering to my feet. Putty, Mina, Rothan Gal, and Rackham had worked their way past their immobile automatic servants and were now making their way toward Apprentice and Dr. Blood.

Dr. Blood scrambled back away from us, up the dais to his throne.

"Surrender," Rackham called. "You've lost your army."

Dr. Blood glared down at us, looking tiny up there on his enormous throne. "You are cowards! You would rather let Napoleon's armies overrun this planet like a plague of cockroaches than fight. I will not." He jabbed a finger at Apprentice. "Kill them! Kill them all!"

From Apprentice's cloak, a cloud of metallic beetles rose, and as he stepped forward, they darted toward us, pin-sharp jaws spread wide in the air.

— 23 —

Run!

I scrabbled away, but there was nowhere to hide from the clockwork beetles. There were too many of them, and they were too fast. They dived through the air, legs like tiny knives jutting forward. I threw up my hands.

Mina jumped in front of us.

"No!" she shouted. "Don't do it."

Apprentice's mask clicked, and the beetles came to a halt in the air, suspended by their beating wings. Apprentice's head tilted to the side, as though he were asking a question.

"You can't," Mina said, walking toward him, through the cloud of beetles. "You're not a murderer. I know you're not." She reached out a hand and scooped one of the beetles from the air onto her palm. I flinched, expecting it to bite or slash, but it didn't. "Don't you remember? You made these for me when I was a kid. They were toys. I thought they were the most wonderful things in the world." She lifted her other hand and held her finger an inch in front of the beetle. "They didn't bite. They were beautiful. Then you went away, and when you came back, you were changed." She shook her head. "I don't care if he's our father. Look what he's done to you. Look what he's made you."

"I have raised you up," Dr. Blood shouted. "You were nothing. Look at everything I've given you."

Mina stepped closer to her brother. I stared at him, trying to figure out who he would be most loyal to, his father or his sister. Trying to be ready if he made the wrong choice.

"He didn't give you any of this," Mina said, almost whispering now. "All these inventions, all these wonderful things. They're yours. I recognize them. You drew them for me years ago. All he's done is taken them from you and twisted them into something horrible."

"I will make you into a prince of Mars," Dr. Blood said. "You and your sister were starving. You had nowhere to go and no hope of bettering yourselves. Nobody cared if you lived or died, but I will give you everything there is." He leaned forward. "All you have to do is this one simple thing for me. For your father. All you have to do is kill them."

The beetles churned uneasily in the air.

Mina straightened in front of her brother, staring unflinchingly into his metallic eyes. "You'll have to kill me, too."

"Then do it!" Dr. Blood screamed.

Apprentice turned his head slowly from side to side. He stepped back, a series of clicks emerging from the mask over his mouth and nose. I braced myself.

The attack didn't come. The beetles retreated, reattaching themselves to Apprentice's cloak. He stood aside, leaving Dr. Blood unprotected on his high throne.

"It's over, Archibald," Papa called, stepping past Apprentice and onto the dais. "It's finished."

Dr. Blood ignored him. His face was so red it looked like he was about to pop.

"You're nothing!" he yelled at Apprentice and Mina. "You never were. You're gullible idiots. Your father? Me? You really believed that?" He jabbed a short finger at the two of them. "You're pathetic. You have no idea how easy you were to fool. You did everything I asked, all to please me. You would have believed anything."

Apprentice stiffened. His every movement stilled. He didn't even seem to be breathing. It was as though a switch had been thrown that had turned him from a man into a statue. Then his head tipped back and he screamed. Even through the metallic mask that dug deep into the flesh of his face, I could hear it. It sent shivers spilling over my skin.

His cloak snapped out behind him. Hundreds of metal beetles whirred. Apprentice shot into the air. He burst through the ceiling in an eruption of glass and was gone into the night.

Mina let out a sob. I hurried across to her. Her face was

white and she was trembling. I didn't know what I was supposed to do.

"Come with us, Archibald," Papa said, climbing the steps toward him. "It's over."

Dr. Blood sneered. "You always were a fool, Hugo. Do you think me helpless?"

Thick steel-and-glass walls shot up around the dais, trapping Papa and Dr. Blood in a cage.

I threw myself against the glass, hammering it with my fists, but it was an inch thick and it felt like hitting rock.

Beneath the dais, blades whirred, faster and faster. Slowly, it rose into the air.

Dr. Blood threw another lever as Papa advanced on him.

Up above, something rattled. Chains began to move. A shape fell from the ceiling with a clatter. I whirled just in time to see a second machine drop beside the first. It landed on metal legs, then straightened. The first machine looked like a giant spider with long, hinged legs and a body bristling with spikes. The other was flatter, its body lower to the floor, but it had an enormous arched tail that ended in a deadly sharp point, like a scorpion, and two sets of claws.

"Get back!" Rackham shouted, pushing Putty and Mina behind him. I ran to join them, retreating toward the side of the throne room as the metal monstrosities scuttled after us.

"What are we going to do?" Mina demanded.

"We can get the spider," Putty said, grabbing my arm.

I stared down at her. "We can?"

The spider had two deadly looking pincers where its mouth would have been. Its legs ended in razor-sharp claws. It would be less painful to jump into a pit full of spikes.

"Good," Rackham said. "We'll take the scorpion."

He edged behind an immobile automatic servant. "Now!"

He bent and heaved, lifting the automatic servant and sending it toppling toward the approaching scorpion. It lashed out with its tail. The spike drove into the automatic servant's chest with a spray of sparks.

Putty darted to the left and I followed her. The spider turned and scampered after us, fast over the floor as we ran toward the sarcophagus.

"How exactly is this a good idea?" I gasped as the spider chased behind. Putty was faster than I was in just one shoe. I had absolutely no doubt who was going to be caught first.

"The hose," Putty said, pointing. "That one." Half a dozen thick rubber tubes stretched across the floor to end above the sarcophagus, filtering pale gases down onto the egg.

"What are we going to do?" I demanded. "Spray it?"

"Do you think that would work?"

"No!"

"Then shut up and grab it."

I snatched one end of the hose and wrenched it free from

the contraption above the dragon's egg. Putty peeled off to the side and grabbed a loop of the same hose. Heavy metal claws skittered on stone just behind us.

"What now?" I demanded.

"Run," she said, and jabbed a finger.

I didn't need to be told twice. Running away was my great fighting specialty. I took off, dragging the hose, trying not to think of the giant clockwork spider chasing after me.

"Left!" Putty yelled, and I did what she said.

The hose jerked in my hand so hard it threw me off my feet. I clung on as I hit the floor. The spider had gotten its legs tangled in the hose. It yanked, throwing me about like a fish on the end of a line.

Putty raced around the spider and threw her loop of hose over its back. It reared up, dragging me with it.

"Pull!" Putty shouted.

I rolled my eyes. "Right," I said through clenched teeth as I bounced off the frozen body of an automatic servant and went spinning across the smooth floor. "Pull. Got it."

I was starting to see a problem with Putty's plan.

The spider turned, tugging against the hose again, flipping me across the floor.

One of the enormous, carved pillars loomed up. I twisted my body around and got my feet in place just in time. I hit the pillar with enough force to send judders all the way up my back. I bit my tongue and tears filled my eyes.

For a moment, the hose went slack.

I leaped up, pulling the hose with me, and darted around the pillar. Then I braced my feet and waited.

The spider reared again, its legs flailing as it tried to get its sharp claws around the hose. But this time the hose didn't give. It jerked tight. The spider's legs came to an abrupt halt. For a second, it balanced on its rear legs. Then it toppled backward.

It hit the marble floor with a crash. Something split, and cogs scattered. A spring ricocheted away to ping against the banks of machinery.

I let go of the hose. My arms felt like they'd been stretched to twice their length, and I couldn't feel my shoulders.

"What were you doing?" Putty demanded as she ran up to me. "This isn't a game, Edward!"

I glared at her. "Next time you hold the hose."

Above us, on Dr. Blood's flying dais, Papa had managed to yank Blood off the throne and away from his controls. They were wrestling on the steps.

A crash sounded from the other side of the throne room. The giant scorpion was stalking Rackham, Mina, and Rothan Gal across the floor. They were ducking and weaving between the automatic servants, but they were running out of cover and Rothan Gal was staggering. The scorpion's metal stinger lashed out again, knocking another automaton out of the way.

"Are we going to help them?" Putty said.

I rolled my shoulders. "Why not? If one giant metal insect doesn't kill you, give it another go."

"They're not insects, Edward." Putty sighed. "They're arachnids. Everyone knows that."

A yelp sounded from the throne. I glanced up. Dr. Blood had managed to get an elbow into Papa's stomach. Dr. Blood scrambled free and slapped at a lever on the throne. Papa dragged him back, but too late.

The moment Dr. Blood pushed the lever, a door rumbled open at the back of the throne room. A cloud of steam puffed out.

In clatter of metal hooves, a massive mechanical bull trotted out through the steam. On either side of its head, where its horns should have been, two long, curved swords spun as fast as cycle-copter blades.

"Or we could fight this one instead," Putty said brightly.

The bull lowered its head, still puffing steam. Its red metal eyes fixed on us and it charged.

We ran.

"Any ideas?" I demanded as we sprinted for the cover of the pillars.

"So many."

"Any useful ones?"

Putty grimaced. "Not yet. Although I'm sure I will soon. I'm good at ideas."

"Don't take too long!"

We ducked behind a pillar just as the bull thundered past.

Clouds of steam washed over us. The spinning blades cut the air a foot from me.

Unlike the spider, the bull was a solid lump of iron. Crashing into a pillar wouldn't even slow it, and we could hammer at it all day without making a dent.

"Maybe we could drop a house on it," Putty said as we raced across the throne room. "Or throw it off the platform."

I risked a glance behind. The bull was working up speed, its head lowered.

"You do that," I said.

She wasn't wrong, though. It would take at least that much force, and even then I wouldn't be surprised if it shook it off and got back up again. Maybe if we had a battery of cannons. But we didn't even have a peashooter. Other than Dr. Blood's mechanical nasties, there weren't any weapons in the throne room at all.

Who would build a giant, flying attack fortress and then not leave any weapons around?

Well, no weapons except one. Papa had said that the banks of machinery were part of a weapon big enough to blow up a city. They ought to be enough to deal with one bad-tempered bull.

Of course, that weapon was aimed *outward*, not *into* the throne room.

"Dodge!"

I leaped to the side just as the bull charged past. I stumbled and pushed myself back up.

I didn't know how much longer I could keep this up. My ribs ached where the automatic servant had almost impaled me, and my shirt felt sticky from the cut. My legs were as weak as paper, my blisters burned like wire-wasp stings, and I still only had one shoe.

I staggered toward the throne where Papa and Dr. Blood were fighting. Papa was lying on his back on top of Dr. Blood, pinning him against the steps. Unfortunately, Dr. Blood had his arm wrapped around Papa's throat.

"Papa!" I shouted, over the noise of the dais's propellers. I threw a glance back to make sure the bull wasn't coming. "You said the machinery stores and channels an electrostatic charge? Where exactly is the charge stored?"

Papa tugged on Dr. Blood's arm to suck in air. "Ah. Well. That is quite interesting, actually. You see—"

The bull was ignoring Putty. Its eyes were fixed on me and it was pawing the marble floor. Clouds of steam puffed from its nostrils, and the spinning sword-horns sped up.

"Just tell me where it's stored!" I shouted.

"The glass tubes," Papa managed as Dr. Blood pawed at his face.

"Good."

I turned to face the bull. It lowered its head and watched me through little red eyes. The swords on its head spun faster still. I waved my arms. "Come on, then!"

It broke into a trot. *This had better work.* I turned and ran. Heavy hoofbeats followed. I had to get the bull far away from everyone else. I ducked around a pillar and sprinted for the other end of the throne room.

There! A gargantuan glass tube stretched from floor to ceiling near the main doors. It was filled with some thick, cloudy substance that stirred and roiled slowly behind the glass. I put down my head and raced for it.

Behind me, the hoofbeats thundered closer. Vibrations shook the floor. My shoeless foot slipped and skidded as I tried to push myself on.

"Look out!" Putty shouted.

Another ten feet, that was all I needed. Steam puffed over me. I heard the blades cutting through the air.

This was going to hurt.

I ran straight into the glass tube, twisting my body. I bounced off, falling sideways. The bull's leg crashed into me, sending me tumbling over and over.

Then the bull hit the glass tube, and the tube ruptured. Electrostatic charge ripped out.

I had been expecting a big explosion, but nothing like this. The bull simply disintegrated. Metal and glass scythed through the air. Streaks of lightning crackled and burst across the machinery and up to the ceiling struts. Glass shattered and rained down. I covered my head and hugged the floor.

When I looked up, the throne room was a mess. Bits of broken bull and shattered machinery littered the floor for twenty feet. Broken glass spread all around me. And on the other side of the throne room, the scorpion was still pursuing Rackham, Mina, and Rothan Gal.

I got to my feet, shaking off bits of glass and fragments of cogs. Most of my bones seemed intact, although I couldn't quite be sure under all the bruises. I'd managed to smack my chin against the glass tube when I'd run into it, and from the way it was throbbing, I knew it was going to swell.

Carefully, I picked my way back across the floor, cursing myself with every step for having lost my shoe.

The scorpion slashed at Mina with its stinger. She dodged, but she must have been exhausted, because she was too slow. It caught her a glancing blow that sent her to the floor. Rackham lunged for it. Its great claws slapped him away. The scorpion scampered over to Mina, drawing its tail back for another blow.

I broke into a run and launched myself onto the tail. It whipped forward, carrying me with it. My shoulders screamed in protest. Mina rolled aside. I wrapped my arms tighter and held on. The tail lashed back and forth as it tried to shake me off.

Rackham grabbed one of the bull's swordlike horns that had been blown free by the explosion and attacked. The scorpion's giant claws snapped at him, fending off the sword. Slowly, jabbing and cutting as he went, Rackham retreated, drawing the scorpion away from Mina.

"Anyone got any ideas?" I yelled as the scorpion thrashed

its tail again and my arms slowly began to rip out of my shoulders.

"There's a gap just behind its neck," Putty shouted back. "I can see it. You'll be able to disable it there. Just stick something in."

"Really?" I muttered. "That's great."

How on Mars was I supposed to get close to its neck?

The scorpion slashed at Rackham again. He ducked under its claw and hammered his sword against the scorpion's carapace.

It didn't even slow the monster.

The tail pulled back, then snapped forward. This time, I let go.

I crashed onto the scorpion's body. My fingers slipped on smooth metal. My feet scrabbled for a grip. I slid down. Then I found a crack and held on.

The scorpion spun, trying to reach me with its claws. Its stinger rose above me, glittering and bright in the light of the photon emission devices. It stabbed for me.

Rackham swung his sword into the tail with all his might. The sword shattered, but the force was enough to turn the stinger. It hit the creature's own body to my left.

I grabbed the back of the scorpion's head. I wanted to sob as every muscle in my arms protested. This was agony. It was going to tear my arms from my body and my fingers from my hands.

The scorpion twisted and scuttled, jerking this way and that. Its stinger rose again in a whine of cogs.

I squeezed my eyes shut against tears of pain and heaved myself up. Something popped in my left arm. Pain flared like a foot-long needle. I forced my eyes open and blinked them clear.

There was a gap between the plates on the scorpion's back just below my elbow. I saw cogs whirring frantically in there, and below them, a large spring. Jam that, and I'd ruin the mechanism, but I didn't have anything to put in there except my fingers. The cogs would chop them to bits.

I liked my fingers.

"Catch!" Putty shouted. My head shot up as she tossed a shard of broken metal through the air. Instinctively, I grabbed it. Its edges were sharp, but it was long and narrow.

The stinger came plunging down at me again. With a shout, I shoved the shard into the gap.

Metal clashed and screeched as the shard jammed in the mechanism. Cogs jumped and splintered. The scorpion shuddered under me, bucked, and ground to a halt. Very carefully, I unhooked the stinger from the back of my shirt, where it had come to rest, and let myself slide loosely to the floor.

I was dead. No one could have survived that. Except it didn't hurt this much when you were dead. Did it?

I groaned. Why wasn't everyone gathering around me in

sympathy? I really could do with some sympathy right now. Someone telling me how heroic I was would have been great, too.

The flying platform lurched.

It felt like we'd run into the side of a mountain. I rolled over and pushed myself up. My arm was still in agony. I must have torn something in it. Dr. Blood and Papa were sitting in front of the throne, arms locked, frozen in the act of wrestling.

"What have you done?" Dr. Blood demanded. "What have you *done?*"

"Can't you tell?" Papa said. "Can't you feel it? The electrostatic release has started a chain reaction. It will tear the platform apart."

I grimaced. This was my fault?

The platform shook again.

"Fix it!" Dr. Blood screamed, pulling free of Papa. "I know you can. Stop the chain reaction." He stumbled up the dais steps and onto his throne.

"No, Archibald," Papa said. "It is over."

"Then I'll fix it myself," Dr. Blood raged. "I was always the better mechanician."

He grabbed a lever and shoved it forward. The entire dais tilted down and, with a whir of copter blades, swooped toward the banks of machinery.

Putty darted past me. Instinctively, I made a grab for her,

but she was too fast. She snatched the dragon's egg from the sarcophagus, scattering dust behind her, and raced back. She looked outraged.

"Look what they've done to it!" She thrust the egg at me. The dull scales that had covered it now looked wet, as though oil had soaked into surface. A crack ran from the tip, halfway down one side. "They've broken it." She glared at me. "This is your fault."

The floating dais landed with a *thump.* Its glass-and-steel walls fell away as a larger shock juddered through the platform.

"We need to find a way off," Papa said, clambering from the dais. "Fast. The reaction will grow quickly in strength."

I turned to Mina. "Can we reach the airships in time?"

She looked apprehensive. "Maybe."

"Then let's move. Putty, come on."

With Rackham helping Rothan Gal, we hurried to the doors at the back of the throne room. When we reached them, Papa turned. Dr. Blood had pulled a panel from the banks of machinery and was reaching inside.

"Archibald!" Papa called. "Come with us. There's still time."

Dr. Blood didn't answer.

The platform rumbled. Deep in the workings, a spring burst. The platform lurched again, slipping sideways. Mina stood in the doorway, gazing back at Dr. Blood. I didn't know what to say. She'd thought the man was her father. He'd used her, made her cheat and lie and steal for him, then he'd discarded her. I had thought Mina had betrayed me, but she was the one who'd been betrayed.

Then she looked away, and we fled the disintegrating platform.

— 24 —

Awakening

The airship dropped away from the flying fortress, pushed hard by its propellers. Immense chunks of metal ripped away above us and spun to the desert below as explosions tore through the platform.

By the time we'd reached the docking bay, Dr. Blood's men had made their escape. All I could see of them now were distant shapes against the lightening morning sky as they escaped in airships and fliers of their own.

I was so exhausted and bruised that all I wanted to do was collapse on the seats at the back of the airship's cabin and let myself slump into unconsciousness. Instead, I stood with Mina, flanking Rackham as he guided the airship, looking out for falling debris from the platform and cradling my sore arm.

We came out from under the shadow of the platform as

another great explosion sent it tilting and sliding down toward the rock walls of the valley. The vast propellers that helped support the platform had stopped turning, and it was sinking slowly.

"We're clear," I said, glancing out the side windows.

Rackham angled the airship up, and I watched as we rose past the platform. When we'd first approached it, it had looked like a flying fortress. It still looked like that, but now it looked like it had come under assault from half of Napoleon's armies. Great rips and craters had appeared in it. Smoke and steam rose from gashes torn deep in the metal. The glass dome of the palace was no more than a skeleton, the supports twisted, the glass gone. Even as I watched in the airship's mirrors, another explosion erupted from the platform, tossing metal high into the air.

Rackham leaned on the controls, pushing the airship on faster, away from the dying fortress.

Then the platform simply shattered. One moment it hung there, suspended by its balloons. The next, it was gone. It was as though the platform had been nothing more than an illusion, a cluster of giant flies hovering together that had burst apart as one. Lightning crackled and raged between the spreading fragments of metal.

Chunks of platform rained down on the desert, and we were free, flying through the clear Martian sky.

With a sigh, I retreated to the seats and let myself fall into one.

"Did he escape?" Papa asked, absently polishing his eyeglasses on his filthy sleeve.

I shook my head. I hadn't seen any other flying machines leave the platform. Dr. Blood had still been on board when it had been destroyed.

Papa nodded, then lapsed into silence.

Putty looked like she was about to cry.

"Are you all right?" I asked.

She shook her head and lifted her dragon's egg. She'd wrapped it in the remains of my jacket, but I could see the crack in it had widened and spread, spawning dozens of new cracks across the hard stone surface.

"It's falling to pieces. It was the only one there was, and he ruined it."

A fragment of egg fell away.

"Maybe we can glue it back together?" I said hopefully.

Putty just looked more miserable.

"Are you sure it's breaking?" Mina said, joining us.

Putty gave her a pitiful stare. "Look at it."

Mina peered closer. "I am. And you know what it looks like to me? It looks like it's hatching."

Putty's head jerked down and she peered into the crack. "It can't be. It's almost two thousand years old. It's turned to stone."

"My father—Dr. Blood, I mean—he was going to hatch it."

"He was crazy," I said.

Mina's mouth turned down. "I know. But he was sure he could do it."

"He was right," Rothan Gal said. He'd been sprawled so motionlessly on a chaise longue I'd assumed he was asleep. "I have read many old documents and many ideograms from the dragon tombs." He pushed himself painfully up. "A dragon's egg can last for millennia. It does not die like a common egg. Scholars among my people have known this for a long time, but it was not known how to awaken one, and, indeed, we have done all that we could to destroy any clues. We would not willingly allow the dragon emperors to rise again. Somewhere in Patagonian Mars it seems Dr. Blood found the secrets we had tried to wipe out, and with the information from the tablet in the museum, I do not doubt that he knew how to awaken the egg."

Putty peered closer. "I can't *see* anything."

A *crack* sounded, sudden and sharp in the stillness of the cabin. A section of egg fell away.

Something moved in the darkness of the egg. It curled and stretched, sliding like a snake.

Nervously, I inched back.

Then a head arose on a long neck. Black eyes glittered beneath jewel-bright scales. Two small horns curved from the back of the head. A slim mouth widened, showing tiny teeth as sharp as pins.

Putty gasped in delight and reached out a finger toward it.

"Careful!" I warned. Those teeth might be small, but they'd easily draw blood.

A long tongue snapped out, licking across the end of her finger, then drawing back.

"She likes me!" Putty said.

Papa had joined us. He frowned over it. "It is . . . remarkable."

The tiny dragon pushed its way out of the remains of the egg. Narrow wings ran the length of its body. It stretched them as it arched its back. They looked as delicate as fine silk.

"You can't have her," Putty said, wrapping her arms protectively around the creature as Papa bent over it, squinting. Its tail whipped up, curling around Putty's arm. "She's mine."

"If I were you," Rackham called from the controls, "I would keep very quiet about that creature. The first dragon in nearly two thousand years. People will want to get their hands on it."

"Does that mean someone else will try again?" I said. "I mean, Dr. Blood succeeded. There really is a live dragon now." It felt absurd to say it, but it was true. It was right there in front of me. "Does that mean someone else will try to make themself the Emperor of Mars?"

"They'd better not try," Putty said fiercely.

"From what I have read," Rothan Gal said, "the dragons were fearsome weapons by themselves, but it was not the dragon that would have allowed Dr. Blood to conquer Mars. He could only have done it with weapons like that flying fortress. Dragons were a symbol of the Martian emperors, but if he thought my people would greet him as a new emperor because he had such a symbol, he gravely misunderstood us. It would have set us against him."

"He was mad," Papa said. "He truly was. His was a fever dream."

I peered down at the little creature. "And, um, do they grow fast?"

The preserved dragons in the museum were as big as this airship.

"I believe so," Rothan Gal said. "I have read that they can grow quickly enough for a man to ride in no more than a year."

I stared at Putty. This was going to get . . . interesting.

<hr/>

The water had risen visibly in just the day that we'd been away. The Martian Nile had spilled over its banks and was spreading across the desert in a thin, mirror-bright layer. Rackham's ship still lay aground on the sandbank, but it had risen and leveled out with the water.

"I'll have to anchor it," Rackham said as he swung the airship around and down toward his ship. "Otherwise it'll be carried away."

There were figures on the deck staring up at us as we descended. Olivia and Jane had armed themselves from

Rackham's stores, and I couldn't help but feel nervous as we sank toward them. As far as I knew, Jane had never fired a gun before, and I could see this all ending badly if her finger twitched on the trigger at the wrong moment.

But I needn't have worried. By the time we were in range, they were waving. Soon, the airship was tied above the boat, and Rackham had lowered a ladder. Putty and I climbed down first.

Miss Wilkins was waiting next to Mama. Her eyes were fixed thunderously on Putty.

Putty looked mutinous. "I'm not putting up with it, Edward. Not anymore. I'm going to tell Mama about her letters."

And Mama would have no choice but to fire Miss Wilkins. She'd never get another job. We'd be taking away her livelihood and her chances. Maybe it was stupid of me after how harshly she'd treated Putty, but I didn't want to be responsible for that, not for anyone.

But if she stayed, Putty wouldn't be able to take it anymore. Sometimes Putty needed to run wild. And sometimes she needed someone to hold her back, just a little. Miss Wilkins was completely the wrong person for Putty.

"Just give me a moment," I said. "I've got an idea."

As Papa stepped awkwardly from the rope ladder, I drew him to one side.

"Papa. Putty and I discovered something about Miss Wilkins." I took a breath. "It turns out she is married."

Papa peered at me through his smudged eyeglasses. "I see? Ah." He looked confused. "Should we invite the gentleman for tea, do you think?"

I closed my eyes for a moment. "No!" I sighed. "She can't stay on as Putty's governess."

Papa looked surprised. "Can she not?"

"Put it this way," I said. "Do you want to be the one who tells Mama that Putty's governess is secretly married? How well do you think that would go down?"

"Ah . . . Ah! I see what you mean." He scratched at his ear. "Well. I'm sure you'll figure out something. Now, if you don't mind—"

"I have figured out something. Actually, it was Putty's idea originally. Your business is . . . unstable." I held up a hand. "Oh, I know you're doing well right now, but you have to admit it's all a bit chaotic. You spend so much time in your workshop and so little running the business that other mechanicians are the ones who end up profiting from your work. I think you should hire Miss Wilkins to organize things. If there's one thing Miss Wilkins is good at, it's organizing things." Frighteningly good. "And you'll be able to spend more time in your workshop and at the museum. It'll be good for everyone."

Papa frowned. "I . . . ah . . . will certainly consider it. Only—"

"Excellent," I said. "Here she comes now."

Miss Wilkins was stalking across the deck toward Putty

like a thundercloud that had caught sight of a tea party. I gave Papa a little push toward her.

—◆—

It didn't take us long to collect our small amount of luggage. Within half an hour, we were gathered on the deck, ready to board the airship for the trip back to Lunae City.

Rackham emerged from the depths of the boat, pushing Mr. Davidson ahead of him. He untied the ropes that had bound my former tutor so that Mr. Davidson could climb the rope ladder to the airship, but it was clear that Mr. Davidson was still a prisoner. His head was bowed, and he didn't look up as he passed us.

Mina touched my arm. "Can I have a word, Edward?" She was fidgeting nervously.

For some reason, my breath caught in my throat and my chest felt tight.

"What is it?" I managed. I kept wanting to wet my lips with my tongue, but that would look weird.

"After Rackham has taken you all to Lunae City, he's going to bring back a repair crew to fix his boat."

I nodded. Why was she telling me this? Of course he had to fix it. It had lost its rudder. If he needed money, Papa would help. My stomach felt like it was caught in a whirlpool. I didn't know what was going on. I didn't know whether I wanted to step up to Mina and give her a hug or turn and run.

Mina cleared her throat. "When he does, when his boat is repaired, I'm going to go with him."

I froze. I tried to say something, but nothing would come out. Going? With him? I'd thought . . . what? That she'd stay with me when this was done. Why would she? What was there for her?

"It's my brother," Mina said. "You have to understand. You saw him flee during the fight when Dr. Blood told him to kill us. That means he's out there somewhere. He's lost. He's alone. You saw what Dr. Blood did to him. I know you think he's a monster, but he's my brother. I have to go after him. If one of your sisters was out there, you'd do the same."

I nodded slowly, not trusting myself to speak. If one of my sisters was lost and hurt, I'd turn the world upside down to rescue her. Just like we had for Putty.

Mina came so close I could feel her breath on my cheek. "Forgive me," she whispered. "I did like you. I do. It wasn't all a lie. I hated doing what I had to do. But I thought . . . My father. My brother." She looked down. "You're a good person." Before I could react, she set a quick kiss on my cheek.

"It's all right," I said through numb lips. "It's all right."

―◆―

Putty stood on the small viewing platform just outside the airship cabin watching the high, twisting roofs of the Lunae City approach. She glanced over as I let myself out to stand beside her. Her tiny dragon was nestled inside her shirt. Its long neck twisted out and bright eyes fixed me with an unblinking gaze.

"You were right," I said.

"What?" For once, Putty actually seemed stumped. It wouldn't last long.

"I *was* leaving you out of things. I was refusing to get involved in your schemes. And it wasn't fair."

"I knew it!" Putty's eyes gleamed. Then her face dropped. "But why?"

I sighed. "Because I thought I had to look after the family. Because every time one of you got into trouble or created a disaster, I thought I had to fix it."

"That's crazy!"

I peered over the rail at the still-spreading floodwaters below.

"I know. But when I figured that out, after we found the dragon tomb, I realized I never did anything of my own. You and Papa had your inventions. Jane had her suitors. Olivia had Freddie. Mama had her Society rivals. But I didn't have anything. I didn't even know what I wanted. I was just trying to find something I liked doing and something I was good at. That was all."

She looked at me suspiciously. "So did you find it?"

I glanced back at the cabin to where Mina and Olivia were sitting together talking. "Not yet."

The airship dipped down toward Lunae City as late afternoon faded into evening.

The Inundation had arrived. The floodwaters had risen, covering the fields around the city and seeping into the tunnels that the beetle-vines had bored beneath it. Enormous, brightly colored tendrils were erupting from the ground, throwing sticky streamers across the high, twisted buildings. Even the Flame House was covered. It looked magnificent.

"Then I'll help you find it," Putty said.

I put my arm around her shoulders. "All right."

She grinned up at me. "We are going to have so much fun."

Acknowledgments

Once again I would like to first and foremost thank my wife, Stephanie Burgis, for her support, encouragement, advice, and dedication in reading this book many, many times. I couldn't have done it without you, Steph. Thanks to Jamie for the saber-toothed spiders. Thank you to my editor, Christy Ottaviano, for her unending patience and incisive suggestions. Thank you, too, to assistant editor, Jessica Anderson, and the rest of the team at Macmillan who continue to work so hard every day. I'm also constantly grateful to my agent, Jennifer Laughran, who keeps everything running smoothly and who is always on my side.

Finally, thank you to my family, particularly Ollie and Jamie, who have been unendingly enthusiastic and excited, even when this book has taken up too much of my time. You are great, and I'm writing this for you.